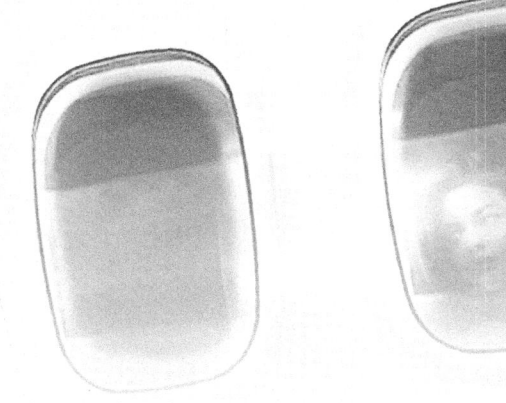

THE
WOMAN
IN THE
WINDOW
A.J. RIVERS

The Woman in the Window
Copyright © 2024 by A.J. Rivers

All rights reserved. Without limiting the rights under copyright reserved above, no part of this publication may be reproduced, stored in or introduced into retrieval system, or transmitted, in any form, or by any means (electronic, mechanical, photocopying, recording, or otherwise) without the prior written permission of both the copyright owner and the above publisher of this book.

This is a work of fiction. Names, characters, places, brands, media, and incidents are either the products of the author's imagination or are used fictitiously. The author acknowledges the trademarked status and trademark owners of various products referenced in this work of fiction, which have been used without permission. The publication/use of these trademarks is not authorized, associated with, or sponsored by the trademark owners.

PROLOGUE

First Week of June: Seminole, Texas

In the first week of June, Seminole, Texas was already hot. Uncomfortably so during the daytime. At four in the morning, when Priscilla walked out of Seminole Gentlemen's Club, the air was cool. She was the last dancer to leave, and the streets were empty except for the occasional critter that darted toward the cover of one of the many dumpsters lining the alleyways along her regular route.

The night's haul of cash had been great. Almost a grand. Priscilla smiled as she lit a cigarette. Her shoes clicked against the broken pavement as she strolled toward home in the middle of the narrow road. She had learned long ago not to walk close to the buildings where anyone could be waiting in the shadow-darkened recesses of doorways, or just to the side of a dumpster, to grab hold of her. The middle of the road was safer at four in the morning. Especially for a stripper just off work and having to walk home.

Walking home. When she had been a child, walking home had been a fun adventure after school, or on a Sunday evening after visiting with her grandmother. As a teenager, it had been a daring adventure on which she chose to embark as part of her rebellious years. The adrenaline pumped as she sneaked out of the house while her parents were sleeping, and then again as she sneaked back in before they woke. At twenty-nine, it wasn't so fun anymore, but owning a car wasn't a luxury she could afford. Not yet, anyway.

If her husband hadn't died a little over a year ago, she wouldn't be walking home at four in the morning. Her kids wouldn't be home taking care of themselves until she got there. They wouldn't have any idea what their mother did for the extra cash. But Dean had died. Dean died and Priscilla was left to fend for their two children all alone.

The day shifts at the diner and weekends at the dollar store barely paid rent and utilities. She tried once to get on food stamps, but the people told her she made too much money. Disenchanted and desperate, she had gone to her shift at the diner. That very same day, Rick from Seminole Gentlemen's Club had gone to the diner for breakfast. He told her she could make quadruple her current salary at his club just by dancing and showing a little skin. She had laughed and told him she didn't make a salary. Waitresses lived by tips alone. Two-thirteen an hour didn't add up to squat at the end of the forty-hour week.

Rick told her that whatever she was taking home in tips and wages for a week, he could guarantee at least quadruple that from his club, if she would work four nights a week. He dropped his card in with a twenty-dollar tip, and walked out.

With that kind of money, she could get out of the crappy apartment on the shoddy side of town, buy a car, and never have to worry about trying to beg help from an unwilling government agency again. It took her until she paid her bills that month to call Rick.

The rest, as they say, is history. She went to work at the club three nights a week from eight in the evening until three or four in the morning. As soon as she walked through the doors at night, her name changed to Prissy—a stage name Rick insisted on. It wasn't easy at first, but counting the stacks of cash at the end of each shift helped her get past the shyness and the awkward feelings of cavorting half-naked in front of strangers.

She had a plan. She wouldn't work there forever. She would work all three of her jobs, save her money, and then, one day real soon, she would take her kids and put Seminole in her rearview forever. Tennessee was in her future. The kids would grow up on a farm with fresh air and animals and trees the same way she had until she graduated high school and left with Dean to strike it rich in Texas.

Though she hated stripping, the pay was great. That was undeniable. And it wasn't like she was a career stripper. No more than she was a career waitress or career retail worker. What was her career? What was her life trajectory? Before Dean died, she knew exactly what she wanted to do, who she wanted to be, and what path she wanted her life to take. After Dean's heart attack, though, her vision of the future became hazy, and then murky, and finally, she was so focused on surviving day-to-day that she forgot to think about the future. The future wasn't something that was abstract and far away; it was only a few days away.

Ironic how a utility bill could bring reality crashing in with the force of a freight train. Who had time to fantasize about owning property and a nice house when there were groceries to be bought, a landlord demanding the rent, and two kids under the age of eleven who needed clothes and shoes and medicine for ear infections? Who has the energy for such thoughts as the future after working seven days straight for the ninth month in a row? Not Priscilla Haun.

She flicked the cigarette butt into the shadows. It hit the brick wall of an abandoned apartment building and the embers made a little sunburst before falling to the concrete. Dean would have scolded her for tossing the butt without extinguishing it first. She smiled at the memories of him. He had been her safe place for so many years that she thought she might never feel truly safe again without him.

There were still several blocks to go before she reached home. Her legs ached. Her body screamed for sleep, but she had to be at the diner for her shift in just four hours. It would be easy enough to drop that job, but she couldn't let it go. The two menial jobs kept her legit and kept her straight. Too many of the other women at the club were messed up on drugs and drank until they were blackout drunk just about every night. She had made a vow to herself that she would never let herself get caught up in that trap.

She had been approached from people on either end of the illegal drug spectrum. She worked with girls who consistently offered her a pill or a snort or a shot to help her through her night, and then she was semi-regularly approached by individuals who offered to pay her twice what she was making at the club if she would agree to just discreetly drop off and pick up a few packages around town a few days a week. She refused as politely as possible, but lately, the latter individuals had been getting more aggressive. As far as she was concerned, she was doing no more sketchy activities than she was already by stripping in front of strangers.

Priscilla stopped and looked at the divergent paths ahead.

She started for the alley, but her gut tightened and a chill rushed over her skin.

"Chicken-heart," she chided herself aloud. "You've walked that alley before, and there was nothing in there but a few rats."

She looked down the middle of the street toward the traffic light in the distance. It was so far away. The alley would shave fifteen to twenty minutes off her walk home. Reaching in her purse for her cigarettes, her fingers curled around the .38 pistol, and she took a deep breath. She let the gun go and took out her cigarettes.

Touching the flame of the lighter to the end of her cigarette, she headed for the alley. Stepping out of the dim cone of light cast by the ancient streetlight, she stopped and let her eyes adjust to the darkness of the alley. She wished there was a streetlight at the other end, but there was only a barely perceptible ambient glow of lights farther to either side of the opening.

She forced her feet to carry her forward, staying close to the left-hand wall. If she could make it past the first dumpster on her right, she thought she would be okay, and that sick feeling in the pit of her stomach would ease. Not like it mattered because she was going through the alley one way or the other. Dean wasn't there to protect her anymore, but his gun was. Sooner or later, she would have to learn to deal with things scarier than an alley in the middle of the night.

Taking a long drag from her cigarette, Priscilla hurried past the first dumpster. She let out a pent-up breath and thought she must look like a scurrying rat. She was in the blind spot, and it felt as though the walls on either side were closing in on her.

"Hey, can I get one of those?" a man's deep voice crawled up from behind her and gripped her spine.

Spinning in fright, she had the gun in her hand, holding it out toward him, her eyes wide as she tried to perceive his features in the darkness.

"Whoa," the man exclaimed, stepping cautiously from the deep shadow near the dumpster she had just passed. He held his hands shoulder-high. "Don't shoot a man for trying to bum a cigarette. I didn't mean to scare you so badly."

Something about his voice was wrong. He wasn't from Texas. He was from somewhere else, but she couldn't place that accent. "What the hell? What do you want?"

He chuckled lightly, keeping his hands up. "Just a cigarette, but if you don't want to share, that's fine, but I could really use one right about now, Prissy."

Great, a perv who'd watched her dance had probably followed her. But that didn't make sense. She would have seen him, or heard him following her, and he couldn't have known she would take the alley. She hadn't even known she would take it.

She held the gun with one hand and tossed him her lit cigarette with the other. "Now, you just stay away from me and leave me alone. My son is expecting me home any minute now, and I'm already running late. He'll call the cops if I'm not there soon." She walked backward a few paces as the man picked up the cigarette, and then she turned to hurry out of the alley. The damnable shortcut. Why hadn't she just taken the main road?

"Why are you stripping if you have a son at home? A good mother wouldn't do that." The man walked toward her. She could hear his muffled footfalls behind her. "He'll be embarrassed by you when he gets old enough to understand what you're doing."

She walked faster, the warm air burning her lungs as she strained harder to pull it in. "Leave me alone, mister. I'm warning you." She turned sideways, still holding the gun. Tears of terror welled in her eyes, and she stumbled a little.

"Why would you leave a son home alone to come out here and make such a slutty spectacle of yourself? Why wouldn't you just be a respectable mother and stay home to take care of him?" His voice changed with every word. It grew harsher, more accusatory.

Priscilla wanted to run, but she was too scared. Fear weighed down her legs and slowed her thoughts. He moved closer. She stepped on the neck of a bottle and rolled her ankle. Pain shot to her knee through her shin bone as she caught her balance. The gun waved erratically.

"You should put that away before you hurt yourself," the man said in a grating voice that sounded as if he were speaking through gritted teeth.

Bracing with her left shoulder against the wall, she leveled the gun at the man. "Please," she said, her own voice hitching. The rest of her sentence was lost in the man's angered, wordless yell as he propelled himself forward. She pulled the trigger.

The muzzle flash was bright. An old-timey photographer's flashbulb in the blackness of the alley that blinded her. She turned and ran, screaming and crying for help, but her voice was thin. Too thin. And the flash of the gun had left her with twin blind spots as she fumbled toward the other end of the alley. The world tried to spin out from under her. Her ears hurt. No one ever tells you about shooting in a closed space and how it's going to hurt your ears, make you deaf for a few minutes, and briefly blind you if it's in the dark.

She had hit the man. She had to have hit him. His body had twisted to the side. Her vision cleared just enough to see the opening of the alley only twenty feet ahead. There were houses to the right. If she could just make it to one of them, she would be all right.

A pain ripped through the back of her skull, and the world went black.

Jody, Anna, I love you both, she thought just before all sensation disappeared. The monster had gotten her. She didn't know how, but he had. And she knew he was a monster because everybody knows that bullets stop humans.

"Prissy," the man said as he slapped her face.

Priscilla moaned and opened her eyes a slit. They refused to open all the way, and the pain in the back of her skull was nearly unbearable. The man stood over her.

"About time. I don't have long. The sun will be up soon." He chuckled.

Priscilla tried to unfold her hands and get her feet under her body, but she couldn't move except to roll from one side to the other. Her hands were tied and so were her legs and feet. The dirty rag in her mouth prevented her from screaming.

One bright beam of light shone down on them from a streetlight at the end of the alley. It was a different alley, and her gut churned when she realized it was one that lay on the very farthest edge of town. No one lived nearby. There were no businesses close by, either. It was an almost completely defunct part of town, and it had been that way since she and Dean had moved there years ago.

No one would hear her screams. No one would know where to look for her. She struggled against the restraints. Jody and Anna were alone at home. Who would tell them that their mother had been murdered in an alley at the edge of town? Where would they go? Who would raise them?

The man shook his head. His eyes were cold steel and his jawline was sharp enough to cut paper. His hands were big and strong and merciless as he slapped her hard enough to rock her head to one side again.

"Little Prissy, such a disappointment to..." He grinned and looked to either side before pinning her with his determined gaze again. "Everyone, right?"

His accent wasn't strong enough to be from the South, the East Coast, or even from the far northern states that bordered Canada. It wasn't flat enough to be Oklahoma or Kansas. A complete stranger from some unknown part of the country had traveled who knew how far just to kill her in an alley.

THE WOMAN IN THE WINDOW

She tried to ask him what he wanted, but the fabric in her mouth stifled the words. She reached to pull it out. The man clamped a hand painfully over her mouth, pressing down until she was sure her skull would break under the pressure.

"You're going to ask what I want, why I'm doing this to you, and then you'll offer me all that cash in your little purse to spare your life, right?" He nodded as he spoke. "Blink once for yes."

She blinked once and then kept her eyes on him. He shook his head and clicked his tongue.

"You have nothing I want." Bringing a hand from behind him, he produced a page torn from some old magazine and held it close to her face. "This," he hissed through gritted teeth. "This is what I want."

Confused, Priscilla looked at the page. It was an old advertisement from a 1950s- or 1960s-women's magazine showing the era's stereotypical idea of a perfect housewife in her kitchen: Campbell's Soup on the stove, a happy boy and a girl waiting at the table, and a smiling man in a suit with the newspaper at the head of that table. There was even a scruffy, loveable pooch sitting to the side of the little boy.

Priscilla shook her head. It was a minute movement under his hand. How else to show him she was confused? What the hell did he want? That mid-twentieth-century lifestyle? Soup? A smiling family? What? And what did any of it have to do with her?

He dragged her bound wrists above her head, leaving her body completely prone to him. Panic coursed through her veins, and she thrashed. Her efforts were useless against his strength. The man attached the thin rope binding her wrists to something that clicked and then ratcheted. Before she saw, she knew he had secured her to the bottom of the dumpster with handcuffs. She screamed loud and hard. The force tore at the inside of her throat as she redoubled her efforts to slip the ropes.

The man whistled and walked a few feet away only to return with discarded empty cans with Campbell's Soup labels. There were three. He set them up across the alley from Priscilla, turned, and pulled a long, thin knife from his back pocket, and knelt beside her.

"Now, let's see if we can't transform you into something a little more appropriate."

She screamed again and shook her head violently. Jody, Anna, she tried to say.

He didn't understand her words, and he wouldn't remove the rag from her mouth. She hadn't told him that she had two kids: a boy, Jody, and Anna, a girl. Ten and eight.

"I know, I know. You have a lot to say now, don't you? I hope you told your son that you loved him before you ran off to your slutty stripping job last night. Do you know how demoralizing it's going to be for your son to learn that his mother, the woman who brought him into this world, was a *stripper*? Do you even care what effect your decisions will have on your son?"

His face grew tighter, redder, angrier with every word. The knife filled her vision. Panic and terror sliced through her brain as he lowered the blade.

Jody. Anna. Would they ever know why Mommy never came home?

CHAPTER ONE

First Week of June: Fairhaven, Maryland

Margot Carter's casefile lay open on Ava's desk. It had been a constant presence on her desk since she returned from Honolulu nearly a month prior. Still, she had no real leads, yet she was expected to clear it ASAP.

Margot's cause of death was labeled as homicide and the means was listed as several knife wounds to her upper torso and neck. The medical examiner said she had been alive during much of the torturous wounding leading up to her demise.

Ava grimaced as she inspected the crime scene photos. In her mind, she could hear Margot's screams of pain and terror during the brutal attack. The staged scene of Margot dressed in a mouse-brown wig sporting victory roll bangs and long, loose curls, a powder-blue vintage dress with a cinched waist and hem that fell just below the knees did nothing to take away from the damage done by the knife. She was left in a sitting position with her head tilted as if she were looking up, and the knife wound across her neck opened like a second mouth. A toothless, bloody maw forever in the semblance of a misplaced grin.

Sal knocked at the open door. "Still no leads on the Margot Carter case?" She wasn't smiling.

Ava sighed and dropped the photo. "No. I called Agent Ellis in San Francisco, though. He has had some cases in which the M.O. is so similar…" She shook her head and glanced at the picture again. "I don't know. This just looks like one of those cases. Margot lived a bit of a wild life; she had a three-year-old son, she liked to go out on the weekends to some wild parties, and some of the interviewees I've questioned said she had questionable morals."

"Judgy, much?"

Ava shrugged. "Their words, not mine. Now, she's been murdered and dressed as a vintage housewife. Her makeup was done, but it was applied over the spatters of blood. This monster even put a wig on her. The medical examiner said he had even taken the time to give her a rough manicure, clipping, filing, and painting her nails."

"Ellis had cases like this in San Francisco?" Sal gave her a dubious look.

"I know. Even he said it's a stretch, but it's too much like those cases for me to shrug off. I just can't."

"So, you're hypothesizing that a serial killer traveled from California to DC, killed a woman for the same reasons and staged her body in the same way as he had all the way on the other side of the country?"

Ava inhaled deeply and let her eyes close briefly as she nodded. "Yes."

Sal took the photo and eyed it with a neutral expression. She shook her head and replaced it on top of the scattered papers from the file. "I'm sorry, but I'm not convinced. Why would a killer do that?"

"I don't know. The cases in San Francisco are in the system. Pull them up and have a look, if you don't believe me."

"I don't have time for that right now. This is your case, and you know the other cases, apparently. I'll trust your judgment for now, but don't get too wrapped up in this. You know I can't get any wild cross-country investigative trips funded right now. Margot was murdered in DC. She was from Fairhaven. You're the lucky one who ended up on the case." She gave an apologetic smile. "Did Ellis have any suspects for the other cases, or were they ever solved?"

"They weren't solved. Every time he gets what he thinks is a solid lead, something happens to prove the suspect's innocence."

THE WOMAN IN THE WINDOW

"I don't envy you this case at all, but I'm glad it's with you. I know you'll figure it out. If you need my help, ask, but don't expect much for the next few days because I'll be dealing with the brass. The politics involved with this job are insane, and sometimes, I just want to be back out in the field."

Ava chuckled. "Wow, you'd rather be facing serial killers and rapists than meeting with the brass?"

Sal chortled and stood. "Sounds bad when you say it like that, doesn't it?"

Ava nodded. "I've got a few ideas how to deal with this case. I'll let you know if I hit paydirt with any of them. Go enjoy those board meetings."

Sal scoffed and walked out. She hadn't said as much, but Ava knew Sal had been hoping for the case to be progressed further than it was. She wanted something positive to report to the board.

Follow your gut. That's what Uncle Ray had always told her to do, and that's just what she was doing. Ava had a gut feeling that Margot Carter's murder and the last three similar cases in San Francisco were somehow connected. If she could prove a connection, even a tenuous one, she might be able to break her case, and perhaps help Jason Ellis break his as well.

What she hadn't told Sal was that she had already began monitoring cities between San Francisco and DC. If her hunch was correct, and the serial killer had traveled across the country from California, maybe he had killed others on his way to DC, or to somewhere else in the United States. There were no hits so far, but there would be. There had to be. Someone twisted enough to do what this killer was doing couldn't just stop. He would have to be stopped.

She picked up the picture of Margot Carter sitting on a park bench with her legs crossed and that powder-blue dress draped perfectly over her blood-smeared legs. The killer had used fishing line to crudely stitch a smile on her once-pretty face by pulling the corners of her mouth back and slightly up and securing the stitch in her hairline behind each ear. He had glued her lips together and tilted her head back as if she were looking slightly up at something.

"At what? What was the point of that?" Ava asked the picture. "Is he living out some screwed-up fantasy where she's looking up at him? Maybe she was supposed to be looking up at the horizon, at God? At nothing?"

For the first time, Ava had trouble putting herself into the mindset of the killer. Every time she looked at the photos, it was as if she was magically being pulled into the victim's perspective. All the fear, pain, panic, and sounds swallowed her, and she couldn't drag her mind from that point of view, couldn't dissociate to enable her ability to see the situation from any other angle.

She put the pictures in the file and shuffled the papers in on top of them. As mad as it seemed, there was always a reason for the staging of a murder; there was always some sort of logic to it in the killer's mind. It was her job to find the logic and pull that thread until it unraveled the tapestry to reveal the murderer.

It had always worked before. Why not with Margot Carter's case?

Pulling up the database, Ava retrieved the information on the San Francisco murders, which Agent Jason Ellis had dubbed the Housewife Murders cases. The evidence in each of the three cases was scant at best, but the photos and autopsy reports were all there, and they were all very similar to the Margot Carter case except that Margot's mouth had been stitched into a smile and the other women's faces had been cut or painted into semblances of smiles.

Two things stood out when Ava looked at the crime scene photos from each case in chronological order: the killer was becoming more violent and was working on the staged scenes with a bit less meticulous care. Especially if she added Margot's photos at the end of the timeline. The first victim probably took several hours to clean, dress, dye and style her hair, pose, and do her makeup. By the time the killer made it to Margot, he didn't bother with the cleaning-up process but instead applied the makeup over the blood. He also didn't cut or dye the hair; instead, he had opted for a wig.

The database seemed to have been altered when Ava got into the interviews and the backgrounds of each of the California victims. She was certain that she remembered Jason telling her that he had two men in custody under suspicion for the second victim, and yet the database only listed one man who was questioned and released. She was also sure that Roxy, the caterer she had interviewed personally in a case, had been killed weeks after Ava had returned from San Francisco to Fairhaven, but the file now said the murder had happened within days. There was evidence of Jason's whereabouts being changed in two of the cases, putting him out of the city during the times of the murders, when she believed he was there.

She shut down the database and picked up her phone. Why hadn't she copied any of the information from the files the very first time she looked at them? That would have made the alterations more prevalent. If the subtle changes had taken place within the files, how would she be able to trust what was left in them? It was possible that other important details might have been changed...

"Or completely removed," she said aloud. She hadn't looked for things that might have been removed.

She pulled up the evidence reports again. Parts of the initial reports about the cases had been completely removed, and empty forms left in their stead. Those reports were not optional, they were required. Who would have done that, and why?

She closed the database again and picked up her phone for a second time. She didn't hesitate about dialing Jason's personal cell number.

He answered on the second ring. "Hello, Ava," he said in a flatter tone than the last time she had spoken with him.

"Hi, Jason. Not a bad time, is it?"

"Not really. I have a few minutes. What's going on?"

"It's this Margot Carter case. I was just comparing it with the similar murders in San Francisco—"

"Again?" he asked, sounding mildly irritated.

She paused. What was the deal with everyone ignoring what was so obvious to her? "Yes, again. I know it's a longshot, but I can't get rid of the feeling they're related somehow."

"That's a stretch. About a two-thousand-eight-hundred-mile stretch, to be more precise."

"Then how do you explain the similarities?"

"I don't know, maybe there are two killers working here. Maybe I've got one in my city, and you just happened to have one in DC."

"Who kill and then dress and stage their victims nearly identically?"

"It's not unheard of. Maybe yours is a copycat."

"How likely is it that a madman on the East Coast heard about and saw your cases and then decided to copy them?"

He let out a long breath. "It's not impossible."

"No, but it's very improbable."

"Okay, don't get all Sherlock Holmes on me. I'm just stating my theories, which, by the way, are a sight more believable than thinking there is a serial killer who travels and kills in similar ways on both coasts."

"There are no coincidences in law enforcement. You know that just as well as I do." The anger rose in her chest at each bit of logic he used to shoot down her theory as if it were juvenile and something only a freshman would come up with.

He groaned. "Okay, okay. Did you call just to vent to me, or at me, over your case?"

"No, as a matter of fact, I called to ask how the database surrounding your Housewife Murders had been altered? Who did it and why?"

"I have no idea. I haven't been in those digital files for a while. I've been busy working just like you, Ava. What do you believe was altered?"

She told him what she had found, and what she had not seen in the files that she was sure had been there before.

"Could it be that you have been so busy this year that you are misremembering what was in the files? I mean, you were nearly hospitalized just a few months ago from exhaustion caused by one of your cases. Then, just when you were about to recuperate, you were sent to Honolulu on that very same case. Now, as soon as you get home again, there's Margot Carter's case on your desk. You had just come from San Francisco, so I know that your Honolulu case wasn't one-hundred-percent resolved."

"That has nothing to do with the database being altered," she retorted.

"But it might be that you are misremembering details. That's all I'm saying. This isn't a personal attack toward you, so don't take it that way."

"So, you're saying that you didn't know the information had been altered within the system?" It had been. Details were missing or changed. There was nothing wrong with her memory. Was there?

"No, I didn't until just now."

A silence drew out between them, and all the miles that separated them became prominent. She couldn't just hop over to his house, or his office, and check things out. She couldn't see his face when he said things in tones that made her wonder if he was angry or upset or entirely unconcerned. Those were long and empty miles between them.

"Could you ask your team if any of them altered the files and then let me know?"

He made a disgruntled sound. "Ava, what exactly are you digging at here? My team didn't alter the files; they would have no reason to do that, and I don't think I'm going to go to the office and accuse them of it."

"I'm not accusing anyone of anything, but information has been changed in those files. I'm sure of it. I'm not misremembering, and I'm not crazy. I know what I saw, and I know what you told me about the cases."

He blew out a long breath again. "All right. Tell you what..." There was a very long pause.

"What?" she prompted after several seconds.

"I'll give it a look as soon as I have time, and I'll get back to you. It'll take me a few days; I'm out of the city on a case right now, and I won't be back for a couple of days at least."

"Thank you." Relief eased in and washed away some of her frantic feelings. "Where are you? Somewhere exotic?" She attempted a stifled laugh but it came out a bit dry.

"Oh, yeah. Real exotic if your idea of exotic is hot, dry, and barren. North Hobbs, New Mexico is about as exotic as a sand dune in the Sahara."

She managed the laugh finally. "I suppose my idea of exotic runs more along traditional lines. Maybe somewhere in Switzerland, or even some Caribbean island."

He laughed with her. "Wouldn't that be nice."

Thankfully, the conversation shifted to more pleasant banter, and any talk of work was avoided for the next several minutes. They fantasized about summer plans, as if either of them would somehow be able to get off work for the Fourth of July. Ava told him about her uncle's award-winning barbecue sauce recipe and Jason promised he'd have to try it sometime.

"Ava, work call. I have to go. Call again anytime, though. Or, I'll call you."

"Sure thing." She was going to tell him to be safe, but he had already hung up.

She laid her phone on the desk just in time for Sal to walk in carrying another file.

"Guess you get a break from the Margot Carter case for a couple of days." Sal handed the file to her. "Just don't let it go completely. It needs to be resolved soon as possible." She raised her eyebrows and pointed toward the ceiling. "They like seeing results, and they don't like hearing theories about a bi-coastal serial killer. Just to be honest, I don't like having to tell them such theories because it's my ass getting lectured about how crazy the idea is."

"What if it doesn't turn out to be just a theory?" Ava grinned sheepishly.

"You have evidence of that?" Sal put a hand on her hip and looked interested.

Ava looked down at the closed Margot Carter casefile. "Nothing that would stand up in court, no."

"There you go, then. Localize your investigation, but the new case needs the lion's share of your attention."

Ava nodded again and opened the file. "Got it."

CHAPTER TWO

Last Week of June: Northport, Washington; San Francisco, California

ORRINE FELDMAN HAD MOVED FROM WALLA WALLA, WASHINGTON to Fairhaven, Maryland a month after her divorce was finalized. Her abusive ex was in prison, and all her family was back east. There had been nothing to keep her or her nine-year-old twin daughters in Washington.

The Feldmans had settled into a routine quickly, and they had certainly believed all their troubles had been left on the West Coast. Corrine had no idea that she and her girls had caught the dangerous attention of an obsessive neighbor until he showed up in Fairhaven. Ava felt certain that Corrine would have reported any suspicious persons or happenings. Victims of severe domestic violence who got out of the situation were always on high alert. Sometimes, for the rest of their lives. But there were no such reports since she had moved to Fairhaven.

THE WOMAN IN THE WINDOW

Tyler Henkel, the Feldmans' neighbor in Walla Walla, had no intention of allowing Corrine or her girls to move so far away. He had broken into Corrine's small, tidy, Fairhaven home in the middle of the night. From the initial reports, Corrine had fought with him, but ultimately lost her life. Her twin daughters, Neelie and Naomi, witnessed their mother's death that night before Henkel abducted them and took them back to Washington state.

Ava and her team had gone after him as soon as Sal dropped the casefile on Ava's desk. It had taken two physically and mentally draining weeks to finally catch Henkel in Northport. Ava couldn't say she was too upset when Henkel was shot and later died of his injuries during his capture. The girls were physically okay, and that's what mattered most to her. It was hard to have any sympathy for a monster like Tyler Henkel. He hadn't hesitated to take Corrine's life in front of her daughters.

Metford met Ava in the lobby of the hotel with his travel bag slung over his shoulder. "You sure you're not going home with us? You have to be just as beat as the rest of us, if not more."

Ava shook her head. "No. I really need to get down to San Francisco for at least a day. I still have the Margot Carter case to work, and there are some records I need in San Francisco."

"San Fran ain't going anywhere. It'll be in the same place next week after you've had some rest."

Ava laughed even though she didn't feel amused, or even slightly happy at the moment. "And until I get those records, there will be no progress on my case. It'll still be exactly where it is, too."

He looked toward the car and Ashton waiting outside for him. "Do you want some company? I could stay, if you want."

"Good Lord, Sal would have a stroke. I just about couldn't convince her to let me have another day."

"They really want the Margot Carter case solved, though. She might be okay with it." He tilted his head and grinned sheepishly.

"I appreciate the offer. Really, I do, but you better get back so you can help the team work on those older cases before they go cold and the whole department has to attend another reaming session with the suits upstairs."

He blew out a long breath. "I guess I'll see you sometime tomorrow, then."

"Yep, barring some catastrophe," she said, giving him a smile of appreciation.

Metford walked to the car and tossed in his bag. Ava raised a hand to him and Ashton as they pulled away from the curb. The help, and the company, would have been nice, but there were far too many unsolved cases back home to keep one of the team just so she felt more comfortable.

Besides, she would be in San Francisco in a few hours, and then on a flight home within twenty-four hours.

An hour before her check-in for the flight to California, Ava called Jason.

"I'm still in North Hobbs," he said shortly.

"I'm getting ready to catch the flight to San Francisco," she said, wondering why he sounded irritated with her. "You said I could visit anytime to go through some of the paper files, right?"

"Yes. Yeah, you can, but the office is a mess. I don't know if you'll be able to find much in a timely manner."

Strange wording, but okay. "I'll do my best. I won't leave the office any messier than it already is. Deal?" She hoped to lighten the mood.

"Please, and thank you," he said in a monotone. "Remind me again why you need those paper files when the system is at your fingertips from anywhere."

"Because the database for the cases was altered. There's missing information and just plain wrong information."

"Oh, yeah, that's right. You think some of it has been changed since it differs from what you recall us talking about. Right, right."

"No, it *has* changed, and it has been removed." She bristled and took a deep breath to keep from snapping at him. He was on a case that was keeping him in New Mexico, which he had already griped about during their last conversation.

"Okay, knock yourself out. If I was there, I'd help, but it looks like I'll be here another few days still."

She chuckled. "No problem. I'm a big girl. I'll figure it out. You just worry about solving your North Hobbs case so you can get back home safely."

He scoffed. "I've already been here two weeks longer than I thought. Keep me updated. I need to go."

"Sure. Why don't we—" The line went silent. "Hello? Jason?" she asked. Pulling the phone away from her ear, Ava saw the call had ended. Had he hung up on her? Did the service just drop the call? Should she try him back?

After a minute or so, she decided against the callback and put the phone in her bag. It was almost time to catch her flight anyway.

About two miles from the office, the road was blocked, and the thick traffic was at a standstill. Horns blared, people yelled, some even got out of their cars and walked ahead to see what the holdup was.

A group of cruisers came past Ava's cab. They drove partially on the sidewalk to get around the crush of unmoving vehicles.

"I hope you weren't on a tight schedule," the cabbie said.

"What's going on?" Ava asked.

"Looks like it's probably another riot. Whole world's gone crazy, and they all came to San Francisco to do it."

"What are they rioting over?"

The cabbie scoffed. "What don't they riot over nowadays? The carpet of used needles on the sidewalks, the homeless addicts shitting in the streets, thieves running in gangs in broad daylight because they know the cops won't do anything to 'em. And then you have all these tech guys coming in driving up the rent. You know my rent doubled in the last five years?"

Ava shook her head. "Jesus."

"Can barely make a living driving either, on account of all those driverless cars. My cousin moved out to Sacramento, and I ain't blame him. I'm tellin' you, If it keeps going this way, this city will be a ghost town in a few years."

"Can't we get around it?"

"Yeah, sure. If we had wings, we could just fly over a few streets to either side and keep going." He scoffed again and shook his head before putting the car in park and cursing under his breath.

By the time Ava reached Jason's office, it was near time for everyone to go home and the office to be locked again. Jason's boss, Julian Garcia, was there, and he was not in a great mood.

"I won't be long. I can lock up when I leave," Ava offered, sensing that Julian wanted to be on his way.

"No. I'll stay until they leave, and then I'll lock it," Julian said without the slightest hint of swaying on his decision.

"Thank you." Ava stepped into the office. She only had twenty minutes at best.

The office was not as messy as she had suspected, but there were boxes stacked everywhere. It was reminiscent of a rat maze in a lab. Some of the handprinted case names on the box labels were turned facing her; others were turned away. It was going to take a hot minute to find the files she needed. What name had he put them under? Were they grouped into a single box, or had he kept individual files in separate boxes? Were the files even in boxes?

Ava dialed Jason's number again. On the fourth ring, it went to voicemail. She looked over the stacks of boxes and sighed. There were no files on the desk, and the drawers were locked. She grabbed the box closest to her and set it aside. It was going to be a long process finding what she needed.

At the back of the room, in an unlocked filing cabinet, Ava found a single folder containing a thumb drive. The accompanying paperwork designated the drive as Jason's assignments and work-related engagements over the last year.

"Hey," Julian called from the doorway. "Hey, are you done? It's time to go."

Ava turned and took a deep breath as she dropped the thumb drive into her pocket. She had moved several stacks of boxes to get to where she stood, and to get out, she would have to move them all again. She grinned sheepishly at Julian around a tall stack of boxes. "It's going to take me a minute."

"Jesus," he said. "I couldn't see you in there. You find what you're looking for?"

She showed him the thumb drive and the papers that went with it. "I think it might be on here. It's a longshot, but I can't find the paper files I was hoping for."

"Let me see that when you get out here."

"Right. Just a minute." Ava struggled with the boxes from her end.

Julian moved stacks toward the wall behind Jason's desk to help clear a path for Ava. "He's going to have to take some of these to the record room. This is a fire hazard. They see this, it's my ass going to get chewed out."

Ava stepped out of the office and smiled. "Why does he have so many in there?"

"Because his name's Jason Ellis, and he eats, drinks, and sleeps this job. Having the best agent on the West Coast has some drawbacks." He held out his hand.

Ava put the folder in it and then pulled the thumb drive from her pocket. Julian looked over them. "These are his personal notes. He approved you taking them?"

"He told me to knock myself out and get what I needed. I just tried calling him again, but he didn't answer."

Julian handed the items back to her and nodded. "I talked to him before you got here but after you spoke with him. He said you'd be coming by and that you needed paper files."

"And?" Ava tried to hold her civil expression. Why had he not said something earlier?

"And what?"

"Did he say where those files might be? I didn't see them in there."

Julian shook his head. "Said he wasn't sure where the files were." He closed the office door. "From the looks of his office, I'm surprised if he knows where the damn floor is."

Julian walked out with her.

"Ellis said you think the database was altered," he said.

Ava nodded. "Certain facts were changed, and some were left out completely."

"Hmm. And you really think someone changed the facts? You didn't just misremember?"

"No, I didn't misremember," she bit.

"He seems to think otherwise but wanted to err on the side of caution. He said to let you alone about it, but I think you need to slow down and concentrate on your own case back home. Don't try to connect dots that have nothing to do with each other. Your case and these are not connected or related."

"What if it's a serial killer?" She stopped and looked directly into his eyes.

"They don't typically travel almost three thousand miles to add to their body count." He pressed the button on his key fob. Headlights popped on, flashed, and the horn booped twice. He pointed at the car with the key. "That's me. You need a ride to the airport?"

"No, I'm taking a cab, but thanks for the offer."

Getting the thumb drive was a win-win. She would be able to better piece together her theories about the Housewife Murders, but she would be able to see what Jason had been up to over the previous twelve months. That glimpse into his life would allow her to get to know him better. Although it felt a bit stalkerish, she couldn't wait to get home and go over the contents of the drive with a glass of wine.

CHAPTER THREE

The Stress of Flying Commercial

THE DRIVE TO THE AIRPORT WAS UNNERVING AS THE CABBIE TRIED to circumnavigate the area of the earlier riot and took them down streets lined with tents assembled from tarpaulins, twine, boxes, and even dumpsters.

At every intersection, stop sign, and traffic light, someone would approach the cab and try to open the door, or they would bang on the windows while shouting, demanding money or sexual favors from Ava.

"I'm sorry," the cabbie said, making brief eye contact with Ava via the rearview mirror. "If I had known it would be this bad, I would have just taken you the opposite way."

"Just get us out of here. I'm already running late, and I can't miss my flight," Ava said, angry and sad at the same time.

THE WOMAN IN THE WINDOW

Why were there so many people on the streets? Where were the cops to clear them out? It had been a devolving scene when she had been in San Francisco on work assignment before, when she had first met Jason Ellis, but it had spiraled even further into the abyss since then. Now, it just seemed unsalvageable.

"I'm doing my best," the cabbie said in a tight voice.

By the time she arrived at the airport, Ava was frustrated bordering on angry.

The airport was busy, crowded, and very noisy with the constant chatter of a thousand different conversations, the announcements over the loudspeaker system, car horns bleating and blatting, and kids crying. Ava thought that if she missed her flight, she might join those bawling kids and just throw a fit.

Ava stepped to the counter after what seemed like hours. "I need to check in and get my boarding pass. I booked, paid, and chose my seat online, but the site isn't letting me check in."

The woman took Ava's information, gave her a tiny, measured smile, and cleared her throat lightly as she looked from her screen to Ava and back several times.

"Is something wrong?" Ava asked.

The boarding call for her flight sounded over the intercom system.

"Your seating arrangement..." The woman clacked away on the keyboard and then gave Ava another strange look.

"What about it? Window seat, over the wing. I already paid the fee and chose the seat. That's my flight." Ava pointed toward the other passengers heading to board.

"I'm sorry, I can't find your seating, but I do see the fee was paid. But it seems there was no seat chosen. I can put you closer to the front of the plane on an aisle seat."

"No. That's not what I paid for. Can you just try again?" Ava pulled her phone out and tried to get on the site again. The little spinning wheel of annoyance in the middle of the screen seemed stuck in an endless loop.

Ava lowered the phone, bit her lip, and looked toward the other passengers heading to their destination with their smiles of satisfaction. Why wouldn't they be satisfied? Everything had gone right for them, apparently. She glanced at the spinning wheel on her phone and then looked back to the departing people. A beautiful woman with bright red hair near the front of the line did not seem to be having a great time, either. Her cheeks were flushed crimson as she pressed a hand to her upper chest. She didn't wear a smile, and she was alone. So, maybe everything didn't go perfectly for everyone else. Was it horrible that such a thing brought a little solace? It was horrible, and it made her feel bad about herself as she looked back to her phone with doubled irritation.

"Oh," the woman said, her eyes registering mild panic before she looked to the other monitor screens on the counter. She looked to Ava and held up a finger. "I'm sorry, my computer just shut down. I don't know what happened."

"God, how long will this take?" She pulled in a breath and held it tightly in her chest.

"Just a moment, I'm sure. It's already coming back up." She smiled nervously.

"I really can't miss this flight." Of all days for this to happen, Ava thought angrily.

After a solid minute, the clerk's eyes brightened. "There it is. Okay, it's back up. Just one more minute while I navigate back..." Her words faded into nothingness as she scrambled to pull up the correct page again. Her eyes scanned the page, and she seemed confused. "Well, I don't know what happened, but here it is as if nothing happened. And it seems that you didn't choose a window seat, Ms. James."

"I did, and I paid for it. There was a fee."

The woman shook her head. "I'm sorry, but it seems you are at the front on an aisle seat. That's what you chose. Maybe you entered the wrong information—"

"I know what I chose, and I know I'm going to miss my flight if this isn't straightened out. Window seat over the left wing. Please. I don't want to miss my flight." She tried to keep a civil tone, but the situation was not making it easy. The plane would leave in less than thirty minutes, and she was stuck at the counter.

"I'm trying, but I can't give you that seat. Another passenger has taken it, and you can't just change your seat. I'm sorry."

Ava blew out a long breath and turned toward the security check line. Shaking her head, she turned back to the clerk. It wasn't the woman's fault. The site had been screwed up. Maybe her seat got changed due to the malfunction on the site. "Fine. I need to go."

The clerk smiled and printed the boarding pass. She held it out to Ava. "Thank you for flying—"

Ava was gone before the sentence could be finished. She hustled to the security check line, dumped everything into the bins, and silently screamed for the line to move swiftly.

Fifteen minutes later, she stood in the body scanner impatiently. Every second seemed an hour long as she imagined the plane rolling away to the takeoff strip.

THE WOMAN IN THE WINDOW

Grabbing everything from the bins, she didn't take time to put on her shoes before she set off at a trot to her gate. As she arrived, the last two passengers were boarding.

"Oh, you just made it," the man at the gate said, grinning as if he had just heard a great joke.

She gave him the boarding pass, dropped her shoes, and bent to pull them on. "Mix-up with the seating," she said.

"Never a good time," the man said. "Looks like you're all set."

Ava hurried to board, leaving the man as he was starting to give further instructions. She didn't need or want the little pre-flight pep-talk.

She walked down the aisle unable to resist glaring at the back of the man's head who had taken her seat at the window over the wing.

After cramming her bag into the overhead bin, a little rougher than was completely necessary, Ava dropped into her unwanted aisle seat. It was uncomfortable, and there was no way to make it comfortable enough for her to get any shut-eye.

Looking over to the passenger at the window, she saw the redhaired woman from the line. Her face was still flushed, and her hand was still pressed to her chest. She seemed out of breath, but her eyes were closed. Either she was collecting herself before takeoff, or she simply did not wish to be bothered with small talk.

That was perfect. If Ava tried to make polite conversation, she would end up grumbling about the seating mix-up, and no one wanted to listen to a total stranger bitch and moan about that for the first hour or two of their flight.

At least there was an empty seat between them. From the looks of the redhead, she didn't wish to be bothered. Maybe she wanted to sleep, too. Her eyes remained closed as the plane was pushed toward the strip for takeoff.

Once the plane was in the air, Ava turned to the woman once more, thinking she might ask if she would mind switching seats, but the woman seemed to have already fallen asleep.

Sighing, Ava looked around, forcing herself to see the silver lining—at least there was no one there to get up and down fifty times and crawl over her to get to the bathroom.

Maybe it wouldn't be so horrible to have the aisle seat after all.

CHAPTER FOUR

A Quiet Death

WITHIN THIRTY MINUTES OF TAKEOFF, THE STRESS AND STRAIN OF the last case caught up with Ava. Her attention refused to stay focused on the Housewife Murders, her odd call with Jason, or the murder case waiting for her back home.

She tensed the muscles in her calves, then in her thighs, then her gluteal muscles. Leaning slightly forward, she continued to tense and relax the muscles up her torso as discreetly as possible. Repeating the process a couple of times helped revive her a bit, and her eyes didn't droop for a few minutes.

Then they did.

The passengers were so still and mostly quiet that it seemed strange. Not one crying kid. No one passing by to go to the bathroom. No attendants walking by offering drinks or snacks with a smile.

Nothing to keep her alert.

Taking another look at the redhead, who seemed fast asleep, Ava yawned. It was a giant, ear-popping yawn. Five minutes later, she used a pillow to prop her head to the side and away from the aisle, but it was uncomfortable to face the sleeping woman. Struggling only a bit, she turned in the seat so she faced the aisle.

It didn't take long for her to fall into a doze, and then into a deep sleep.

Ava was in a dark alley. Confused, disoriented, she ran blindly. The heavy footsteps behind her drew closer. Her heart raced, her eyes darted side to side, up, down. There were no landmarks or visible signs, only more dark and intimidatingly unfamiliar landscape. She shunted to the side to miss a dumpster and her feet splashed in a deep puddle that covered the entire alleyway. She turned around to see who was chasing her, but saw nothing. The sound of the running footsteps continued as she stared into the blackness, the nothingness behind her. Terror pushed her into a dead run. The water under her feet grew deeper with each step until it was at her hips, pulling her, slowing her retreat from the monster at her back.

The bottom dropped out of the pavement, and the water sucked her down, down, down.

She fell with the waterfall. Maybe ten feet, maybe a hundred.

Landing on her feet in a field bordered by lush green trees, she spun to see that she was not alone. A man ran toward her from the shadows behind the trees, but she could make out none of his features. He looked like a charcoal sketch that had been smudged to nearly an unrecognizable smear on the paper. The knife he held was vivid as it glinted back sunlight into her eyes.

He was within arms' distance before she could get her feet moving again. He hit her in the back with the force of a freight train, and she was falling again. The ground rushed toward her with deadly speed, and she braced for impact.

"Oh, I'm sorry," a woman said.

Ava woke with a start, one hand on the armrest, the went to where her gun should have been. The flight. She was on the flight, and the smiling woman who had bumped into her was an in-flight attendant. Pretty, unassuming with dark-brown, loosely-curled hair, and light makeup.

She was safe. There was no pursuer with a smudged body and big, sharp knife glinting sunlight in her eyes.

Had she screamed?

Ava blinked a few times to clear her vision and looked around, but only a couple of the men seated close by seemed to have taken any notice of her at all. She exhaled deeply, glad she had not humiliated herself, and relaxed into the seat.

It took a couple of minutes for her heartrate to slow, but it finally did. A quick check of the time, and Ava was shocked to see that she was already nearly halfway through the flight. She hadn't meant to sleep that long but did feel more alert.

The redhead was still asleep as Ava made her way to the restroom. Upon her return, she noted that the woman was still asleep but her posture was odd. Wrong, in fact. After settling into her seat again, Ava turned and looked more closely at the woman. Nothing about the way she looked was normal. Her skin was ashen, and her head rested at too sharp of an angle.

"Hey, are you okay?" Ava asked in a low voice, not wishing to startle her from sleep.

The woman remained motionless.

"Ma'am? Are you okay?" she asked a bit louder.

There was no answer again.

Shifting in her seat, Ava reached across to gently shake the woman by the shoulder. "Hey, are you—"

The woman's head lolled so that she faced Ava. Her gorgeous red hair fell over one eye and cheek like a curtain. Her lips were pale red, and there was dried drool and what looked suspiciously like dried vomit down her chin, neck, and on the top of her blouse.

Every instinct screamed for Ava to call for emergency services—anyone who could help—doctors, nurses, medical personnel of any kind. But she was on a plane, soaring above the clouds in a metal tube full of regular, everyday people who might panic. It didn't matter. The woman was dead, and she had been for a while. Maybe ever since Ava had fallen asleep.

She looked around to see if the two men who had noticed her being startled awake had also taken notice of the situation. They had not. Expecting the worst, and hoping for the best, Ava put her fingers to the woman's neck to check for a pulse. Nothing but slightly warm, lifeless flesh met her fingers. She checked at the wrist just to make sure, but she knew there would be no pulse there even before she pressed her index and middle finger to it.

Leaving the woman sitting there was wrong, but what to do? Had any of the flight attendants dealt with a death during a flight before? Would any one of them not freak out and cause a panic among the passengers?

A slight and familiar odor wafted from the corpse. It was a smell that caused Ava's insides to recoil. Not decomposition, but something else. Something that caused a trauma response in her whole being. Was it the dried vomit? Where had she smelled that odor before, and what was it?

THE WOMAN IN THE WINDOW

Ava eased into the vacant middle seat, leaned a bit toward the woman, and inhaled slowly. Again, her first instinct was to recoil, but she didn't. She closed her eyes and inhaled again.

"Bitter almonds," a voice in her memories said. It was the voice of a doctor. *"Your grandma's breath smells like that because she is in diabetic ketoacidosis. Do you know what that is? Has anyone explained that to you?"*

Ava opened her eyes. Bitter almonds. Not the sweet almonds that were safe to eat, but the kind that could kill a person if ingested raw because they contained a chemical that the body broke down into cyanide.

Had the woman died of diabetic complications, as Ava's paternal grandmother had all those years ago when Ava was only seven and only slightly capable of understanding what had happened?

She looked at the woman's face. It had been completely flushed when she was alive. She had pressed her hand to her chest and acted as if she were having a difficult time breathing. She had not presented as a person with a severe headache, thirst, or severe stomach discomfort, and she had not gotten up to go to the restroom.

Ava remembered that her grandmother had made several trips to the toilet and had complained about the frequent urination. She had even made a joke or two about it that day while Ava was in the kitchen eating the chicken nuggets Grammy Andie had given her. Then the confusion had hit Grammy. She couldn't remember what she was doing from one minute to the next, where Grandpa was, or why Ava was there. That's when Ava became scared enough to use the phone without permission to call her mother.

The woman in the window seat had not seemed confused at all.

Grammy Andie had worn a medical alert necklace due to her diabetic condition.

The redhead wore no such necklace or bracelet. That didn't mean she wasn't diabetic, just that she didn't have a medical alert necklace for it. Many people refuse to wear them as they think it's an outward proclamation of some weakness.

Reluctantly, Ava leaned close enough to check the woman's fingertips for signs that she often checked her blood sugar levels. She saw nothing but a slightly chipped fingernail on her left pinky.

There was another possibility, but Ava didn't want to think about it. Surely it wasn't necessary.

She eased back into her own seat and glanced casually around at the other passengers. They were all absorbed in their own activities. She kept looking to see if anyone glanced in her direction. No one did.

Flushed face. Shortness of breath. Possible weakness that had mimicked exhaustion. Dried vomit and drool. The distinct bitter, fruity odor.

Cyanide.

Why would someone poison the pretty redhead with cyanide? Could it even be possible? Really?

CHAPTER FIVE

Risky Revelation at 36,000-feet

NONE OF THE PASSENGERS LOOKED GUILTY.
Would a killer even still be on the plane?
Every passenger looked like a normal person going about their normal lives. But there were only three ways to introduce cyanide into a human body: gas, injectable, and a powder/crystal form to put in foods or drinks the victim would ingest. If the poison had been introduced through a gaseous form, there would have been more than one victim. Ava would not have been alive to analyze the situation given her proximity to the redhead. As for injections, the woman would have noticed someone injecting her, and she would have put up some sort of fight, or she would have immediately alerted everyone.

That left the powdered or crystalized form in food or drink. Something the victim would have ingested willingly.

Turning to scan the redhead's seat again, Ava noted that there were no signs of a drink or snack anywhere. Her purse sat on the floor, and the top was slightly open. There were no signs of food or drink in it, either.

Ava held a tissue and reached for the woman's purse, but she stopped while her hand was only inches away from it. If it was cyanide poisoning, she didn't want to touch anything. The poison could be absorbed through the skin.

Her insides tightened and fear prickled along her skin in the form of cold chills. She had touched the victim's neck and wrist to check for a pulse. Had she inadvertently come into contact with a poisonous substance? By trying to do the right thing, had she doomed herself?

Grabbing hand wipes from her pocket, Ava scrubbed at her hands as she tried desperately to keep her racing mind in check.

The four flight attendants—three female, one male—seemed like normal people, with the exception of their jobs.

She rolled the handwipe in the tissue and then placed both inside the plastic wipe container.

Motioning to the attendant who seemed to be the oldest and have the most professional poise, Ava moved to the back of the seating area, hoping no one would notice the dead woman.

The attendant looked her up and down quickly. They were trained to make snap judgments about situations and people. Ava did the same thing, made the same quick assessments in her job every single day.

"Yes? May I help you with something?" the woman asked politely.

Ava looked to her nametag. Riley. She nodded and stepped close. "Riley, I need to speak to you about a situation. I'm a federal agent, and something has happened to the lady seated with me."

Riley's eyes widened, and she peered over Ava's shoulder. Ava took Riley's arm and blocked her view with her body.

"Please, don't draw attention. The woman in the window seat..." Ava moved her farther from the passengers, lowered her voice to a whisper, and said, "That woman has died, and I need you to keep calm. We don't want to panic the others."

Riley struggled for only the briefest moment, but she caught her composure admirably quick under the circumstances.

"The captain," Riley stammered in a whisper. "We need to tell him. Now."

Ava agreed. "Let's go."

Captain Bryce Sparks took the news better than Riley had, but only slightly. "I've been a pilot for almost twenty years, and I've never dealt with this personally. We need to inform the passengers and then move the body."

"No," Ava said. "If there has been foul play, if this is a homicide, the body shouldn't be moved."

"I can't leave a corpse in the passenger seating area. That's ridiculous. We'll preserve the seating area and do what is necessary to—"

"I can't do that, and I can't allow you to do that," Ava said. "She might have been murdered. That means the murderer could be one of the passengers. If we move the body, the killer could compromise any evidence of his or her crime."

"You mean there's a murderer on the plane?" Riley asked, her voice rising in pitch with the onset of fear.

"I'm saying that I don't know, but we need to leave everything just as it is to keep from contaminating a crime scene."

"Are there signs of foul play?" Captain Sparks asked. "Blood, visible wounds...Why do you think foul play, Agent James?"

For a terrible moment, Ava was torn between telling them what she really thought and just playing the FBI card to try bullying her way through the situation. Which would be worse? Which would cause the most panic and fear? The crew needed to be as calm as possible and have as much information as possible for the safety of everyone.

"I think she might have been poisoned. Possibly before boarding, but I can't say for sure," Ava said in a rush.

The captain's eyes widened to comical proportions and then immediately dropped back to normal as he shook his head. "That's ridiculous. She probably had a pre-existing medical condition. Most likely, it was a heart attack or a stroke, but not poisoning." A touch of humor licked the comment.

"Yeah, who poisons anyone these days?" Riley asked, trying on a scathing half-smile of disbelief that didn't match the concern in her eyes.

"You'd be surprised," Ava said. She could have added that people are downright genius at coming up with strange and unusual ways of killing each other. The human race had gotten it down to an art form millennia ago. "We're not moving the body unless it becomes absolutely necessary. We can move some of the passengers to empty seats farther away so they don't have to be close to it."

"Move passengers around?" Captain Sparks asked as if he had never considered such a thing.

"Yes. I'll stay close to the body to make sure nothing is touched," Ava said.

Sparks heaved a sigh and rubbed his cheeks. "Fine. Tell the other attendants while I get the crew up to date and then we'll tell the passengers. I have to call my superiors for instructions as well."

"Take care of your business, and Riley and I will take care of the attendants and any preparations we might need to make in case of a panic situation," Ava said, looking to Riley for confirmation that she was behind the plan.

Riley nodded.

Sparks agreed, looking as if he had aged twenty years in five minutes.

Riley led Ava to the other attendants and motioned for them to follow her back into the first-class section and into the galley.

"Everyone, this is Agent Ava James. She's with the FBI. We have a situation, and we need to keep very, very calm." Riley looked to Ava.

"What's going on?" the male attendant asked in a low voice.

"Are we being taken over by terrorists?" a woman with long, straight, black hair asked. Her nearly black eyes grew round and filled with terror.

"No, no," Ava said, holding out her hands to quiet the group. "Please, we need to be completely calm. A passenger has died, and I believe there might have been foul play. I can't stay here long. I need to be back there with her, so please, get hold of yourselves."

Oddly, one of the attendants asked no questions, and she made very little eye contact. She seemed to shrink in on herself. She had bumped Ava earlier and made a quick apology as she moved away.

"She was murdered?" the man asked in a shocked whisper. "I'm just training. I didn't sign up for flying with a murderer. I don't think I can do this."

"We don't know for sure, but the captain is going to be out soon so we can make the announcement to the passengers. I need all of you to keep your cool and help calm them. Also, we need to move some of the closer passengers to the empty seats elsewhere on the plane."

"There are over a hundred passengers on board," the man said. "twelve are already in first-class."

Ava nodded. "We need to move the passengers near her. Just get it done as per the captain's orders when he comes out. I need to get your names as well." She pointed to the man.

"Terry Carr."

The black-haired lady was next. "Asa Berry."

"Tanzy Bruner," the nervous woman said without making direct eye contact.

"I'm Riley Moss."

Ava nodded again, looking at each attendant and silently repeating their names. "I need to get back to my seat for now. The captain will be out shortly. I need you to gather sheets and cords so I can make a blind around the scene after the announcement. Leave the items here in the galley within easy reach." She headed back to her seat, hoping the attendants would keep their wits and not provoke an all-out panic. With so many passengers, it would be disastrous.

As she walked down the aisle to her seat, she felt eyes on her. People wondered what was up, what was going on that took all the attendants out of their sight, and a slight rumbling of whispers spread behind Ava as she sat again.

CHAPTER SIX

Crime-Scene in the Sky

F IFTEEN MINUTES AFTER THE PASSENGERS LEARNED ABOUT THE dead woman, Ava helped the last woman who needed to move.

The elderly lady gripped the tops of the seats with gnarly, arthritis-riddled hands as she moved forward a few inches at a time. "I've been flying this route for years, and I've never seen this kind of situation. I'm sixty-two in a few months, and I don't move so fast anymore." She exhaled deeply and turned her head away from the dead woman as they passed. "Terrible, terrible business," the woman grumbled as they slowly made their way forward.

"Yes, it is terrible," Ava agreed. At least the old lady would be able to fly the rest of the way in the comfort of first-class, and Ava was pretty sure she could mark the woman off the suspect list.

THE WOMAN IN THE WINDOW

Back at the scene, Riley and Terry stood in the aisle holding sheets and canvas straps.

"This is all we could find," Terry said, handing her the straps.

"It will work. Thank you." She took the straps and laid the sheets on the arm of her seat.

Terry tied the strap quickly and in silence. One end was tied to the overhead bin so the sheet could hang down like a curtain. His ashen face belied the stress swirling under the surface of his professional composure.

"It's going to take at least four sheets. Be sure they hang all the way to the floor, and don't flap them. We don't want to disturb any evidence."

Riley helped with the sheets, and in a matter of minutes, the scene was covered, and hopefully would remain unchanged until they reached their destination.

"Riley, did the captain say where we were landing?"

She shook her head.

"Who's getting the passenger list for me?" Ava asked.

"I think Asa was getting it," Terry said.

Riley nodded. "She is. Tanzy is collecting herself, probably in the restroom."

The captain appeared behind Terry from the first-class section. He motioned to Ava. "Could you come to the cockpit for a minute?"

"I shouldn't leave the scene unattended anymore."

"Riley can watch it," he said. "It's important."

Ava looked at Riley. "No one can touch anything behind these sheets. I don't even want anyone walking past. Instruct them to use the other aisle if they try."

"I'll do my best. Please, hurry, though."

Ava followed Sparks to the cockpit. He shut the door. "My superiors instructed me to land in DC as planned."

"Okay," Ava said, making it sound more like a question than a statement. She had left the crime scene under the watch of a flight attendant after the passengers all learned that there had been a possible murder on the plane. Chaos could erupt at any moment, and Riley wasn't trained in how to handle such a situation. None of them were, with the possible exception of Captain Sparks, who presented as an ex-military man whether he was or not.

"There will be federal agents at the airport when we land. They're waiting for the body."

"Wait, how did they even know who she was? Who called the FBI?"

"I told them who she was, but I didn't call them. They contacted me right after I informed my superiors of the situation."

"You know the dead woman?"

"No, but I have access to the passenger names."

"Did they give their names? Metford, Rossi, Dane, Santos, Ashton? Any of those ring a bell?"

Sparks shook his head as she spoke the names in rapid succession. "They didn't give names."

"I want to speak with them. Maybe it's my team," she said. "What is the dead woman's name, anyway? I'm waiting on a list of names, but if you know it..."

"Covey Cahill."

"And did the FBI say why they were so interested in Covey Cahill?"

He stared at her for a moment and then gave a slight nod. "I think it's best if you spoke directly with them. That's why I wanted you to come in here." Sparks raised the airport in DC and asked to speak with the federal agents. He nodded and thanked someone, and then turned to Ava. "They'll contact me in a few minutes."

Only a minute passed before they contacted him and he handed over communication to Ava. "Hello?" Ava asked.

"Is this Special Agent Aviva James?" a man asked in a monotone.

Ava gave him the required information to confirm her identity.

"Do you have more information for us, Agent James?" the man, who introduced himself as Tyler Bale, asked.

"No, I was hoping you could fill me in on what's going on. Captain Sparks said you were waiting at the airport in DC for the dead woman."

"That would be correct, Agent. What is there to fill you in on?"

"Why are you so interested in Covey Cahill? How did you know she was even on this flight? In short, what's going on? I think I should know given I am also FBI, and I'm trying to contain and assess this situation alone."

Bale cleared his throat, and for a minute, Ava thought he was getting ready to give her the details. "Agent James, I can't give any details at this time. Just know that we are here, waiting to take possession of the body and to fully investigate the situation. What we need from you is that you do everything in your power to keep the scene secure and closely watch the flight attendants and the passengers."

"And that's all you're going to tell me?"

"That's all I can tell you for now."

"If I'm keeping the scene secure and watching everyone aboard the flight, is it safe to assume that you believe Covey Cahill was murdered?"

The silence was long enough that Ava thought he might have disconnected.

"Agent Bale?"

"Yes?"

"Is there a murderer aboard this flight? How much danger are we in?"

"The victim was in peak physical condition, and it's likely she was murdered because of the trial she was set to testify at. That's really all I can divulge. Keep the scene secure and watch everyone. Everyone on that flight is a potential suspect at this point."

"Everyone? You realize that's like a hundred people, not including the pilot, co-pilot, three attendants, and one in training, right?"

"I do. We'll speak further once you arrive in DC."

She and Sparks made eye contact, and she groaned. "I guess you heard that?"

He nodded. "Dire lack of details from them, but it doesn't surprise me."

"Those details might have come in handy. I'm moving forward under the assumption that a killer is among the passengers. How long until we land?"

"About ninety minutes now," Sparks said as he returned to his seat.

Frustrated with the lack of information, Ava headed back to the scene. Bale had said she needed to watch everyone, including the attendants. What kind of trial had Covey been set to testify at? Who was of such high profile that they would resort to poisoning a witness to prevent her from testifying? Many criminals might wish to do such a thing to save their own skin, but having the reach, the power, the money to actually carry out the deed was in a whole different league.

CHAPTER SEVEN

The Last Leg of the Flight

AVA SAT ACROSS THE AISLE FROM COVEY CAHILL. THE PASSENGERS sat subdued in their seats. The atmosphere inside the cabin was tense. If she stood and turned around, Ava could see almost everyone with the exception of the ones in first-class and some of the crew.

She looked toward the white sheets shrouding Covey's body. The name meant nothing to Ava. She had heard of no high-profile cases, either, but there had to be one. And soon.

Was Covey Cahill even the victim's real name? It was possible that she had been in witness protection whereby she had been issued a new identity. That opened a door to even more possibilities. Not good ones. If she was in witness protection, someone had known where she would be, what she looked like, and/or which flight she would board. How else had the poison been administered?

None of the passengers had been affected by whatever means was used to kill Covey, and Ava couldn't be a hundred-percent sure that means was poison, although all the current evidence pointed to that conclusion.

Ava stood to look over the passengers. If one of them was the killer, surely something in their expression or body language would give some hint. She scanned faces of men and women, young, old, and every age in between. Each person wore some kind of expression ranging from fear to agitation mixed with suspicion. Given the news they had received only a short time before, it was no wonder.

Asa Berry came down the aisle clutching papers to her chest. Her smile twitched when she stopped. "The list you asked for." She held out the papers.

"Thank you."

"It won't be perfect." She cocked one eyebrow and pursed her lips.

"What do you mean? I thought the seating was with the names." Ava looked at the list and saw that they indeed were there.

"But you moved more than a dozen people, and we didn't think to record which passenger went to which seat, so it's only going to be partially correct. And there was such confusion for a while…" She shrugged. "Who knows if anyone else moved seats?"

"It's fine, Asa. Really. If I need to know who someone is, I'll just ask them to see their ID. This was just a way to get their names and seats without causing them more stress than they're already under."

Asa looked doubtful but nodded anyway. "If that's all you needed, I'm going to go around and offer drinks and snacks. We still have a while before we land."

"That sounds great. Thank you, Asa. Just no alcoholic drinks."

Asa shook her head. "No. I think the last thing this whole situation needs is for the passengers to be getting lit right before we land."

Grinning, Ava nodded. "Right, you are."

A couple in the middle row of seats about midway from the back intently watched the exchange between Ava and Asa. Their keen interest waned only a little after Asa walked away and they kept their eyes on Ava and the paper.

She made a mental note of the couple, if they were indeed a couple, in their thirties in the center of the cabin.

A bald man at the back broke eye contact with Ava as soon as she glanced up at him. He dragged his palm down his cheek and across his mouth as he turned his head to the side.

Ava looked at the list. His seat was listed as unoccupied. He was one of the relocated passengers.

Her gaze flitted over the couple, and they were staring at her closely again. Despite her instincts screaming for her to make direct eye contact, she did not. She continued until she found their names. Simone and Dino Hunt. They were a couple.

Tanzy emerged from the restroom wringing her hands. Her gaze darted and flitted everywhere as if she were searching for someone. No one looked at her, or even in her direction except Ava, and it seemed that the attendant purposely avoided looking back at her. Tanzy adjusted the neck of her blouse and then tugged at the blazer. Her face was ashen, but her hands were ruddy.

From the incessant wringing, Ava thought.

Why was she so nervous? What had taken her so long in the restroom? Was she sick? Had she been exposed to whatever chemical had killed Covey. Ava was certain in her own mind that Covey had been somehow poisoned. If, as she suspected, the killer dosed Covey with cyanide, was it possible that he had put it in food or drink that Covey had been exposed to? If so, perhaps Tanzy had been inadvertently exposed by handling the item.

That didn't work. Tanzy would have shown symptoms much sooner, and they would have been more aggressive than a pale face and a bad case of nerves. Tanzy was nervous-natured, obviously. Most likely that was all that was wrong with her.

In addition to the overtly nervous and hyper-alert three passengers, there were three who seemed to have no emotion at all about the goings-on. A man in his late fifties near the front, a much younger man, possibly in his early twenties seated near the back, and a woman in her mid-to-late-forties at the front. The paper had them listed as Ralph Cox, Garrett Cobb, and Fran Mills, respectively.

Ava placed a dash next to their names to represent their lack of emotion. Beside the Hunts' names, she placed two dots each—a device so she would remember that they were hyper-vigilant. The bald man in the back was the only suspicious party to which she couldn't immediately fix a name.

If she asked to see his ID, she would need to ask several other people to see theirs. If he was the killer, she didn't want to tip him off that she was onto him, or give him any reason to think that she suspected him of anything untoward.

For the moment, she searched the seating chart for seats that should have been vacant but were not and made notations. Afterward, she moved to first-class and noted the passengers who had moved there. Three of them, she remembered, because she was the one who'd moved them. Going back to the chart, she put names with the new seating arrangement.

A man in the row closest to Ava and the victim motioned.

Ava folded the papers with the writing to the inside as she approached him. "Yes, sir?"

"Are we going to land on-schedule? I have an appointment soon after arrival."

"We are approaching the airport within the next thirty minutes," she said. Which was technically true. But that didn't mean that the passengers were going to be free to leave as normal. They'd be held for who knows how long to ensure everything was clear.

Telling him that he was going to miss his appointment would likely cause an uproar with most of the passengers getting involved and yelling about missed appointments and how they had nothing to do with the death. Then there would be the inevitable groans of unfair treatment of the innocent. No one wanted to be delayed indefinitely, but it would be unavoidable. Everyone on the plane was a suspect until the FBI could clear their names with certainty.

Ava gave him a measured smile and stepped back to her seat, where she perched on the edge and faced the aisle.

"Do you know who killed her?" a woman asked from the far side of the cabin. Although she was standing when Ava looked over, the woman's head barely cleared the backs of the seats.

"Ma'am, please remain in your seat until we land."

"We just want to know. We have a right," a man from the other side interjected.

Agreement rumbled through the group. The Hunts didn't add anything, but they simultaneously looked from Ava to the short woman who still stood in the aisle. The emotionless woman at the front gave no sign that she even heard what was going on. Her attention was on her hands in her lap.

"She's in the same boat as the rest of us," Graham Cobb spoke up. "She doesn't have any idea what happened. The woman probably just had a heart attack, or a stroke."

"That doesn't happen from normal travel," an older woman scolded. "She's been murdered."

"Did you see someone kill her?" Cobb asked. "No, you didn't. None of us did."

"Don't be rude, young man," a man in his forties warned. He turned in his seat to eye Cobb.

"Why don't you piss off and mind your own business?" Cobb retorted, glaring at the man.

Ava stood. "All right, everyone. Let's stop. Fighting and arguing isn't going to help anyone. This will all get sorted out after we land." She nodded to the short woman. "Ma'am, please sit."

"Who are you to tell any of us what to do?" Cobb asked snidely.

"I am Special Agent Aviva James of the FBI, Mr. Cobb, and I am asking you to refrain from instigating any further upheaval."

"Screw you, Special Agent. I didn't instigate anything, and I'm pretty sure I still have a little right called Freedom of Speech."

"I didn't say you couldn't talk. I don't want you causing any trouble." What happened to his unemotional poise all through the situation? Where was that calm, stoic exterior that seemed to not register there had been a death a few seats from him?

The captain came across the speakers to announce their approach to the airport.

The attendants made their way to the front of the cabin, asking that every passenger take their seats and belt up for landing. Tanzy made her way into first-class, and Riley went in behind her.

Ava waited until all the passengers were in the process of complying with the instructions before she sat and belted up. It was a relief that she would soon have backup.

CHAPTER EIGHT

Landing

FEDERAL AGENTS AND UNIFORMED COPS CAME ABOARD AS SOON AS the plane landed. Most of the passengers were angry upon finding out they were going to be detained. Just as Ava had foreseen. Some of the passengers were pale and quiet as they followed orders.

Ava remained with the body even as the captain and co-pilot filed out the door.

A stern agent in his late thirties made his way toward Ava. His gaze flitted to the makeshift blind. "You're the agent I spoke with earlier?" he asked as his cold, analyzing gaze roamed the scene and over Ava.

"Special Agent Aviva James, yes. And you are?" Her gaze was as cold and analyzing as his. He was armed, his body was stiff as if ready to pounce into action, and his demeanor was less than welcoming.

"Special Agent Tyler Bale." He nodded toward the blind. "That's Covey Cahill?"

"Yes." Ava moved back so he could approach the body.

"What happened?" He stood in the aisle to appraise the body. "Did you touch her? Move her?" The three questions were rapid-fire and without eye contact.

"I thought she was asleep and then I realized something was wrong, so I nudged her arm. That's when she slipped to the position she's in now. I checked for a pulse at her neck and wrist. Other than that, she wasn't touched while I was awake."

"You were sitting here?" He pointed to the aisle seat.

"Yes."

"No one in the middle seat, correct?"

"The seat between us was empty."

"And you didn't see anyone touch her, approach her, and she never got up to use the restroom?" He glanced at Ava with an expression of disbelief.

"No."

He nodded once. "I need you to come with me." Motioning for her to walk out first, he stepped into the middle row of seats.

Outside, the other passengers were being corralled inside the airport. "Where are you taking them?" Ava asked.

"We have a waiting area cordoned off with agents and local police standing watch so no one leaves before they are questioned. Everyone must be interviewed."

"I have the seating chart, and I've marked a few passenger names of people who acted out of the ordinary after finding out about Covey's death." Ava showed him the paper as they walked toward the entrance of the airport.

Taking the paper, Agent Bale sighed. "Thank you. I already have all that information, though. I'll look at the passengers you marked first. Why did you mark them? What did they do to make you suspicious in the first place?"

"Some were hyper-vigilant, nervous, and even a bit combative while others were cold-fish about the entire thing. I just noticed their emotional reactions didn't match with what seemed in the normal range at the time and under the circumstances."

"Right." He put the paper in his pocket. "Let's get you questioned first. I have a feeling we'll be needing your help to expedite this situation." He turned the corner and pointed to a room. "Just go on in there and I'll get started out here."

Ava stepped into the room and gave her statement.

After twenty minutes, she stepped back out and looked for Agent Bale. Not seeing him, she approached another agent. "Agent Bale?" she asked.

"Bale is with the CSI team. They're getting ready to work the scene." He pointed outside to the plane.

Ava hurried out to meet them. Bale spotted her and held up a hand to motion her over.

"This is the agent who sat with her," he told the older man with the CSI unit.

"Doug Loudon," the man said, holding out his hand.

Ava shook with him. "Aviva James."

"Would you accompany me to the scene so I can get a better overview of what happened to the victim?"

"Of course." Ava walked ahead, and Bale walked behind. She stopped at the seat.

"Did you put up the sheets?" Loudon asked.

"Yes, I thought it would be a way to keep the passengers calmer and to preserve any evidence."

Bale walked past them in the other aisle to first-class.

"Good thinking. People have a real aversion to staring at a corpse for hours while they're trapped in a plane." Loudon stood much as Bale had earlier—in the aisle—to inspect the scene.

"I wasn't too keen on it myself," Ava admitted.

"Tell me what happened."

Ava related the story to him. "I fell asleep for a while, so I can't be certain no one came near her during that time, but when I woke up, I noticed something was very wrong with her. I think she was probably poisoned."

Loudon's eyes widened. "Oh? Why do you think that? From here, most people would assume heart attack, or some other medical problem."

Ava looked at Covey. "I don't think it was just poisoning. I think someone gave her cyanide. When I got close to her, I smelled the odor of bitter almonds. That's cyanide, right?"

Loudon blinked at her for a few seconds and then nodded. "Yes. Yes, it is, but most people can't smell that, and if they do, they don't know what it is, or they figure it's just something the person ate leaving the smell. How did you know what the smell was? Have you been around someone poisoned with cyanide before?" Loudon's expression registered suspicion.

"No. My grandmother was diabetic, and I was there when she went into diabetic ketoacidosis one time. The doctor told me what the smell was. As I got older, I learned that cyanide smells like bitter almonds..." She pursed her lips, hating that she was on the spot for having random knowledge that most people didn't possess.

"Then why wouldn't you think the victim died of diabetic complications instead of poison?"

"I wasn't sure why she died. I looked for a medical alert bracelet or necklace, and I didn't see one. That's what started my suspicion."

Bale came back from first-class. "Process the entire plane. We don't know but the perpetrator might've been aboard the whole time. If it was cyanide, there will be at least a trace somewhere. Everything in the galleys and bathrooms needs special attention. Agent James, I need to speak to you as soon as you're done here."

Loudon nodded but glared at the back of Bale's head as he made his way off the plane. Once he was out of earshot, Loudon blew air between his lips and shook his head. "That man can be infuriating telling me how to do my job, and I've been doing it since before he was out of diapers." He shook his head again and headed for the door. "We're done, Agent James. I'm going to get the team in here now. You can go see what he needs, if you like. Thank you for your insights."

"You're welcome. If you need anything else, just yell." She saw Bale walking toward the airport door again and jogged to catch up with him. "You wanted to talk to me?" she asked as she fell in step with him.

"You need to call and let anyone know where you are?"

"Just my boss," she said.

"Do that and then come find me inside."

Sal answered on the second ring. "Ava? Don't tell me you're going to be late coming back. We had an agreement, you know."

Ava pulled in a deep breath and braced. "Sal, I am going to be late but—"

"I need you here, Ava. I don't want to explain this whole situation to the suits just to get my ass chewed again." She groaned quickly and then added, "What happened? Are you all right?"

"I am, and I am in DC. At the airport—"

"Then what's the big deal? Of course, you'll be back in the office on time. You had me worried."

"You didn't let me finish. I'm going to be stuck at the airport for a while, looks like. There was a death on the plane, and it just happened to be the woman sitting next me."

"So, let DC police deal with it. Why's that going to detain you?"

"Because I think she was poisoned with cyanide, and she was a witness in some big, mysterious case. I'm with Special Agent Tyler Bale. It's one of his cases the victim was supposed to testify in."

Sal was quiet for a few seconds. "Okay. Okay, we can deal with this. Do you know what case?"

"No, Bale is pretty tight-lipped about all of it. I'm not even sure of the victim's real name. I suspect she was in witness protection."

"They didn't do a real good job, apparently. Okay, listen, keep me updated."

"I'll call you when I can. Thank you."

They hung up, and Ava went to find Bale inside. She didn't like chasing him around like a lost dog to find out what he wanted. Why couldn't he have just said it before she called Sal?

CHAPTER NINE

Getting the Low-Down

Agent Bale stood outside one of the impromptu interview rooms reading a paper. His jaw was set, his eyebrows bunched down and almost met over the bridge of his nose, and the deep lines in his face seemed even deeper.

Either the job had gotten to him and turned him into the sour-looking man who stood before her, or he had always looked like an angry person. Being part of the Bureau, Ava didn't find it hard to believe the former was true.

It didn't take too many years of dealing with the worst of society for it to leave its mark on an agent. She had plenty of marks, but so far, she had been lucky enough to avoid the wrinkles. Her marks were in the form of scars.

He glanced up as she approached. "That didn't take long. Done with all the phone calls so we can get to business, Agent James?"

After an extremely short internal debate on how to react to Bale's remark, Ava nodded. "Otherwise I wouldn't be standing here, right?" She pasted on a tight smile that she was certain looked more like a smirk. So be it. She had done nothing to earn Bale's sarcasm.

A short dry chuckle escaped as he nodded and made eye contact. "And she bites back. Good to know you have a backbone about you, Agent James."

"Likewise, Agent Bale," she said, holding back on other words that wanted to come out.

He tilted his head to indicate the passengers sitting in the waiting area across the corridor. "I would like to ask you to help interview the suspects. You were on the plane, although asleep through a good part of the flight, you still were there and might have some insights that will help us with the investigation."

Was that another jab? It wasn't camouflaged very well. "Then ask away," she said without a smile. If he was going to take jabs, she was going to insist on being asked to join the investigation.

"Don't be an ass. Either you will help, or you will not."

Another agent walked up to Bale and whispered something in his ear. Bale nodded.

Ava bit down hard to keep from retaliating.

The other agent walked away. Bale turned his attention back to Ava. He raised his eyebrows in question.

"What's the process? What are we concentrating on during the interviews?"

"Standard. Get their info, why they were on the plane, and find out if any of them saw or heard anything that might help us find Ms. Cahill's killer. We're running their background checks now, but it will take hours to get them all back. As the background checks come in, we'll clear them to leave if nothing stands out."

"Just let them walk out?"

"Yes. Is this your first rodeo? If there's no evidence pointing at them, they walk. We have nothing to hold them on, and we'll have all their info at that time. Pretty simple task."

"I was clarifying whom and when I should just let people walk out of the airport. I know my job as well as anyone else."

"I'll clarify for you: I will be personally clearing and releasing each and every suspect who is now seated across the hall from us. Each and every one." His voice was low, even, and almost monotone.

Was he being sarcastic again? Blunt? It would be a nightmare to work with him every day. "Thank you. Who do you want me to question? What's the order?"

He handed her a list of names. "I have divided them into groups of ten. I have men working these first two. You take the third group. When you finish, report back to me. If there are more to question, I'll assign you a new group then."

She took the paper. "What is really going on here? What trial was Covey Cahill going to testify at? I mean, if she was so important to the trial, why weren't there any agents assigned to her on the flight?"

"This isn't the time, Agent James."

"It's the perfect time," she said with conviction. "The more I know and understand, the more insight I'll have, and the better I can tailor my questions."

Bale stepped back and into the room, motioning for her to step inside. "Don't just stand there, get in here."

Ava stepped inside, and Bale shut the door behind her. "I'm just saying that it seems like Ms. Cahill might have had a better chance if there had been an agent with her."

He motioned for her to hush. His expression registered understanding and irritation simultaneously. "Jesus, do you always ask so many questions and give so many personal opinions?"

"Most of the time, yes." She crossed her arms, still clutching the list of names in one hand.

"What I tell you cannot leave this room. Do you understand?"

"Of course," Ava said.

"It's a case against a big crime syndicate here on the East Coast, but that's not the entirety of its reach. They're at least nationwide, and I suspect global, to an extent."

"Crime syndicate? Which one?"

He shook his head. "A very big one. Covey Cahill was our key witness. She was going to testify to things that would have taken the syndicate down. She knew things about the men and women who run the syndicate." He pointed upward. "All the way to the top. Do you know how rare that is?"

"Yeah, she's a unicorn. Or, she was until someone killed her," Ava said. "Which crime syndicate? How did she know so much?"

"Jesus, you and the questions. This isn't the Spanish Inquisition."

"Why was she in California when the trial was set on this coast? Where was the trial going to take place, anyway?"

"Here. In DC. And she was in California because that was as far away from the people she was going to testify against as we could possibly get her without leaving the country. We could keep her relatively safe out there."

"So, she was in witness protection?"

He nodded. "And we did kind of have an agent with her." He cocked one eyebrow at her.

"Well, who was it? Because he didn't do a thorough job."

He pointed at her.

"Me?" she asked. "I wasn't assigned to anyone or anything. I was on my way back to Fairhaven. To my field office and my job." Mild panic crept into her core. Had someone screwed up and not given her the orders?

"No, you weren't officially assigned to the case, but I had your seat changed so that you were sitting with Ms. Cahill and no one was seated between the two of you."

Ava was apoplectic. "What?" she asked angrily. "You mean, you're the reason I almost missed my flight completely? And you didn't even tell me what was going on? Why?"

"We wanted you there for Ms. Cahill's protection. Even though it obviously didn't work out as we had planned. We thought she would be safe on the flight as long as you were there. What agent would allow anyone to be harmed? We didn't think about all the ways someone could be killed, though. We expected outright retaliation against her. That's the syndicate's usual way of handling business. They hire someone to take out a target and make an example of them."

"That was a ridiculous and careless mistake. I should have been informed before I reached the airport even. Why would you just stick a random agent next to a key witness in a big case and hope for the best? Why wouldn't you send one of your own agents? You know, the ones who knew the whole story and maybe could have prevented her death?"

"Because we think there's a mole in the agency, and we wanted to keep it on a need-to-know basis. Someone keeps leaking vital information, and now, it seems they have leaked even the flight Ms. Cahill was going to be on. How else would she end up dead? I'm sure it wasn't a heart attack, or any other natural cause. She was in great health. After the incident that led up to her turning on the syndicate, her health has been monitored regularly by doctors who do periodic checkups to make sure she isn't having any issues."

Ava shook her head. "What incident? What issues could she have developed?"

"It's a long story, and we need to get these suspects questioned before I'm old enough to retire." He motioned toward the door. "Remember, this all stays confidential. I don't know who the mole is, and I don't want them knowing how much you know, or you could become a liability to the case." He held the doorknob and looked at her.

"What?" she asked, still upset that she hadn't known she was Ms. Cahill's protection.

"Do you understand?"

"Yes, I do understand. I also understand that if you had informed me, if I had known, or even had a clue that I was supposed to be protecting Ms. Cahill, I might have kept the woman safe. She might not be dead." She glared up at him.

"You're not wrong. You didn't keep her safe, and that's as much my fault as anyone's, but the next best thing you can do is help us catch whoever killed her. Right?"

Without a moment's hesitation, Ava nodded.

He opened the door. "Good. At least we can agree on that."

That was one thing they did agree on. Outside of the job at hand, there wouldn't be much else she would agree with him on. He was a disagreeable person from what she had seen, and there were so many holes in his plan to keep Covey Cahill safe that she didn't see how he could make such rookie mistakes.

She looked at the names on the list and headed across the way to the seating area.

CHAPTER TEN

Gathering Information

Ava was glad to see that Buck Perron was first on her list of interviewees. The nervous, bald man from the back of the economy seats who had raised her suspicions early on. His overtly nervous demeanor had not calmed any since getting off the flight. If anything, the fidgeting had grown worse.

"What are we doing here?" he asked as soon as they were in the room. "I didn't do anything wrong. I'm a good person. Mind my own business and make sure to follow all the rules. I don't understand this."

"Mr. Perron, a woman died on our flight—"

"And I'm real sorry about that. I am, but I had nothing to do with it, and I have a family waiting on me at home. I've been gone for work for over a week now. I don't understand why I'm still here and being questioned about something I had nothing to do with. It's not right."

"Actually, it's procedure. If you had nothing to do with the death, then you have nothing to worry about. We're just following procedure here. We have to question everyone who was on that flight."

"What about you? You were on the flight, too. Yet here we are on opposite sides of the table."

"I was questioned already, Mr. Perron. I understand you want to get home to your family, and answering my questions honestly and quickly will ensure that you are cleared soon so you can be on your way."

He nodded aggressively and made a rolling gesture with his hands. "Then, let's get on with it. I can leave after this, right?"

"As soon as your background check is cleared by Agent Bale, yes."

"How long will that take?" he asked incredulously.

"I don't have an answer for that, but the sooner we're done in here, the sooner your information will be run through the system."

"What do you want to know?"

"Why were you on the flight from San Francisco to DC, Mr. Perron?"

"I told you, I was coming home from work."

Ava continued to ask questions, and Buck Perron continued to spit out short, sharp answers. Hopefully, every interview would go as smoothly.

"We're done?" he asked at the end.

"Yes, we are, but remember, you have to wait for Agent Bale to tell you it's okay to leave. It might take some time yet for that to happen."

"What you're saying is that I'm going to be here a while?"

"Unfortunately, that might be the case." She walked out with him and called the next person.

Garrett Cobb, Mr. Combative Smart-Mouth himself was next on her list.

Garrett sat heavily in the seat and looked at her with disdain. "You can't keep us all here like this. It's not legal."

"Actually, it is, Mr. Cobb. We're investigating a death. We can do what is necessary."

"I didn't know that woman, and I had nothing to do with her dying on the plane, so why am I being questioned like a suspect?"

"Because you are a suspect. Everyone on the plane is a suspect right now, if that makes you feel any better about your situation."

"It doesn't. The last thing I need is to be questioned by another suspect." He pointed at her. "Last time I checked, you were right there with the rest of us, so why are you questioning anyone?"

"Because I'm a federal agent." She could have been softer with the answer, but she didn't feel it necessary given his proclivities toward incivility. He had caused enough trouble on the plane, and she was not going to allow it in the interview room.

"Well, little miss Agent, you will all be hearing from my lawyer if I'm not out of this airport in the next half-hour." He gave her a haughty look as if he had just administered the threat that would make her quake in her shoes.

"That's your privilege, but it will do you no good. You're stuck here just like everybody else: until we get your background cleared."

"What does my background have to do with anything?"

For the first time, that high and mighty expression of his quivered and almost vanished.

"Got something to hide, Mr. Cobb?" She smiled.

"Absolutely not," he said as his voice lost volume steadily. His gaze dropped toward the table. "No, I don't have anything to hide."

"Well, then you have nothing to worry about." She asked her questions quickly, without giving him time to think overly much about them. What did he have to hide? Something would show up on his background check, she was sure of it.

"Now, Mr. Cobb, did you see anyone approach the victim at any time?"

"You mean other than you and the stewardesses? No, I didn't see anyone do anything to her."

"Which flight attendant approached her, and when?"

"I don't know who she was. It was the brunette. You were in the seat. Didn't you see her? Were you sleeping that hard?"

Ava recalled Tanzy bumping into her with the cart and making an apology as she hurried away. "What did she do exactly?"

"I don't know. I was coming back from the bathroom. I saw her lean over you, stand back up, and then I was in my seat again. Next thing I know, there's a ruckus about a dead woman."

"Thank you, Mr. Cobb." Ava's mind raced. Why hadn't Tanzy said anything about Ms. Cahill? Had she seen the woman was dead? Had she simply panicked? Had she done something to the victim?

Ava had moved to the door with her mind running in high gear. She opened the door. "You can take your seat out there now."

"We're done? Just like that?" He stood, scoffed, flipped his suit jacket into place and strode out.

Ava made notes about Tanzy and included every detail she recalled of the situation. She called the next six interviewees. Two of them saw Tanzy lean over Ava, but no one saw her actually do anything to Ms. Cahill.

The ninth and tenth suspects were flight attendants. Riley Moss and Asa Berry.

"Riley?" Ava said, motioning for her to come to the room.

"I've already been questioned," Riley said as she caught up. "So has Asa."

"Who questioned you?"

"Agent Lin." She pointed toward one of the other interview rooms. "He's in there, if you need confirmation."

Ava shook her head and sighed. What happened to following the list and the marked groupings? "He questioned both of you?"

Riley nodded. "I was first, Asa was next. She's been done for about forty minutes now."

Ava stopped just outside her door. "Wait here. Do you mind if I ask you and Asa some questions? Since your interviews are already done, I just have a few questions that I think only you two and Terry could answer."

"Terry was just taken to one of the other rooms, but I'm okay with answering more questions. Anything beats sitting out there listening to everybody moan and gripe about being stuck here."

Ava called for Asa and took her back to the room. She agreed with Riley: anything was better than sitting out there with the grumpy passengers.

"I just wanted to ask about Tanzy Bruner. How well do either of you know her?"

Riley and Asa exchanged a brief look.

Riley leaned forward. "She's not new, but she's new to us. Or, rather, we don't know her very well. She exchanged flights with Melissa Rockford, our regular third attendant."

"I think she might still be training, or something," Asa added.

"She's not," Riley said. "She's just a nervous klutz. I wish Melissa hadn't agreed to switch with her, to be honest."

"Do you know her story? Anything else about her at all?" Ava asked.

"Just that. And, she's very quiet and private. She never speaks unless spoken to. I know a lot of people like that sort of thing, but not me. It's annoying, and I have to wonder how well she's taking care of passengers when I'm not standing there prodding her to conversate and smile at them."

"Why all the questions about Tanzy? Did she do something?" Asa asked.

"Did either of you see her check on the victim at any time during the flight?"

THE WOMAN IN THE WINDOW

"I saw her bump you with her cart," Asa said. "I wanted to say something about it to her, but it's not my place. Besides, she took the cart to the other galley and stayed in there for a long time. When I walked back there, she was pale as milk. I figured she felt bad enough for what she did. She seems awfully shy. I don't know how she does this job with her personality."

"Okay, thank you both," Ava said. "I'm sorry, but I have to toss you back out into the crowd of upset passengers now."

Both ladies huffed as they stood, but before they left the room, they wore nearly identical expressions of poise, confidence, and friendliness. It came along with being in the service industry, and it inspired Ava's admiration.

Looking over the interview notes, no one stood out. It was a bunch of people who were going about their normal everyday lives when something out of the ordinary happened and catapulted their routines into chaos.

Opening the door to take the notes to Bale, it seemed that routines weren't the only things thrust into chaos. The passengers had become even more agitated. Many of them stood even though the officers asked them repeatedly to take their seats.

"Hey, everybody hold it down," Ava said loudly as she approached the spiraling situation. "Nobody's going anywhere just yet. We'll have your backgrounds cleared as soon as possible, and you'll be released according to the order in which we receive them."

"Yeah, well, nobody here killed anyone," a man said.

"So, why are we having to wait? We already gave all our information," another man said.

"It's not like you don't know where we live, work, and eat," a woman said.

"We have jobs, believe it or not," another said.

"None of us even saw the woman in distress," a woman yelled from the back. "Some of us didn't even see her at all. She probably died peacefully in her sleep from some medical issue."

"Heart attack, most likely," another said.

"And there was obviously no gunshot or knife attack," someone else yelled. "So, you can't really keep us when you don't even know how she died."

"And we know all this. But, yes, we can, and we will keep you here for a while longer," Ava said loud enough to be heard clearly over the din of grumbles. "This situation is stressful enough, but if you don't cooperate, it's going to get even more stressful. Keep in mind that this is a federal investigation and that each of you is a suspect in a murder until we clear you. Act accordingly. This will be over soon enough, and you can get on with your lives."

The crowd settled, but only very slightly.

CHAPTER ELEVEN

The Searches

B ALE HAD FINISHED WITH HIS INTERVIEWS AND HAD GONE TO THE other room where the computers were set up. A two-man team was on the computers.

"What is it, James?" Bale asked when she knocked at the open door.

"The interviews." She held out the papers.

"Is there a problem with them?" Bale walked to her and took the papers.

"No. I finished my group. The last two had already been questioned by Agent Lin, but I asked them some follow-up questions."

"Why would you do that? That's wasting time we don't have to waste."

"The last two were Riley Moss and Asa Berry, two flight attendants—"

"What does that have to do with anything? Did you find out something about them you want to share?"

Now who was asking questions like it was the Spanish Inquisition? "I had questions about the other female flight attendant. Some of the passengers saw her lean over me before she bumped me with the cart and woke me up. I wanted to know what her story was and what they knew about her."

"And what did you find out?" He pursed his lips and tilted his head.

"That she was very quiet and private. She's a bit of a nervous klutz, and she wasn't even supposed to be on that flight. She switched flights last-minute with Melissa Rockford."

Another agent walked into the room holding out papers. "I'm finished with the last on my list, boss. What do you want me to do now?"

"Agent Lin, this is Agent James," Bale said. He moved to the doorway. "Now that we all know each other, let's go into the other room."

Ava and Lin followed Bale into his interview room where he shut the door and offered them seats.

"You didn't see anything during the flight?" Lin asked Ava as they sat.

"Nothing out of the ordinary, no. Nothing. I almost missed my flight because my seating was messed with." She shot Bale a glance. "I was the last one on the plane, and I barely made it. I think whatever happened to Ms. Cahill happened just before she boarded, or just before I boarded. It's a pretty short window of opportunity."

Lin scowled at the floor. "A short window of time is all that's needed in most cases." He looked at Bale.

"Especially to administer a poison," Bale said.

Ava looked at him sharply. "You think she was poisoned, too?"

"We've discussed it," he replied, nodding to Lin.

"Are you familiar with the case of Richard Kuklinski?" Lin asked.

"The Iceman?" she asked.

Lin nodded. "That's him. He didn't need but a few seconds to kill someone, and he would do it in public. Didn't matter if it was day or night, or the setting."

"He claimed he used cyanide solution spray and it was his favorite method of killing," Ava said.

"Right," Lin agreed. "He only needed to get close to the victim, and the deadly poison was introduced within seconds. He could keep on moving past them, and virtually no one saw what happened. The victim would mysteriously die soon after, and he was long gone from the scene."

"Do you think that's what happened to Covey Cahill? The crime syndicate hired a hitman to do the same thing to her?"

"We're working on the details," Bale said.

"If the cyanide was in spray form, wouldn't someone else have gotten sick or died, too? I was right there in the seat. If she had been sprayed, the mist would have floated in the air and likely would have come into contact with me, the person directly behind Ms. Cahill." She bobbed her shoulders. "Spray doesn't make sense in this situation. Especially if it was administered on the plane. The killer wouldn't want to risk breathing in the mist himself, or getting it on him."

"We're working on it," Bale said. "We asked the attendants—all of them—and no one gave her a drink or a snack on the plane. That leaves injection and spray as the likely path of introduction."

"I agree with Agent James that the spray would have been too risky once they were on the plane. The medical examiner will look for injection sites on the body, and we'll know as soon as he does."

"Injection isn't the most likely way she was poisoned, though," Ava said. "I know it could have been done prior to me taking my seat, but wouldn't the victim have said something? If someone jabbed me with a needle, I'd make a scene."

"It would be a short scene," Lin said.

"But still a scene. Someone would have taken note, right?" She looked from Bale to Lin and back again.

The men exchanged another look and both nodded.

"But if it wasn't spray or injection, that leaves gas, and nobody would do that. That is more of a risk than any other variation," Lin said.

"Cyanide is at its deadliest in gas form," Bale added.

"What about powder form?" Ava asked.

Both men exchanged another look and shook their heads.

"She didn't eat or drink anything," Bale said.

"I've seen cyanide poisoning up-close and personal during my time as an agent," Lin said. "It was only once, and it was way back twenty years ago when I first became an agent, but it's still vivid in my mind's eye. Kind of thing a man never forgets. If Covey Cahill wasn't poisoned to death with cyanide, then it's something so similar it can pass as cyanide; right down to the odor it leaves behind."

"We are going aboard the plane to search all the carry-on bags and every inch of the plane while the background checks are running. I want you to come help us, Agent James," Bale said.

Ava agreed. "Do you have anything specific in mind that we're looking for, or just any evidence?"

"Possibly be on the lookout for any type of small vials, hypodermic needles, anything that could be used to carry the poison," Bale said.

"Just remember that you don't open any of these things," Lin said. "No kind of baggies or containers. Leave that to the people who are trained in poisons. Cyanide is much more potent and deadly in gaseous form, but you don't want to risk getting any liquid or powder on yourself, or anyone else, for that matter."

"I understand. What about the passengers?" she asked.

"What about them?" Bale asked.

"Are you going to inform them that we're going to search all their bags?"

"They don't have a choice in the matter," he said.

"I'll inform them as we head out," Lin said.

"Don't know why," Bale said. "They're just going to kick and scream about it, and we're still going to do it." He moved to the door and pulled it open. "Agent James, you're with me. We'll let Lin be the good Samaritan, and he can deal with all the objections while we get started with the search."

Lin smirked at Bale as he exited the room. Ava walked with Bale.

The objections started before Ava and Bale reached the turn to the doors.

"And there it is," Bale said. "Just as I predicted."

"It's better for them to understand we're going through their things," Ava said.

"I disagree. We could have told them afterward. Like I said, they don't have a choice in the matter."

"They do until it's proven Ms. Cahill was murdered," Ava said in a lowered voice.

"Which we will know soon enough," he replied confidently.

It took Ava, Bale, and Lin the better part of two hours to search all the carry-on luggage and the whole of the plane. It was tedious work, but it was also the kind of thing most agents enjoyed on some deep level. It was in their marrow to get down to the nitty-gritty and really get into the small details of an investigation. Few agents would admit to enjoying that part of their jobs, though. Most preferred to say they liked being out physically running after the bad guys, the shootouts, the standoffs, and the stakeouts more than anything, but Ava was of the inner circle, and she understood how much they really enjoyed the detective work that went with the day-to-day of the job.

Coming off the plane with no more proof than when they started, Ava stretched mightily as they walked back toward the terminal.

"Now for the fun part," Bale said.

"I shudder to know what you call fun," Ava said only half-joking.

THE WOMAN IN THE WINDOW

"Has anyone checked the passengers themselves?" Bale asked.

Ava and Lin were silent.

"That's what I thought," Bale said. "They're going to have to turn out their pockets. If the container wasn't on the plane, it must be in someone's pocket. Lin, I want you to make sure every trashcan between the doors and the seating area is checked as well."

"Got it, boss," Lin said, veering to the right as they stepped through the doorway.

"When they start objecting, just remember, they don't have a choice. We need to find the container," Bale said.

"But they do have a choice," Ava reminded him.

Bale stopped. "I expect this out of the suspects, but not from an agent. If you're going to help, help. If you're going to hinder, sit it out, Agent James."

"Don't shoot the messenger," Ava said, holding her ground.

"Don't give me a reason," Bale said, turning toward the suspect pool.

Everyone balked at the idea of turning out their pockets. Most of them were still mad about the luggage search. A small portion of them were okay with the luggage search as they just wanted to be set loose, but those same people were fighting mad over having their person searched.

Not finding anything suspicious in anyone's pockets, Bale and Ava concluded the search. Bale walked off as people yelled at him, demanded answers, and asked how much longer they were to be detained.

Ava answered as many questions as she could before she joined him, but the passengers were tired, hungry, and understandably angry at the whole thing. They felt they had no control, and as long as Bale was running the show, they didn't. He could have eased their minds a little just by answering a few questions. It wasn't in his nature to be caring and humble and understanding, it seemed.

Ava worked to acquire bottled water and pastries for the passengers while Bale remained aloof and mostly absent for the next couple of hours. When Ava had done all she could for the people, she sat in her interview room.

She wasn't in the room more than five minutes when the passengers' voices rose in complaint again. The sound quickly morphed into a cacophony of chaos. She jogged from the room to see Bale approaching the group.

He held up his hands to quiet them, but it didn't work very well. "Do any of you want to go home before tomorrow morning?" he yelled.

The group quieted, but some were still grumbling.

"Good. Your background checks have all cleared. You can all pick up your luggage at the usual place. Your carry-ons will be there as well. Go home, people." He nodded to the guards and turned away.

"That's it?" someone asked. "No information at all?"

Bale shook his head and kept walking toward his room. "James, clear any of your personal items from the interview room."

She followed him into his room. "What was that?" she asked.

"What do you mean? They're all free to go home, or go wherever they were headed. Their backgrounds are clear."

"I thought you were going to release them as their backgrounds cleared. One or two at a time. That's what I kept telling them because that's what you told me."

"Well, it didn't happen that way. It would have taken much longer for me to release them one or two at a time, and there would have been more moaning from the ones who didn't get to leave. I don't have time for that. When you think you can do a better job, be my guest. Is your room cleared?"

She turned on her heel and walked to her room to collect her few items and fume in peace. She hated that she had lied to all those people even though it wasn't her fault. People were easier to work with when there was a bit of transparency and truth right up front. They became combative and uncooperative when they felt as if they had been lied to or manipulated, though.

CHAPTER TWELVE

Time to Go

Bale met Ava outside her room. "Looks like there's nothing left for you to do here, Agent James. You should go on home, too."

She wasn't going to argue the point that there was a lot to be done yet. It would do no good, if she did. Not with Bale, at least. "When will the preliminary results be in from the autopsy? Any idea?"

He shook his head. "It'll be finished much sooner than usual. I put a rush on it. We need to know who's running loose out there with access to deadly poisons and the will to use it on people, if that's what happened to Ms. Cahill, which I'm almost one-hundred-percent sure of."

Ava nodded. "I'm right there with you."

"We have to be certain before we can form opinions like that. Those uninformed opinions are frowned upon by the powers that be."

His tone was so sarcastic that it was impossible to know if he meant the words he spoke, or if he was merely saying them. Had his superior reprimanded him for forming an opinion of how Covey Cahill had died?

"This is very true. If you need anything else…"

"I won't hesitate to call for you," he said. "Thank you for your help thus far."

"Anytime," she said as she turned to leave.

Maybe everyone else had to be certain of how Ms. Cahill had been killed, or that she had been killed at all, but Ava was certain. Her heart and her gut told her that Covey Cahill had been poisoned with cyanide. The why was obvious, but the who was elusive.

Covey had been one of the first people to board the plane. Maybe even the first. Everyone else had boarded behind her, and that made them all suspects. That weighed heavily on Ava's mind as she made her way to get a cab.

So, where could she have come into contact with the poison? It couldn't have been on the ride to the airport, that was too long a time. She would have died in the terminal.

Ava replayed her time in the terminal before boarding the flight. She had noticed Ms. Cahill boarding, and had seen the woman seemed flustered and upset. Her face had been red, and she seemed as if she were having an anxiety attack because she pressed her hand to her chest and kept it there.

Had she been sitting with anyone in the waiting area? Had anyone passed through the area who seemed suspicious or out of place? Had anyone approached her while she waited? Being a key witness in such a big trial, Ms. Cahill would not have been very social. She would have been withdrawn, probably scared, and would not have interacted with anyone of her own free will.

Any other time, it would have been simple to recall if anything out of the norm had happened while she waited for a flight, but she could not remember much of anything other than arguing with the clerk about the sudden and unexpected seating change.

The only thing to do now was wait and see what happened.

It wasn't her case. She had her own waiting for her in the office.

Sal needed to know what was going on. She answered the phone sounding slightly annoyed. It was not a new development. Sal had seemed irritated a lot over the last several months. The stress of the job eventually got to everyone. Even Sal, who was usually even-tempered.

"Sal, it's me. I just wanted to call and give you an update."

"What's going on? Any progress?"

"Absolutely none. They are waiting on autopsy and tox-panel results so they know for sure what killed her."

"Does that mean you're back home? You're done with that case?"

"That's what it means. I'll be back to work in the morning."

"Great because we really need to get some of these older cases moving through the system in July."

"I thought we were doing okay with them."

Sal exhaled. "Did you find out anything that would help with the Margot Carter case?"

"I haven't had time to look through the thumb drive files yet. I'll do that as soon as I get home," Ava said.

"There are other cases you need to be looking over, and there are sure to be new ones landing on our desks. Don't let the Carter case get lost in the shuffle, but you're not going to be able to devote much time to it. If it's unsolvable, you need to move on to another case for a while. Put it on the backburner so we can get through the slush pile of old cases that can be solved."

"Okay. That's what we've been doing, I thought." Confused, Ava had to wonder if something had happened during her absence.

"There's talk, Ava. Talk about a handpicked agent they want to put in our unit to help us get through the cases we haven't solved or moved yet. I've checked out his background, and he's not someone we want on the team."

"What? Wait a minute. How long have they been talking about putting him in the unit? This is the first I've heard about it. Does the rest of the team know?"

"No, no one on the team knows but you. They've been talking about this agent for over a month now. I kept thinking, or maybe hoping, that we would be able to get through these cases on our own and show them that we don't need someone else involved—especially because we seem inept at our duties—but it's not working out like I thought; like I hoped."

There had been talk of perhaps finding another team member, but that had been nearly a year prior. To hear that the suits had chosen someone of their liking to force into the unit was a shock. If he had been chosen by Sal's bosses, it was likely because he was someone the team wouldn't get along with, and that was done on purpose as a sort of threat to the team: Buckle down, get us results, or else.

"We're not inept at our duties. We'll get through this, Sal. Even if I have to work from home every night I'm there. I'm sure if the others knew, they would feel the same way."

"Or, they might not. Either way, they'll be pissed about it, and I don't want them to know yet. This is just between me and you for now. I need you to help motivate them without telling them about this. Not yet. Got it?"

"Yes, but I don't understand why."

"I don't want to say anything unless I have to. If they stick us with this new agent, and I know it's going to happen for sure, then, and only then, I'll make the announcement."

"It's your call, Sal. I'll keep it to myself. And we will get through those cases."

"I hope so. Get home safe, and I'll see you in the morning."

Just when it looked as if things were going to settle back to semi-normal, someone had to go and throw a monkey-wrench in the works.

CHAPTER THIRTEEN

A Chat with Uncle Ray

AVA PACED THROUGH HER HOUSE, THANKFUL TO BE BACK, BUT uneasy because of all that had transpired since the last case. Finding out what had obviously been bothering Sal did nothing to calm her.

Taking out her phone, Ava dialed Uncle Ray. He was the one person she could talk with about her work and not worry about over-stressing him. Her parents had enough to deal with, and she never liked venting to them. Uncle Ray, on the other hand, mostly welcomed the opportunity to stay in the loop with what was going on in her life.

"Hey, kiddo," he said in his usual cheery tone.

"Hi, Uncle Ray," she said as a smile eased onto her face. She could feel the tension melting at the sound of his voice, and she quickly took a seat on the nearest chair.

"What's up? It's been a hot minute since I heard from you. Everything okay?"

"Yeah, it's been a while. I've been busy. You know how it is with the work. How are you?"

"I'm fine. So is Aunt Kay. She's staying busier than I am these days with the charity having events all the time. Sometimes, we only see each other two or three nights a week. I thought we were getting close to the age when we're supposed to start slowing down a little." He chuckled lightly. "That was nice, by the way."

Ava's own chuckle cut off. "What was nice?" She hadn't done anything.

"The way you avoided answering my question. Smooth. Almost so smooth that I didn't even notice until I was distracted by talking about myself and Kay."

"I didn't avoid any question." Had she?

"I asked if everything was okay. Is it?" His tone was more serious.

"Oh. Yes, I guess so, but maybe not. I'm not sure. How's that for an answer?" She scoffed. "I just don't know how things are right now." So many things felt as if they were not okay: the lack of progress on the Margot Carter case, the way Jason had acted on the phone, the Housewife Murders files being messed with, the Bureau wanting to force another member into the unit, and Covey Cahill's murder. Everything seemed about as far from okay as it could possibly be.

"All right. Let's narrow the scope of the question. How are your parents? I haven't talked to them in a while."

"Mom and Dad are doing... okay. Mom is still having issues, but it's nothing new since we found her and brought her home."

"Alcohol still?"

"Mm, yeah. It's not like she's a raging alcoholic, but it's not good, and that worries Dad. I try to talk to her as much as I can, but it seems as though I'm beating my head against a wall for all the good it does. And you know how sick Dad was with his stomach."

"I do. Is it flaring up on him again?"

"Not that he admits, but if he keeps worrying about Mom, it will."

"Elizabeth is self-medicating with the wine. It's not uncommon in situations like she went through. You keep talking to her gently. Kay has spoken with her a couple of times about it, too. Maybe if the two of you keep at it, she'll snap out of it before too long. If it's really bad, though, you might want to talk to her about getting help. I know it'll be difficult, but it's better to get it under control, or keep it under control, in the early stages before she can turn into a full-blown alcoholic."

THE WOMAN IN THE WINDOW

"She doesn't think she has a problem. She says she can quit anytime she pleases. I don't believe her, though."

"Then challenge her to stop for two days. Tell her to prove to you that she isn't as addicted as you think."

"I might, but usually that's a topic that's off-limits every time I try to bring it up."

"Going through what she went through to find Molly and then not having her job afterward… She always processed stressful events by working harder at her job, or throwing herself into some other activity that required a lot from her. Not having the job has thrown her off-center, I'm sure. Maybe you could help her find another cause to occupy her and keep her from drinking so often."

Often? Over the last several months, there had not been a single time that she wasn't drinking when Ava went to visit. It didn't matter if it was before lunch or after dinner or right before bed. She always seemed to have a half-empty bottle of wine nearby.

"That's something I might be able to do without her getting defensive," Ava said.

"Right. Just don't mention the why, only the activity that you think she would enjoy. Anything from tennis to starting an advocacy group to, I don't know, cleaning up the park. Just something to put her focus into."

Ava laughed. "Mom playing tennis. That's hilarious. She hates tennis. If I suggested that, she might take the racket to my backside."

Ray laughed. "Agreed. But you get the general idea. Just give it some thought. You'll figure it out, and if it is worse than you're telling me, it's time to get professional help. In that case, I wouldn't delay, and I wouldn't care if she got mad. After the problem is dealt with, she'll understand."

"It's not that bad. I promise. If it was, I would have already called in the professionals." She tried to keep her tone light. It was a subject she didn't enjoy discussing.

"Now that we have your parents squared away, how are things at work?"

Ava groaned. "It's a lot right now. I have a case involving a murdered woman. I think that case is related to some West Coast murders, but apparently I'm the only one, which doesn't matter because I'm going to figure it out. But then on my way home I opened up a whole other can of worms."

"Sounds like a real shit show."

She summarized the days' recent events for Uncle Ray, who listened attentively without interrupting.

"So, she what, died or got killed on your watch? I'm confused, Ava," Ray inquired.

"Yeah, you're not the only one. It was on my watch, but I didn't know it was my watch because no one ever informed me of the situation. I thought she was just sleeping. I had no idea she was in any distress."

By the end of the story, Ava felt a bit better.

"If I had known her situation... I didn't even check on her. If I had checked on her earlier, she might have lived. If I had stayed awake instead of sleeping..." She sighed and put her hand to her forehead. "Bale should have told me. It's as much his fault as it is mine. No," she said firmly. "It's more his fault than mine, and I don't usually blame someone else for bad things that happen."

"Come on. Ava, it's not at all your fault. Are you listening to me?"

"Yeah, I am listening. And I get why you would say that, but—"

"You're listening but are you hearing me? Are you understanding that there is no way any of this is your fault? How can it be? Because you didn't take it as your duty to check on a complete stranger on a plane just because she happened to be sitting next to you?"

"I know it's not my duty to check on strangers, but—"

"But what? Bad shit happens all the time, kiddo. I know that sucks. I know firsthand how much that sucks. You can't be responsible for all the bad shit that happens. You can't save everybody."

Her breath hitched once, twice, and then she held it until the tears prickling at the corners of her eyes were gone again. Gone, right along with the urge to cry. Ray was right. She knew in her heart that he was, but it was hard to let it go.

After the phone call ended, Ava pulled up the interviews from the passengers. She had access to all of them, not just the ones she conducted. That and the access to all the background checks made for a broader, fuller picture.

After two hours of scouring the interviews and backgrounds, she had them all in order according to last names. The background checks were with the interviews of each person. She printed them. Even as she was watching the printer spit out sheet after sheet of information, she wondered why she was doing it. It wasn't her case. It wasn't her responsibility.

And just as Ray had so eloquently reminded her: she couldn't save everybody.

But she could do the next best thing and help find the killer.

To do that, she needed access to the big case that Covey Cahill was set to testify in, and that was the one thing she did not have access to.

But she knew someone who might be able to help her out. If Bale didn't give her access or the information she requested the next day, she would speak with Ashton.

CHAPTER FOURTEEN

Finally in the Loop

At nine the next morning, Ava sat in her office going over the Margot Carter casefile. She had not gone over the files of the thumb drive from Jason Ellis' office as she had told Sal she would because the dead woman on the plane wouldn't get out of her head. It was not easy to concentrate on anything else.

She knew how Margot Carter had died, and it had been horrible, but she had worked the case long enough that she knew the chances of finding anything big to help solve the case were slim to none, and in her opinion, slim had left town. At least for a while. The thumb drive was still at the forefront of her mind, and she wished she had opened it, but she had not.

At nine-thirty, she picked up the phone and rang Agent Bale's number.

THE WOMAN IN THE WINDOW

"If you want to know the whole story, or as much of it as I know, meet me in Upper Marlboro. Know anything about the area?"

"Some, but I have GPS," Ava said.

"Good. Meet me at Rosaryville State Park. I'll be at the first set of picnic tables you see. Agent Lin will be with me. Don't bring anyone with you. There's a mole, and I still don't know who it is. Lin is the only other agent I trust right now. Can you meet me there at eleven?"

Ava looked at the clock. Nine-forty-five. "I can. I just have to take care of some things at the office first."

"If you're not there by eleven-thirty, I'll call you back and we can set another time and place. I have to get back to DC early to be in court for a case, and then I have to go to Culpeper, Virginia after that. I don't have a lot of time to spare for this, but I think you could help us."

Ava stood and held the phone between her ear and shoulder as she gathered her things. "I'm leaving now."

"See you at eleven." Bale hung up.

"You're leaving to go where now?" Sal asked from the doorway, her smile barely perceptible.

Ava startled and her phone slid from her shoulder to bounce on the desk. She grabbed for it, muttering.

"Are you all right?" Sal asked. She stepped into the room and walked up to the desk eyeing Ava suspiciously.

Ava held up the phone and nodded. "Yes. I'm fine. You startled me. I didn't know you were there."

"Yeah, so I gathered." She laid a folder on the desk and put her finger on top of it. "Where are you headed?"

She couldn't lie, but if she told the whole truth, Sal would stop her. "To meet someone in Upper Marlboro about a case." She picked up her bag and made a point to let the top sag open to show the files inside before she closed the flap. "Why, did you need me to do something while I'm out?"

Sal scrutinized her for a moment, finger tapping idly on the new folder. Could she see the deception? Could she sense it somehow? It sure felt that way under her direct gaze.

"Are you still working the Margot Carter case?" she finally asked.

Clearing her throat, Ava nodded and pushed her hair away from her face. "I am." She pointed to the folder under Sal's finger. "Is that a new case, or one of the older ones that needs moving?"

"One of the older ones. Can you work it while you're out doing whatever it is you're doing?" She held up a hand to halt any interruption. "If you're on some wild goose chase, get off it. I need you on the Margot

Carter case, and this one. It's almost eight months in with no progress after the first and only suspect was questioned. It's going to require some good old boots-on-the-ground work. You and Metford are the best at getting results with that type of work, so I expect the two of you will deliver on this one." She picked it up and held it out to Ava. "Sooner rather than later."

"We'll do everything we can." Ava took the folder and shoved it in her bag with the others.

"I know you will. Keep me in the loop."

"I always do," Ava said, relaxing a little as Sal walked out again.

Ava gave Sal a minute to get settled back into her office, and then she hurried out to the bullpen to talk with Metford about the case Sal wanted them on.

"I'll just ride along with you," he said, grabbing his jacket from the back of his chair as he stood.

"No," Ava said, remembering what Bale said about not taking anyone else to the meeting.

Metford looked like someone had slapped him. "What do you mean? Why not? I can help you with that murdered woman case you've been working on."

"I can't take you with me," she said lowering her voice. "I can't explain right now, but I need you to do me a gigantic favor. Just for today." She winced and made a face. "Maybe just today."

"You're doing something Sal would have your head over, aren't you?" He lowered his voice to match hers.

"It's not that. I just have to do this today alone. I need you to work the case she just dropped off in the office. She wants us both working it, but I really need to do this other thing right now, and if I don't, I might not get another chance for a long, long time." She pulled out the folder and handed it to him. "Walk me to the car?" She glanced over her shoulder to make sure Sal was still in her office.

He took the folder. "Tell me you're guilty of something without saying you're guilty."

"Huh?" She urged him to keep up with her pace.

"Glancing over your shoulder like someone making a drug deal in front of a police station, the whispering, the secrecy. Hey," he held up a hand and smirked. "I'm not judging. Just be safe with whatever crazy thing you're doing now."

"It's not crazy. I promise, just as soon as I get the all-clear, you'll be the first person to know all the gritty little details of what I'm doing." She cocked her head to the side and raised her eyebrows at him as she armed the door open. "Deal?"

He grinned. "Deal, but I want all the deets. Every single one of them, nothing left out, and I want to be the very first to hear the story."

"That's what I just said, Metford. I'll even throw in the newest heart attack in a wrapper from Wendy's."

"Oh, you had me at heart attack in a wrapper." He laughed and opened his car door.

"Thank you," Ava said, walking past him and toward her car.

"What are partners for?" He shut the door and the engine revved to life.

When she climbed into her car, it was fifteen after ten. If she ran into thicker-than-normal traffic, or any more delays, she wouldn't make it to the park in time to meet Bale and Lin. It was technically about a thirty-minute drive, but with traffic and the lowered speed limits near the park, she would be lucky to get there by eleven.

Rosaryville Park was busy with cars and people in the parking area. The weather was great for hiking or just having a nice day in the park grilling burgers and hot dogs with the family. Why had Bale chosen that park? Was it really because he was already in town, or was he worried about his and Lin's safety? Did he think being in a public place would be safer for him, or maybe for her? The victim on the plane had been set to testify against a big crime syndicate. Could the danger be that real? That imminent?

The fine hairs over her upper arms and neck prickled as she headed toward the picnic table area. Suddenly, the shadows and the smiling, happy people walking around didn't look so safe and pleasant.

A little boy ran by pointing a finger gun back over his shoulder and yelling, "Bang, bang, bang, you're dead, Tommy. Bang. Fall down dead. Bang."

Ava's stomach knotted as the boy's voice rang out right beside her, startling her.

Another boy, presumably Tommy, ran after the first kid laughing. "Your wimpy little gun can't kill me, Jakey-boy."

The whole encounter happened in five seconds. Her nerves were on edge lately. She prided herself in not being jumpy, and she had jumped at stupid things twice in as many hours.

Someone whistled. "Agent James," Bale's familiar voice called.

She turned to her right and saw him with Lin. Their table was situated in a small alcove of tall trees that threw everything below into shadows. She made her way over to them.

"I almost passed you up. It's bright out there on the trail, and it's so dim in here." She exhaled and sat on the opposite side of the table from them. She straddled the bench so she could get up quickly if the need arose. Lin sat the same way on his bench.

"One of the most private spots I could think of," Bale said.

"Yeah, it was that or Popeye's in town," Lin said.

Bale shot him an ill-tempered look and then turned back to Ava. "You know Covey Cahill is not your responsibility, her death wasn't your fault, and you don't owe her anything. It's my case, not yours."

"I know all that, but…" She shrugged and her gaze slid down toward the table.

"You still feel somewhat responsible for her death," Lin said.

"Yeah, I do. And you said something about a mole in the agency." She looked at Bale. "I need to know who that is just as much as I need to know who the hell would poison Covey Cahill on a plane full of people."

"I get it," Bale said. "As much as it pains me to admit it, I do need your help if you've got the time and you're willing."

"I'm here, aren't I?" She pulled a notepad and pen from her bag.

"I need to check you and that bag before we talk," Bale said.

"Seriously?"

He nodded.

She pulled the front of her blouse out, tilted her head down, and said, "He knows I'm wearing the bug. I think my cover is blown." She smirked and let her shirt drop from her fingers.

"I still have to check." He stood.

"Of course, you do," she said, mildly agitated.

He finished with her and moved to the bag. "Clean," he said, dropping the bag on the edge of the table.

"I try," Ava said.

"Anyone ever tell you that you're a smartass, James?"

"At least once a week. Are you going to tell me anything about the case before you have to leave back to DC? I have a busy day to get on with, too." She pulled the paper and pen back in front of her.

"Glad to hear it. After this, I daresay your schedule will get busier. The woman on the plane was Covey Cahill, age twenty-eight, red hair, freckles, five-five, weighed a buck-twenty, Irish descent, raised by a single mother, and to say the least, they didn't have much money."

"What changed? She looked like someone who had money to me. The way she was dressed, her makeup, her hair, her bag—it was a wealthy woman's combo."

"I was getting to it. Once upon a time, young Covey delved into the dark world of drugs, as do many girls who aren't very well-supervised by a single parent who works fifty or sixty hours a week just to keep a roof over their heads. While in that world of sex, drugs, and rock-n-roll, Covey got the idea to start running drugs for cash. She worked her way up and became a low-level runner all over DC, and trust me when I say she had plenty of customers," Bale said.

"All the drug-runners have a lot of customers in DC," Lin added.

"But she ran for the lower-income customer base mostly. It was when she met a man who had some money, and he liked her, that she deigned to bump her status in a city that doesn't like that sort of thing very much. When her name started coming up to the bigger suppliers, that's when she began her real journey. She met Callum Horne. Fourth man under Porter Ambrose."

Ava wrote furiously, and then looked up expectantly. "And?"

"You don't know Porter Ambrose?" Lin asked.

She shook her head. "Should I?"

Bale and Lin exchanged a strange look.

Bale shrugged. "He runs the Emerald Block, which is a crime syndicate. They have their fingers in everything illegal."

"How did it get the name Emerald Block?"

"Most of them are of Irish descent, and they started out small. Like very small. One block in north DC. The whole thing started in the sixties when Porter's father figured out there was money to be made in drugs. And when I say he started out at the bottom with nothing, that's not an exaggeration. It only took him twenty years to expand the business and become one of the biggest names around. In the late nineties, Porter took the high seat and expanded the business even further."

Ava nodded as she wrote. "And how does that lead us to Covey Cahill being killed? You said she got involved with..." She consulted her notes quickly. "Callum Horne, and that he's fourth under Porter Ambrose."

"Callum was supposed to recruit Covey or get rid of her. She was hurting Emerald Block's bottom line by taking their drug clients. When he met her and made an offer, she saw dollar signs and couldn't say no. That's what she told me in her own words. She said she was making more money just by helping Callum than she ever dreamed possible. And then they started dating."

"But it wasn't just drugs they were running then," Lin said. "By the time Covey came onto the scene, Emerald Block was running guns and ammo, had their stakes in illegal gambling, and there were rumors that they had access to some politician slush funds."

"We don't know about the slush funds for sure, but all the other rumors turned out to be true. Ms. Cahill told us."

"Why did she turn against them so easily?" Ava asked. "If it was such a money-loaded life, why would she turn on them?"

"When she had been in the syndicate's business for a couple of years, she started seeing things that scared her, and they scared her bad," Bale said. "Their gun and drug trades didn't always go smoothly, as they had in the beginning. People were starting to lose some of their fear of Emerald Block as a whole, and they didn't always play nice when it came time for business. We arrested her during a federal raid on a gun trade they were conducting in the basement of a hotel right in the city."

"There was underground access for delivery trucks, service workers, and the like," Lin added. "Emerald Block had set up the deal, and we had found out about it. Ms. Cahill was shot in the ankle while attempting to get away, but it wasn't us who shot her."

"Someone from the syndicate?" Ava asked.

Bale nodded. "Callum Horne himself. He was getting into his vehicle and turned to see that she had fallen. He was set to shoot her because he didn't want her giving us any information. Lucky for Ms. Cahill, she saw what was about to happen, and she scrambled back just far enough that the shot hit her an inch above the ankle."

"If Callum hadn't been distracted trying to save his own ass, she would have been dead right there," Lin said.

"No love lost between them, I imagine," Ava mused.

"She had been wanting to get out for a couple of years, but she couldn't. She knew if she tried to disappear, they would just find her and kill her, so she did the survivalist thing and she stayed," Bale said. "She said she kept hoping something would happen that would let her know it was safe for her to run to us, or the cops, but Emerald Block has so many of the cops in their pocket that she couldn't even trust them. So, when we took her into custody, she was more than ready to flip on them and give us whatever we needed to put Callum, and hopefully Porter Ambrose, in prison for the rest of their lives."

"All she asked in return was that we promise to keep her safe no matter what it took," Lin said. His gaze fell to the table. "And we promised her." He exhaled deeply.

"We did what we could," Bale said, more to Lin than to Ava. "We sent her all the way to California. How were we supposed to foresee that any of the syndicate picked up her trail and would try to kill her in broad daylight on a plane full of witnesses?"

"I don't know, but we didn't keep our promise, did we? She held up her end of the bargain. We should have been able to do more to keep her safe," Lin said.

"We can't do anything about it now," Bale said sharply. "Except take down the syndicate, or as many of the big dogs as we can."

"Does Emerald Block still only operate in the DC area?" Ava asked.

"Unfortunately, no," Bale said. "They are headquartered there, but their reach is nationwide. Ms. Cahill said she was sure some of the deals she saw were with foreign nationals. Most of those deals were for guns. Some were for drugs, but she didn't have firsthand knowledge of them." He pulled out his phone and tapped a few times on its screen. He turned it toward Ava. "Scroll down. Those are pictures of deals gone bad. We had to pull cleanup duty more than once."

Ava scrolled through the pictures. The aftermath of the mayhem reminded her of the Cornbread Mafia killings she had dealt with the previous year. The Emerald Block's messes seemed more localized, more concentrated, and much bloodier. And, unlike the mess she had worked before, Emerald Block, as far as they knew, was not tied to any worldwide trafficking rings. She wanted to bring them down, stop them for good before they did make that leap. It wouldn't be a big leap for them to unite with one of the worldwide rings. They were already into every illegal thing under the sun. What would it bother them to start dabbling into human trafficking? If they weren't already, which was a distinct possibility.

She handed the phone back to Bale. "Why haven't they been taken down before now?"

Bale shrugged one shoulder. "I figure their ties with law enforcement must run pretty damn deep and wide. Every time one of them gets into trouble, he's out before the judge hangs up his robe for the day."

"Give me names, ranks, hangouts, meeting places, any information you can about the syndicate, and I'll do everything I can to help you take them down," Ava said.

"I'm going to see that you have access online to the case against them. Everything is in there that we know. Just remember: no one knows about the details of the case but the three of us. Anything you find out; it comes straight to me or Lin. Nobody else."

"I can do that."

"Good. We have to go now. I'll be in touch."

CHAPTER FIFTEEN

Jason on Her Mind

Ava's phone rang as she got into her car to leave Rosaryville Park. She answered without looking to see who it was.

"James here," she said, shuffling the notebook and bag into the passenger seat and fumbling her keys.

"That's funny because it's James here as well." Her father laughed.

"Oh, hi, Dad. Everything okay?" She leaned as far over the console as her ribs would allow and hooked her keys with one finger from the passenger floorboard. As she righted herself, her elbow caught her coffee cup and dumped it in the cupholder and on her leg. She swore and picked up the cup.

"Sounds like I should be asking you that question."

"Yeah, everything's just peachy-keen. No use crying over spilled coffee, right?"

"I didn't call to cause catastrophe; I just thought you might want to grab lunch with your old dad if you're still close by. Want to meet at Founding Fathers on Pennsylvania Avenue?"

She stopped swiping at the coffee on her thigh. "How did you know I was anywhere close by?"

He laughed again. "I have connections, eyes everywhere, don't you know? You were in Upper Marlboro, right?"

"Yeah, but how did you know that?"

"Your boss answered the phone when I called your office. She said that's where you were headed when you left. I just thought you might still be there."

Ava let out a breath that she hadn't realized she was holding. It was her turn to chuckle. "I am. I was just about to leave, though."

"So, you don't have time to get lunch?"

"I can. Yes, that's great, actually. I haven't eaten today, and my stomach is letting me know about it." Funny how not one thought of food had crossed her mind until he mentioned getting lunch.

"Well, I'll be at Founding Fathers a few minutes after twelve. I have a couple of things to do on my way out, but I won't be much later than twelve-fifteen. We can catch up. Haven't seen you in forever."

"I'm sorry, Dad. I've just been so busy. And I got caught in the middle of a big case during my flight home from San Fran the other day. That's an ongoing mess. Not to mention, we're catching it at work because of the number of older cases that are balanced on the precipice of going cold, and the case I was supposed to be working."

"Never a moment of peace, is there?"

"Not really. Not lately, at least." She started the car and buckled up. Hitting the Bluetooth button on the phone, she connected it to the speakers in the car and adjusted the volume before pulling out of the parking spot.

"Then I believe you deserve to take a few minutes and get lunch. It will be an opportunity for you to slow down for a while. You keep going like you do, and you'll end up with ulcers. Trust me."

"I know, but there's really nothing I can do about it. The bad guys keep being bad, and the cases keep coming in."

"I know. I just worry about you. Your mother and I both do. I hear that you've switched the call to the car system, so I'll let you go. I don't want you to be distracted while you're driving."

"Okay, Dad. I'll be at the restaurant in about forty or forty-five minutes."

"See you there." He hung up.

Although she had another small lead on the Margot Carter case, it would be nice to have some time with her dad. It had been too long since they just sat and chatted. It might be good to get her mind off work for a while.

Hank met her outside Founding Fathers with a huge smile. He hugged her hard. "It's good to see you. Come on. Let's get in there before all the tables are gone."

"Good to see you, too, Dad." She followed him inside.

The contrast between the park and the city was stark and jarring. The constant grind and hum and rattle of the city and its traffic was enough to give her the start of a headache. The crush of people hurrying to wherever they were going was enough to make her want to retire back to her office, or better yet, her house.

Thankfully, once they stepped inside the restaurant, much of the noise was dampened. They got a decent table near the side.

In the middle of their chat, Ava remembered the digital files she had gotten in San Francisco again. That memory dragged all the memories of Jason right along with it.

"What is it, Aviva?" Hank wiped his fingers on the napkin and pushed his plate to the side.

She shook her head. "I just remembered some files I have to go over still for my case. I got them from Jason's office after I came off the last case. That's why I stayed in the city while the rest of the team flew back that morning." She sighed. The files would have to wait until she followed up with the next lead in the case. Suddenly, she was itching to be done with lunch and get back on the road. "There are never enough hours in the day," she said, feeling as if she were parroting a phrase both her parents used all the time.

He grinned. "And if we had forty-eight instead of twenty-four, we would surely find ways of making them too full. Human nature, I'm afraid." He rested his arms on the table. "How is Jason?"

"I don't really know. I didn't get to see him when I went to his office. There were riots and traffic jams. I barely made it there before his boss left for the day. Thankfully, he agreed to let me in for a while so I could look for what I needed. I don't think he was thrilled about it, to be honest."

"Eh, the closer it gets to the end of the day, the less anyone likes any delay." He smiled and gave her a strange look. "You didn't even talk to Jason?"

"What are you grinning at, Dad? What's going on? You're not that interested in how Jason's doing. You've never even met him. What's really on your mind?" She pushed her plate aside and scooted closer to the table, keeping her eyes on him.

"I was wondering how much longer it's going to be before I do meet him."

Shocked, Ava sat back in the seat. "What? Who? Jason?"

"Wow, that wasn't the reaction I was expecting, but yes, Jason. When am I going to meet him?"

"Why would you meet him? He's based in San Francisco, Dad."

"I know where he's based. I also know that Molly hinted that you might be interested in him in more than a professional way. She seems to believe you are… romantically involved."

Ava scoffed. Molly. Of course, she would think that. "We're just friends, Dad. That's all it is. We worked a case together, we get along, and we agreed to keep in touch for the sake of work." Mostly, she wanted to add but did not. "We barely talk, let alone see each other."

Hank smiled knowingly and nodded as if he completely understood. "And?"

"There is no 'and.' That's it. We're friends, or at least I like to believe that. We help each other with cases, and…" She let her voice trail and looked up sharply at her father.

"I knew there was an 'and.' Why do you look so shocked and disturbed? It wouldn't be the end of the world, you know."

"Now, you sound like Mom."

"Are you interested in him, or is it just professional?"

"Just friends and professionals. Really." Making eye contact was easy; holding it was impossible. She had never been able to lie successfully to her dad.

"Right, right. I understand, but I also see it in your face, in your eyes."

She shook her head and opened her mouth to deny it again, but he spoke and cut her off.

"It's fine, Aviva. Don't worry, I won't breathe a word of it to your mom. I'll let you do that, and I'm not responsible for anything you say to Molly that might get back to her."

"Thanks," Ava said, unable to continue denying it to him. Could she keep denying it to herself, though? How long before that was wholly impossible? "It's nothing serious, though. I can swear to that. We are just friends, whether you believe me, or not."

"But he's a friend you could get used to being around a whole lot more. A friend you want to see more often; talk to more often, and not always about some case you're working."

She scoffed again. "You are impossible." Her cheeks burned. They were red, and she hated knowing it. She looked at her watch. "It's one-thirty, don't you need to get back to work?"

"Are you trying to get rid of me?"

"No, but I need to go. I still have a ton of work to get done before quitting time."

"You go ahead. I'll get the bill. I still have some time before I'll be missed at the office. They might not even miss an old dog like me for the rest of the day."

Ava stood. "You're not an old dog, and yes, they would definitely miss you. The place would crash and burn if you weren't there." She walked to him, and they hugged briefly. "Thanks for lunch. I enjoyed it."

"We need to do it more often. You should come to the house every now and then, too. Your mom misses you, too."

"I'll try to get by soon. Love you."

"Love you, too." He smiled sadly as she turned away.

If she had her way, she would have stayed and talked longer, but she could not afford to get any farther behind on the cases. Sal needed her to pull her weight and then some. The whole team needed her to do it; they just didn't realize it yet, and hopefully they would not have to find out.

For the next several hours, Ava worked, but Jason occupied her mind most of the time. She couldn't concentrate on the case because of it. Thanks in large part to her father making such a deal out of him at lunch. There were unanswered questions in her own mind about her relationship with him, but she had done a marvelous job at keeping that separate from her work for months.

Where was Jason? Had he finished with his work in New Mexico? How was he doing? Was he safe? Those were all questions that she allowed at the forefront of her thoughts because they could be explained away with her professed friendship with him. Just one friend wondering about another.

At home, glad for the end of the day, Ava lugged her bag with the casefiles and notes into the house. She set the styro carry-out container from Mandy's Burger Shack on the kitchen table next to her laptop. It was time to finally go through the files she had brought from Jason's office. If she learned nothing new, at least maybe it would get him off her mind so that she could concentrate on her work better.

She scrolled through the files while she ate, and what she found was upsetting from the beginning.

While she was in Honolulu working the Kelly Winters case, Jason had told her he was in Fairhaven at a work conference. She recalled the conversation they had beforehand, also because he was going to be speaking at the event and had asked if she would attend. She had agreed. They were going to go to a bar afterward and grab food and drinks while they caught up. At least, that had been the plan until the Winters case took her off to Honolulu unexpectedly.

According to what she saw in the electronic files, Jason was in DC at that time, not Fairhaven. Was it a big deal? When she returned and he carried on with the story of being in Fairhaven, had he been purposely lying to her for some reason? What reason would he have to lie about it? Fairhaven and DC weren't worlds apart, and he could have driven from one to the other in under two hours even in heavy traffic. So why keep making a point to tell her he was in Fairhaven during that time?

Telling the truth was part of his nature, not just his job. Or, she had thought so until she saw the lie staring back at her from the computer screen.

His hotel, room number, and the case he was working were noted right there. She hadn't even known he had been working a case in DC. Which of his cases brought him that far from home? He had never mentioned it. Of course, she had never asked. How could she when she didn't know about it?

She shut the computer and stared down at her cold burger in the styro tray.

"Maybe I misunderstood something when we were talking," she conjectured, still staring at the now-unappetizing food. She pushed it away and covered it with the lid. She wasn't in the habit of not finishing burgers, but that one would be the next day's crow food.

Her phone rang, and for a moment, she thought to ignore it. The whole Jason situation was devouring her mind, plaguing it with questions.

Exclaiming wordlessly, she slammed her hand over the phone and jerked it to her ear. Why was someone calling her at the worst possible time? Why couldn't they just leave her alone for a few hours?

"Hello," she snapped, unable to even pretend to be civil.

"James? This is Bale."

She pulled in a deep breath and closed her eyes as she pushed the laptop closed again. "Yes? What is it?"

"Sorry if it's a bad time, but the prelim on the autopsy and tox-screen are ready. The ME wants us in his office tonight. Can you make it?"

She looked up at the digital clock on her stove. "Right now?"

"Yeah. I told you I put a rush on it, and he's been working hard to get it done. He says it's important."

"It's seven-thirty. I need forty minutes to get there." She stood, glad that she hadn't already taken off her shoes and changed into her night clothes.

"See you there. I'll wait outside if I get there first."

"Me, too," Ava said.

They hung up, and she pulled the thumb drive from her computer. She put it in her pocket and headed back out the door she had so recently entered. So much for a relaxing night of getting Jason off her mind.

Then again, maybe the Covey Cahill case would be just what she needed to get him off her mind. Work always did the trick. Or almost always. If something bothered her in any way, she could always bury herself in her work to get away from it for a while, and eventually, it would work itself out, or she would figure out a solution.

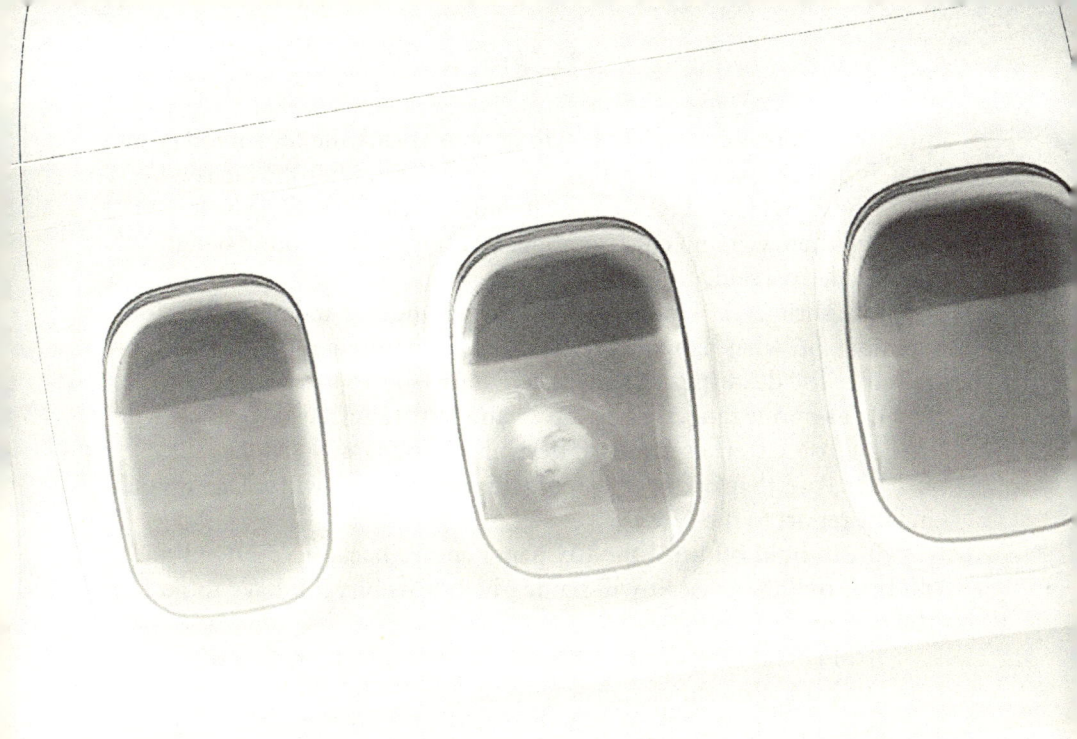

CHAPTER SIXTEEN

Findings

Dr. Ethan Pate was a large man with a permanent expression of suspicion. His brows never relaxed back to their places but stayed scrunched toward the middle as if he were scowling all the time.

Dr. Pate looked at Bale. "You said you wanted this kept quiet, no matter what I found, and that's what I've done, hence the after-hours meeting." He handed Bale the report. "I haven't even put this in the system yet. She was poisoned, and it was homicide. It wasn't some accident."

Bale held the paper to let Ava read it along with him.

"Cyanide," Bale said, looking back to the doctor.

Pate nodded. "We have to wait on the full tox panel to come back before we can announce anything officially, but it was cyanide. There wasn't any on her face or hands, so I concluded that it was administered, probably in powder form, and on food or in a drink she consumed immediately before boarding the plane, or immediately after she boarded."

"She didn't have anything to eat or drink when I took my seat next to her, and there were no cups, wrappers, or trays when I found her already deceased," Ava said.

Pate shrugged. "I'm just giving you my findings and my professional opinions on what happened and how. Just working off what the body tells me. The dead speak loudly if you know how to listen."

Bale's phone rang. He held up a hand to Pate and Ava. "Gotta take it." The call lasted thirty seconds at best, and he hung up.

"Dr. Pate, thank you for keeping this quiet. When will you be uploading the report to the system?"

"I can hold off until the tox panel comes back, if you need me to do that. But after that, it will be nearly impossible. It'll have to go into the system."

"Hold off as long as you can unless you hear from me again."

"Will do." Pate shook hands with Bale and Ava.

Bale turned to leave. "We need to get back to the plane."

"This late?" Ava asked.

"Yeah. My team found something, and if I don't miss my guess, it's something to do with the cyanide. I told them we'd be there in a few minutes." He held the door for her. "Unless you need to be elsewhere."

"No. I don't have anywhere else to be except home." She went to her car. "I'll follow you in," she said without looking at Bale.

"See you there."

Agent Lin met them outside the plane. "Airport's having a fit because the plane's still grounded. I told them it was a federal investigation, and that we would be done soon enough if they stopped calling about it so we could get our jobs done."

"Good. What did you find and where?"

Lin nodded at Ava. "We found a small glass vial and lid in the toilet waste tank. I called forensics in to test the vial. They said it held cyanide. I pulled our team out and forensics is testing the whole lavatory now. They should be done in a few minutes."

"That confirms what we just learned at the medical examiner's office," Bale said.

"What was that? Is the autopsy done?"

Bale nodded. "That's where we just came from. His unofficial finding is that Covey Cahill was poisoned to death with cyanide. He believes it was introduced to the victim via food or drink, and he believes it was in powder form."

"How would he even be able to guess at the form?" Lin asked. "Liquid could have been dropped into her food or drink."

"Powder is easier to control; it stays in place better on food, and she didn't have any residue from, say, a liquid spray. He's sure she ingested it, so that rules out the gaseous form of the poison."

"We already figured that. If it had been any sort of gas or spray, at least one or two others would have been exposed. We'd be investigating several deaths instead of one," Lin said.

"And it was definitely targeted," Ava added.

Bale and Lin nodded.

A man in a hazmat suit stepped out of the plane and headed toward them.

"What did you find?" Lin asked.

"There was powder on the rim of the toilet and on the floor of the lavatory."

"Good God," Lin exclaimed. "Did any of our men get exposed? There were at least three of us in there at different times." Lin started for the group standing near the tail of the plane.

The man in the hazmat suit stepped in front of him. "No, no one else was exposed. Ted is with the men who were in there. He'll have them strip and wash off. If there's a chance anyone else could have it on their clothes or shoes, I would suggest you send them to Ted immediately, and tell them to keep their hands away from their faces until they have washed off. Ted will give instructions and supervise the whole cleanup for your men."

Lin turned to Bale. "I didn't shake hands with you when you walked over, did I?"

"No. Why, are you contaminated?"

"I was in there. There's a possibility that I got it on my shoes and clothes."

Bale and Ava took two large steps back from Lin.

"Agent Lin, I need you to walk over there to the van," the man in the hazmat suit said, pointing and urging Lin to move. "Immediately. For your own and others' safety."

Ava felt sick to her stomach watching Lin walk away. She would be terrified if the tables were turned.

"He'll be fine," Bale said, but the look in his eyes belied his deep worry.

"Yeah, yeah. He'll be fine," Ava said. Lin would be fine if he had not accidentally breathed in or ingested any of the poison. She did not need to say that aloud; Bale already knew.

"What did you do with the glass vial?" Bale asked the suited man.

"It's safety sealed in evidence, but it won't be good for anything other than letting us know that the killer was on the plane. It's useless as far as fingerprints or DNA, if that's what you were hoping for."

"It was. But when is anything ever that easy?" Bale smirked. "Thanks. Let me know if you find anything else."

The man nodded and turned away.

"Whoever did it tried to get rid of the evidence," Ava said.

"Probably as soon as they realized Ms. Cahill was dead."

"I don't understand about the cyanide being on the plane, though," Ava said as they walked back toward their cars. "What happened? Did the killer administer the lethal dose in the terminal somehow and then carry the evidence onto the plane?"

"She could have been dosed on the plane."

"There was no evidence of that," Ava reminded him. "Did you bring a copy of the medical examiner's report?"

"Yes. It's in the car. Why?"

"It will have Ms. Cahill's time of death."

"We know she died within the first two hours of the flight. That's pretty spot-on already."

"But Dr. Pate would have also been able to tell about when she ate last. Maybe we can tell if it was before or after boarding."

He shook his head. "It was cyanide, James. It's not like her breakfast was dosed. It had to be within minutes of her death." He turned and held out both hands. "Either ten minutes before boarding, or ten after. Not much wiggle room with cyanide." He turned away. "But the report is right there. Knock yourself out." He pointed to his front passenger seat.

She ignored his pessimism and picked up the report and read it. "It says here that her last meal was Coca-Cola and a donut."

He shrugged.

"It says she ate the food immediately before she died; within ten minutes. Also, she had only taken a couple of bites of the donut, and she only drank approximately four ounces of the soda."

"Oh, you think she had that in the terminal before boarding."

"Exactly. Maybe she was worried about the food on the plane, or she simply didn't like plane food, and she was grabbing a snack in the terminal to avoid eating and drinking on the flight."

"So, we're back to the killer dosing her and then carrying the poison onto the plane to make sure the job was done. He brought it with him in case she didn't die; so he could finish the job." He scowled toward the plane and shoved his hands into his pockets. "Maybe he wasn't sure of the dose?"

THE WOMAN IN THE WINDOW

"Doesn't sound feasible to me. If someone was going to off someone with cyanide, I think they would know it doesn't take much to get the job done. Besides, how the hell would they sneak it through the security checkpoints? I would think a small glass vial with white powder would get someone detained."

"Yeah, you're right. It would raise an eyebrow or two, but that doesn't change the fact that it happened."

Her next thought was bad. "Maybe one of the security team at the airport was in on it."

Bale blew out a heavy breath and his shoulders slumped forward briefly. "God, I hope not. I'm hoping it was just an oversight, a careless mistake."

"Wouldn't it have been simpler for them to wait until she reached DC to kill her? If they wanted her dead that badly, why not wait until she was within easier reach?"

He chuckled humorlessly. "Because we were waiting for her here, and the bad guys knew she would be under twenty-four-hour protection until after the trial."

"The mole," Ava said flatly.

"The mole." Bale spun his keys around his finger and stared toward the plane. "Come to my office tomorrow morning as soon as you can. If I need to officially request your help, consider it done. You and Lin are the only two agents I can trust, and I need the help on this."

"Put in the request, and I'll be there. You have a plan?"

"Yeah. We need to narrow the suspect list. The killer was on that plane, and I want to know who it was before they can do any more damage to the case against the syndicate. They hoped killing Ms. Cahill would put that case in the dirt, but they're wrong. I want to know who killed her, and I want to rip every person in Emerald Block a new—"

"Okay, I'm in," Ava said. "I want to find the killer and take down as many in the syndicate as possible, too."

He pulled his gaze back to her. "I'm going to hang around and make sure Lin and the others are okay. You go on home. It's late. I'll see you tomorrow."

She nodded and went to her car.

CHAPTER SEVENTEEN

Process of Elimination

B™ EFORE THE MORNING MEETING, SAL OPENED THE DOOR AND walked into Ava's office.

"Good morning?" Ava asked after seeing the expression on Sal's face.

"You're going to DC, Ava."

"You talked to Bale?"

"I did. He told me a few things, but not much. Says you are one of the only two people he can trust to work this case. What's that even mean? He wouldn't elaborate. I told him I needed you here, but my boss overrode my decision."

Ava adjusted in her seat, which had become very uncomfortable suddenly. "I'll still work on the Margot Carter case, Sal. I won't leave you in the lurch."

"Did you ask Bale to let you help on the Cahill murder?"

"No, but I did tell him I would if he needed me. Did he tell you there was a mole in the agency leaking information about the case against Emerald Block?"

"Emerald Block?" Sal's eyes widened.

"Yes. That's who Covey Cahill was set to testify against, and Bale believes they are the ones who had her killed to prevent her testimony."

"How the hell was she mixed up with them?" Sal put a hand on the back of the empty chair as if for balance.

"You know who they are?"

"They're bad news, but I didn't know there was a case against them. Didn't you know them?"

"No, I didn't."

"How was the victim involved with them?" she asked again.

"She was dating a guy in the upper echelon of the syndicate. She witnessed a lot of their dealings, and she knew enough to put people away for a long time; forever, in some instances."

"Can the case carry on without her? Is there a chance to take down the syndicate without her testimony?"

"Bale seems to think so."

Sal fidgeted and then ran a finger over her left eyebrow and breathed out slowly. "If that's true, do whatever it takes to finish that case. Make it your priority. Hand the Margot Carter case over to Metford and the others for now."

"What? I told you I could—"

"No. I said hand it over to Metford. Do it when you leave."

Why was she taking it so personally? Why did she seem so strange after learning who the original case was against?

"Yes, ma'am. I'll get it ready and give it to him after the meeting."

"No, do it now. You need to get to DC as soon as possible. Just get the files and notes together and I'll give it to him." She held out her hand and made a 'give me' gesture with her fingers. "Come on. I know you have it right there. Put your notes with it and give it to me."

Ava moved papers on her desk and retrieved the notebook she used for the Margot Carter case. She held it out to Sal. "Is everything okay, Sal?"

"Fine. Yes. Now, go help Bale. Keep me updated on your progress, but don't worry about the cases here until you're done with that one." She leaned forward and lowered her voice. "Take those bastards down. As many of them as you can, and don't ask me why because I'm not ready to talk about it. I haven't talked about it in years. Maybe one day, I'll be ready, but not yet, so don't ask." She turned on her heel and stalked out of the room stiffly.

Ava left the office with one more reason to throw herself into the Cahill case. If someone had wronged Sal, even in the distant past...

Bale rang Ava's phone as she was pulling out of the parking space. She told him she was on her way.

A little under an hour later, she walked into Bale's office. "I'm here," she announced.

Bale looked up from his desk, nodded, and pointed to a rolling chair nearby. "Grab that and let's get to work." He lifted a stack of papers and let them drop to his desk again.

"What's that?" She pushed the chair to the short side of the desk and sat.

"Interviews, passenger list, background checks. In short, everything we have so far. Let's go through this and figure out how best to narrow our suspect list."

It looked like a Stephen King novel manuscript had been dumped on his desk. It would take all day to go through them. "What about if we go through and eliminate anyone who had no connection to Covey Cahill or Emerald Block?"

"Logical. Very logical, James. Don't know if I was expecting that from you, or not." He pushed half the papers toward her.

"What's that mean?" She picked up the papers and tapped them into a neater pile.

"Your reputation is for thinking outside the box, unorthodox methods to get fast and reliable results."

"I have a reputation? Right."

"You do." He tapped the desk. "Put connections here. Anyone who doesn't have connections, put them here." He pointed to an empty file box a bit farther toward the edge of the desk.

After two hours of relentless reading and analyzing, Ava dropped her last interview into the box. "Well, that was a bust," she said, looking at the empty spot on the desk where the connections pile was supposed to be.

Bale put his hands behind his head and stretched back in his seat. "Process of elimination just eliminated every passenger."

"We need new parameters is all."

"Pray tell, what would the new parameters be?"

"Let's eliminate by proximity to the victim. Let's figure out who was close enough to poison Ms. Cahill without her or anyone else noticing."

Bale pulled out the seating list. "That's easy enough on the flight. There's only two people seated close enough that they might have been able to slip the poison in her food or drink."

Ava groaned. "But there was no evidence that she even had anything to eat or drink on the flight. Even the attendants denied bringing her anything."

"Well, that's another bust anyway because one was a woman in her sixties who has difficulty moving around, and the other was you."

"What about in the terminal?"

"What about it?" Bale tossed the seating paper aside and looked disgusted.

"Let's work under the idea that the poison was administered in the terminal. Let's request the video surveillance footage from the San Francisco International. Let's get it from two hours before the flight boarded until an hour after."

"She was dosed no more than ten minutes before boarding," Bale said. His tone of exasperation was annoying.

"We need the broader range of time to look for possible perpetrators. We want to know when a person showed up, where they went, what they did before Ms. Cahill came along and ate or drank poison, right?"

"Moot point if we see the culprit spiking her food, right?" he asked through a smirk.

Didn't matter, he was already reaching for the phone. It took twenty minutes to get an agreement about the footage. He put the phone back on the cradle harder than necessary.

"Figure out something else?" he asked.

Ava had taken the papers from the box and tapped them straight again. "We can dig deeper into the backgrounds, but first, I think we should eliminate all the women from the pile, and only keep the names and backgrounds of the men between the ages of twenty-five and forty-five."

"Why only those men?"

"Because most killers—serial or mass or mercenaries or regular killers—are white males between those ages."

Bale seemed to consider it for a moment before an impressed expression crossed his stern features. "That's pretty good, but what if it's none of them? What if it was a woman? Or a grandfatherly old man?"

"Or someone's ten-year-old kid? Come on, Bale. Work with me here unless you have a better idea."

He held out his hand for a stack of papers. Ava grinned and gave him about half. When they had sorted through, she picked up the stack from the desk and counted them.

"Eighteen," she said.

He laughed. "Eighteen? That's still a lot."

"It's better than a hundred." She handed him half of those papers. "Now, let's dig deeper into the backgrounds of these *eighteen* men."

"Hope you plan on getting dinner in DC."

"I know a great Chinese takeout place here. Ping's. Know it?"

"Every agent who's ever pulled a late night in the office knows Ping's."

"You're paying, right?" she asked without looking up.

"If you're not."

They worked until five in the evening, digging into the backgrounds, arrest records, divorce records, high school discipline records, and even the immunization records of the eighteen men.

"You ready for dinner yet?" Bale asked as he laid down his last paper and flipped off his computer.

"I am. Do you have pictures of the Emerald Block members?"

"Of course, I do. They're here." He handed her the folder with the casefile on Emerald Block. "What did you find?"

"I'm not sure, but I think maybe a connection, maybe not."

Bale's phone rang and he spoke to someone for a few seconds. He hung up and turned on his computer again. "Surveillance footage arrived."

Ava dropped the files and scooted her chair closer to see the screen. She pulled the pictures over with her. "Did you order dinner?"

"You know I didn't." The video filled the screen. "But I will."

"That would be great. They do delivery," she said while she pulled the pictures from the folder.

"I know. I use them a lot." He called and ordered their food. He didn't give them a card number to run but insisted he would pay with cash upon delivery.

"You still use cash?" she asked, slightly amused.

"You give out your card number over the phone to strangers?" He shook his head. "Good way to invite trouble you don't want or need."

"I use a prepaid card so there's never much money on it. Less than a hundred at any time. I just move money over to it when I need something."

"Well, color me impressed." He shook his head with finality. "But count me out. Sounds like too much of a headache. I like cash. They hand me the product, I hand them the cash, and everyone walks away happy and secure. Quick, clean, simple."

She pointed to the screen. "We can look for these mugs in the footage. The killer was probably one of them." She tapped the photos on the desk.

"Might be someone they hired, too. Someone we don't know about, but..." He flourished a hand toward the screen. "...process of elimination."

CHAPTER EIGHTEEN

The Footage

THE FOOTAGE SHOWED COVEY CAHILL ENTER THE AIRPORT AND take a seat in the waiting area. She sat on the end seat where she was exposed to foot traffic beside her and directly in front of her.

"Horrible choice of seats," Bale said.

Soon, the waiting area was nearly full of people waiting to board their flights. The airport bustled with activity, and it was difficult to follow any one person's movements because of the crowding.

Covey Cahill remained in her seat.

Ava leaned close to the monitor and put her finger against the screen as she squinted. "She has a bottle of soda sticking out the top of her purse right there."

Bale leaned in. "Her open purse, at that. It's on the seat beside her. Why would she leave it so exposed?"

"Maybe she just wasn't thinking. It's not easy for everyday people to think like criminals, or to think like we do. They can pull it off for a while, but not continuously."

"Well, Ms. Cahill was not an everyday person. She thought like a criminal because she was one for much of her life, and she should have been able to think ahead a little. How hard is it to think that someone might do something to an open purse sitting beside a person?"

"Did she think someone would poison her, though? I mean, really? From the photos you showed me, Emerald Block has a tendency to work with a much messier method. She was probably looking out for a gun or a knife, hence sitting where it was most crowded with foot traffic and leaving the open purse beside her. She probably felt pretty safe in the airport because it's almost impossible to get a gun in there, and if someone did, they might shoot her, but they would be caught quickly."

"Sure, but she knew how dangerous they were. We moved her to San Francisco to heal from her wounds and to keep her safe. As soon as the hospital released her, she was gone from here. She knew how vital she was to the case against them, too."

"I don't think she got herself killed on purpose. A good man told me that shit happens and you can't save everybody," Ava said.

"I don't think she did, either, but she should have been more alert and careful. I'm not blaming her; I'm just mad at the whole situation. Emerald Block has been getting away with their shit for far too long. It was time to put it to an end, and now…" He pointed to the screen and scoffed. "By the way, that was good advice."

She nodded but kept her gaze on the screen. The video playback was set to twenty-five-percent faster than normal. Groups walked by and blocked Ms. Cahill from view several times. Each time they moved on, Ava squinted to see if Covey acted any differently. She did not. She ate a few bites of the donut she had, and then she took it to a trashcan and tossed it in before sitting again.

"How did no one steal her purse or carry-on when she did that?" Bale asked. "She just left all her things sitting there like we live in a good and honest world, or something. I'm figuring out how she got involved with those people."

"I thought you knew already."

"I mean her mindset. She's careless and way too trusting. I think that bottle of soda is probably how she got dosed."

"I am leaning in that direction, too," Ava said.

Bale and Ava watched as an unknown woman took a seat behind Ms. Cahill and struck up a conversation. After a short exchange, Ms. Cahill pulled her purse into her lap and pulled something out and handed it to the woman behind her. They continued to chat.

"Could you tell what that was?" Bale asked.

"Nope. Video quality isn't that good." She stopped the playback, put the speed slower than normal, and replayed the event. "Still no good. I can't be sure what it was, just that it was small."

"Might be another option for introduction of the cyanide."

A group walked by and blocked the view of both women. "Can't even see what the other woman is doing," Ava said.

When the group cleared, the unknown female was gone.

"The woman disappeared," Bale said. "I can't see her in the walking group."

"Ms. Cahill looks just fine. She is putting whatever that was back into her purse and doesn't seem to be in distress at all."

Bale sped up the video again. "It's getting closer to our window of time." He pointed to the timestamp.

A tall woman who looked to be middle-aged walked in with another small crowd. They stopped in front of Ms. Cahill. The middle-aged woman turned to face Covey, and it seemed maybe they exchanged brief pleasantries. Suddenly, the older woman bent forward as she dropped something beside Ms. Cahill's purse. She quickly retrieved the item, and pulled it close to her, and moved away with the group.

"What did she drop and pick up?" Ava asked.

Bale rewound the footage and slowed it down. They watched it three times. It was no use; the video quality was not good enough to see details on something so small.

"Whatever it was, she hid it in her hands and walked off with it," Bale said.

"Could have been anything, though."

"Including another way to introduce the poison," Bale reminded her.

"We need to get the information on both women and check out their stories," Ava said.

Ms. Cahill stood when the rest of the group did. She shouldered her purse and pulled her carry-on.

"They're boarding."

"Window of opportunity closed," Ava said. "Let's pull up the first woman and get her info."

Bale did. It didn't take long to get her information.

Bale smiled and held up the paper on which he had scribbled notes. "Halle Westerville. She wasn't even a passenger on Ms. Cahill's plane."

"Is that her address?"

"It is. Right here in DC."

Ava stood and grabbed her bag. "Come on. I'll drive."

"Right behind you. I'm not going to argue. God knows I hate the traffic this time of day. Everybody trying to rush home for the day as if they're not going to be coming right back out in the morning to do it all again."

"Traffic will thin out soon. It doesn't bother me most of the time. She only lives fifteen minutes away."

It took almost thirty minutes to slug through the traffic to the apartment building at the southern-most end of DC. Bale and Ava took the elevator to the eighth floor. Apartment 8C was the first unit to their left after exiting the elevator.

"Posh enough place. Guess working in finance here pays great," Bale said.

Ava knocked on the door.

Halle opened the door but left the chain lock engaged. "If you're delivering food, try two apartments in the opposite direction. Hobbs is the one who orders takeout. Eight-G. I'm Eight-C." She started to close the door but stopped when Ava and Bale held up their badges.

"We're not delivering anything, Ms. Westerville?" Ava asked.

"You're the FBI and you don't know my name?" She started to close the door again.

"Ma'am? You flew in from SFO recently—"

"Gold star for Columbo there, but no, I didn't fly from SFO to DC, I flew from San Fran to North Carolina, and then I flew here after I took care of my business. So, why is the FBI interested in my flights over the last week?"

"A woman you were seen speaking to ended up dead on her flight," Bale said.

Ms. Westerville's eyes flew wide and she shook her head. "No. No, you are not involving me in any investigation. I didn't have anything to do with anyone's death. I know nothing about it."

"May we come in and ask you a few questions? You might be able to help us clear up this matter," Ava said.

She opened the door but didn't move past the short entrance hall. "We can talk right here. You won't be here long."

"Ms. Westerville, you sat behind a woman at the airport. In the waiting area," Ava said. "You spoke with her, and she handed you something from her purse."

Halle nodded emphatically. "And?"

"Did you know Ms. Cahill?" Bale asked.

"No," Halle exclaimed. "I didn't know her at all. I just sat for a minute behind her because I had a terrible headache. She turned around when I sat down, and I said hello. It seemed like I startled her, and I didn't want to be rude."

"What did she hand you?" Ava asked.

"A travel size bottle of Tylenol. I told her I only sat because my head hurt, and she offered the Tylenol."

"And you took Tylenol from a complete stranger?" Bale asked.

"I did. It was just Tylenol. I took two of them, thanked her, and gave the bottle back. I realized I didn't have a drink to swallow them with, so I went to get one. When I got back, she was gone. My flight was called, and I boarded without seeing her again. Is she the one who's dead?"

Bale nodded.

"I'm really sorry for her, but I don't need to be embroiled in some murder case. I didn't even know the woman, and I don't need to be in the middle of some investigation. That could kill my career and my reputation. Without those two things being pristine, I'm sure you realize it's almost impossible to work in DC. So, whatever happened, I'm sorry. I'm not part of this, so kindly leave me alone."

"You said you flew from San Francisco to North Carolina, correct?" Ava asked.

"Yeah. I was in Asheville for a business day trip, and I caught another plane from Asheville and was home late that night. Feel free to check it out. I just don't want to be associated with this case. Don't ruin my life."

"Ms. Westerville, that's not what we're trying to do at all," Ava said.

"And remember, a woman lost her life. She was murdered," Bale said. "If the tables were turned, you would want us to check every lead we have. Just so happens that you turned up as one of our leads today. If we need anything else, we will be in touch."

He turned and motioned for Ava to leave in front of him.

Ava got behind the wheel. "It's almost seven. The company she works for won't have anyone in the office, but I'll check her story first thing in the morning."

"I don't understand how people can act like that. She was more worried about her reputation and her career than a woman who was murdered. A woman she talked to and took a Tylenol from."

"That's really eating you, isn't it? That she took those pills from Ms. Cahill."

"Yeah. She felt safe enough to take them; Ms. Cahill was considerate enough to even offer them in the first place. Now, none of that matters. It's just, 'don't bother me with this.' It's sickening."

"People are self-centered, but it wasn't like she knew the victim. She has a right to be unaffected. As bad as it is, she has that right." Ava started the car and drove away from the posh apartment building.

CHAPTER NINETEEN

No Laughing Matter

Bale was outside his office the next morning. "You check out Westerville's story?"

"It checks. There was even security footage of her entering and leaving the building in North Carolina. I confirmed that she was on the flight from Asheville, and that she arrived and got off that plane in DC at eight that evening. She's clean."

He walked into the office. "I ran her background. Clean and shiny. Too clean. She never even had a moving violation. Can you believe that? In DC, and never even got a ticket."

"We can take her off the suspect list, in my opinion," Ava said.

"No. No, we can't. We still don't know for sure how Ms. Cahill was poisoned. Westerville had contact with her during the crucial window of time when we know the poison was introduced. No matter how clean

THE WOMAN IN THE WINDOW

her story and background are, we can't completely dismiss her as a suspect." He sat at his desk. "She's still on the list."

"Okay. Makes sense, but—"

"No buts. She's still a suspect."

"I was going to say that we need to look at the airport footage again and home in on the tall, older woman. She bent down next to that purse and did something. Maybe she didn't just drop something and pick it up."

Bale tapped at the keyboard of the computer and nodded. "She was bent there for a hot minute, wasn't she?"

"She was." Ava took her seat.

"I passed it off because of her age. Maybe she was just slow." He queued the video.

"But she walked away without any trouble. She seemed to have no problems walking in with the group, either."

The video played from just before the tall woman appeared. Bale zoomed and slowed playback. They watched as she seemingly dropped something. Ms. Cahill only glanced in her direction as she bent to pick it up again.

"There," Bale said. "There's too much arm movement for her to be just picking up something she dropped."

Ava watched again. "It does look like she's doing something else, but she has the purse blocked. Covey doesn't seem to think anything's up, though. Look at her. She's watching more people coming in from the main hall."

"There goes the tall woman," Bale said. "She's heading for the public restrooms across the hallway."

Ava watched as she walked into the restroom alcove. Bale centered the scene on the screen, and they both watched intently for the woman to come out again.

The video clip ended.

"What?" Bale asked, rewinding it again.

"That's the end. That means we watched for almost an hour for her to come out of the restrooms again, and I never saw her."

"I'm watching again. I don't believe that. No matter how old she might be, nobody stays in the restroom at an airport for a damn hour."

The video played at fast speed until the woman entered the bathroom alcove again, and then Bale set it to play at normal speed. Again, they never saw her exit.

"One more time," Ava said. "I want to see if I can get some good stills of her face."

As she navigated through the scene of the woman, she took a few stills of the screen, but none showed her clearly.

Bale looked over the stills. "Look at that. Not a single one that's any good. But I can see how big her hands are. She's a big woman. At least six feet tall, maybe more."

"It's almost like she knew where the cameras were and avoided getting her face on any of them."

"Yeah, but she stands out, for sure. Did you see her while you were there?" He pointed to Ava at the counter.

"No, I don't remember seeing her at all." A woman of her stature would have stood out. She would have been memorable. "See if we can get at least a couple of stills that are better than these."

They worked together to tweak the shots as much as they could, but the resulting images were low-quality. Bale took two more that showed how tall the woman was compared to other people in the airport.

"These only show her from the side and from behind, but they're good comparison shots. Surely somebody will have some memory of a middle-aged woman who looks like she towers over all the other women," he said.

"I'm going to call SFO and see if I can get a video call with the security who were on-duty that day."

It took almost two hours to get the call going. Ava introduced herself and had the men on the other end do the same as she wrote down their names. Finally, she held up a shot of the woman's face. It was a profile shot that was less than great, and better than crap.

"Do any of you remember seeing this woman at the airport?"

They leaned in close and took turns staring at the picture and then shaking their heads.

"I need you to look very closely and be sure. As you know, a woman was poisoned and died. We believe the poisoning might have happened in your airport." She held up another profile picture. It was slightly clearer than the other one.

Again, the men looked closely, but they shook their heads and denied having seen anyone like the picture.

"She was very tall. We estimate that she was at least six feet tall. Maybe more, though," Ava said as she readied another picture.

One of the men laughed. "Maybe she was a ninja granny."

The other chortled and added, "Maybe it's all an international intrigue, and she was a master of disguise—not a granny at all." He made woo-woo gestures with his hands, and they all laughed.

THE WOMAN IN THE WINDOW

Ava did not laugh. How could they joke about the situation? Did they not realize how serious the situation was? She cleared her throat, and the men settled back to stare at the screen again. A couple had the decency to look chagrined.

"This is no joking matter, gentlemen," she said flatly as she held the picture up for them. "This woman is seemingly missing. She seems to have gone missing in your airport, under your watch, and you think it's funny?" She put the picture down and brought out one of Covey Cahill. It was her driver's license photo, which did little justice to her beauty in life, but it sufficed. "This, gentlemen, is the woman who lost her life. She's dead. She doesn't have the luxury of laughing at your jokes. She'll never laugh again. Now, did any of you see anything that might further this investigation?"

The man who made the first joke looked down at his hands clasped on the table. "I didn't. If I had seen her, I think I would remember her, Agent James, as would any of my men."

The one who made the international intrigue joke nodded and leaned forward. "We didn't mean anything by the jokes. Just breaking the tension is all."

Disappointed, she nodded.

One of the younger officers raised his hand shyly and stammered, "I do remember seeing a really tall woman, but she was far away from me. I didn't get a good look."

The other officers turned to look at him.

Ava held up the last picture of the older woman again. Excitement surged through her chest. "Was this her? Try to remember."

"I'm sorry," he said, shaking his head. "I didn't get a good look at her. Like I said, she was far away. I was down the hall, and she was near the seats. It could have been her, yeah."

Could have been was not good enough. "Thank you," Ava said. The whole meeting had been a let-down. "If anyone remembers anything, give me a call. Doesn't matter what time it is." She gave them her number.

"Did you check to see if the people up front might have checked her in for her flight?" The young officer asked.

"Yes. No one remembers her. Thank you, gentlemen."

Ava shook her head as she headed back to find Bale.

CHAPTER TWENTY

Still No Laughing Matter

B ALE WAS ON THE PHONE WHEN AVA FOUND HIM. HE HELD UP A hand to her, and she nodded, hoping he was having better luck finding a lead than she had.

He hung up and turned to her. "Any luck with airport security?"

"No. Was that Lin?"

"Yeah. Nobody saw anything at the airport? That woman should have stuck out to somebody."

"One officer remembered seeing a really tall woman, as he put it, but she was too far away for him to be certain it was our woman. The others seemed disinterested at best."

"Did they look at the pictures? Really look at them?" Bale's eyes narrowed and his brows drew down farther. "Or, did they just brush it off and act like they looked?"

"No, they looked. They looked at a few pictures, and then a couple of them made jokes. One woman is dead, another missing, and they had jokes like some stand-up comedians. The audacity of people rubs me the wrong way." Clamping her mouth closed against the tirade that wanted to escape, Ava drew in a long breath and looked away.

"Audacity?" He chuckled.

Ava's blood boiled. "What is it with people laughing today? Am I the only one who can't find the humor in the situation? First, the security officers, and now, you?"

"Don't get in twist, James. It's not every day you hear someone use that word. Especially not in our line of work." He moved closer, still grinning. "You gotta learn to laugh sometimes, James. You're going to end up with an ulcer the size of Texas. This job will drive you nuts if you don't learn to compartmentalize. It's okay to laugh."

"So says the man with a permanent scowl."

"Touché." He walked by her. "Might I add that maybe you should look in the mirror sometimes?"

"I don't scowl," she said a little too defensively even for her own liking.

"Right, right. So, security made a few tasteless jokes, you're upset, I understand, but we need to get on with it."

"It doesn't even matter. They were being callous jerks. They didn't care that a woman might have been poisoned in their airport, or that the other one might be missing. Who knows? Maybe there were two victims."

"It might matter. We still don't know for sure how many people were involved. How would the killer get the poison aboard a plane? How did the vial get on board? Maybe the jokes were just jokes, but maybe they were an attempt at redirecting the focus of the investigation. What were the jokes?"

"One said that maybe she wasn't a granny at all but some sort of master of disguise and that's why no one remembered seeing her. That's why she wasn't on the footage ever leaving the restrooms..." Her voice trailed off as her mind jumped to several different possible reasons.

She headed for the computer.

"What? You just thought of something." Bale was right behind her.

"What if he was right?" She pulled up the footage taken from the airport.

"First you're mad and now you think maybe he was right?" He scoffed, but there was a barely disguised chuckle in the sound.

"What if she came out of the restroom area looking totally different than when she went in? We were still looking for her." Ava tapped a printed still of the tall woman. "We were looking for her hair, her clothes, her everything. Did you look to see if anyone came out that resembled her but was dressed differently? Had different hair?"

Bale laughed without trying to disguise it. "That's a hoot, James. When they said you think outside the box, they didn't say just how far out in left field you went sometimes." He patted the top of her chair and walked away laughing.

"Laugh. That's the right way to approach a possible lead, Bale." She played the footage fifty-percent faster than the normal speed.

"Sometimes, it's the only way to react to such an idea." He spun toward her again, his laughter gone. "It's not really the idea, but the way you swung from being so pissed about the officers and their jokes to believing that there might be something to it. Even Emerald Block doesn't go to such extremes. Master of disguise? This isn't a movie; it's real life, and in real life, things like that just don't happen."

"Usually," she said, mostly ignoring her own urge to react to him and defend her decision. The tall woman appeared on the screen, and Ava slowed the playback, leaned in close, and squinted at her. Who was she? Was she wearing a wig? "Her hands," she said in a low voice.

"What about them?" Bale asked.

"Nothing. They're just big for a woman." The woman headed for the restrooms. Ava zoomed as much as was possible and barely blinked while people were entering and exiting. There was a constant small crowd in the area of the restroom entrances. The little alcove was never empty, and it made seeing each person difficult, and sometimes, impossible.

"The whole woman was big for a woman, in my opinion," Bale said from across the room.

At the end of the footage, Ava sighed and thumped back in the chair.

"Anything?" Bale asked.

"Useless." She shut down the playback screen and pushed away from the desk.

Bale chuckled good-humoredly. "I'm sorry it didn't pan out the way you'd hoped, but if you're done playing double-oh-seven, we could go over some of the other interviewees' backgrounds in deeper detail. You know, like real-world detectives." He grinned and held up a paper.

She smirked at him and then nodded. "How many did we get back already?"

He counted papers. "Five."

"Out of eighteen, we only have five?" She rolled her chair to his workspace and sat again.

"It's a slow process when you're getting more details. The farther back the report goes—"

"The longer it takes. I know the drill. I was just hoping for more." She held out her hand.

Bale handed her two of the papers. "Do any of them have connections to Emerald Block?"

"Well, seeing as how I just got these printed and handed you two of them, I can honestly say that I know as much as you do for now."

"Let's check. It doesn't matter how long ago it was, or how tenuous the connection was, we need the information. We need their arrest records—"

He shook the papers in his hand. "Part of the background checks, James."

"You didn't let me finish. We need their records from juvenile to present. I want to even check their families' arrest records, warrants, anything that would be a red flag to investigate further. If someone's auntie was busted twenty years ago for buying a dime-bag from a dealer who later ended up tied in with Emerald Block, I want to know about it."

"James, I must say that I wholeheartedly agree with you on this one," Bale said. "I don't know that I would have gone so far out on the branches of the family tree thing as you are, but it's a good idea."

"Emerald Block could be holding anything over anyone's head. At least, that's the assumption I'm working from. I put nothing past them. In my mind, they would do anything necessary to get the results they want and not have it lead back to them. What better way than to exploit someone with a tenuous past connection?"

He nodded. "Nice. I can appreciate that kind of curved thinking."

"But not searching for a disguised woman leaving the restrooms kind of curved thinking, huh?" She smirked again.

He shook his head. "That's a little too movie-world for me." He looked down at his papers. "Maybe something to check out later, when we've exhausted the more realistic possibilities," he muttered as if it had to be said but he didn't really want her to hear it.

"Later, then," she said.

His words were an admission that he didn't think she was being totally flaky about the disguise theory. For the time, that was good enough.

CHAPTER TWENTY-ONE

One Step Back, One Step Forward

Three hours later, Ava tossed the papers onto the desk and shoved away. "Okay, this is ridiculously slow, Bale. Are you getting anywhere?"

He looked up and shook his head. "Not far, but this is how it goes in the real world, double-oh-seven."

She made a disgruntled noise and scrubbed her palms up and down her cheeks. It was like being slowly devoured by quicksand. Sitting in the chair for another minute was out of the question. She stood.

"I know a faster way to get the information we need," she said, thinking of Ashton.

"I'll listen to any suggestion short of consulting a psychic." He laced his fingers behind his head and rocked back in his chair.

"I want to call in my team to help speed up the investigation," she announced with confidence. It felt wonderful just to say it aloud. The thought of actually having her team there felt phenomenal.

He rocked forward and brought his hands down in one motion. "Absolutely out of the question, James." He pulled a paper to him and started clacking away at the computer keyboard as if that was the end of the conversation.

"My guy would make this his priority, and he is twice as fast as anybody I've ever worked with on getting information over the computer."

He slammed the paper onto the desk and looked up angrily. "I said no, and that's final. You know the boundaries of this investigation. Counting me, Lin, and you, there are only five people actively working this case who have any details. Do you understand that there is a mole in the agency, James?"

"I understand that, Bale. You've made it abundantly clear that someone is leaking information, but I can personally vouch for every person on my team. None of them is the mole."

"Well, gold stars for you. I don't know them; therefore, I don't trust them. Drop it. It's not happening."

"This is the age of technology. I wasn't the best in my class with the tech side of the job, but I know someone who was top of his class. We're not working in the 1970s. The wheel was invented a while back. We're not huddled around a fire in a cave anymore." She blew out a breath in frustration and turned away.

"The case remains as it is," he said gruffly.

"Even if one of my team could expedite the information on backgrounds, arrests, and anything else you need to help solve the case faster than the speed of smell?"

"No, James. No way. No can do. The five on the case are the only ones I trust, and I don't want to have to warn you, but I find it might be necessary. If you go behind my back to use anyone else, speak to anyone else about the case, or give out details of it, I won't hesitate. Don't test me on this. Don't make me regret trusting you. A key witness is already dead even with all our careful measures in place. Remember that."

"Have it your way, Bale," she said. What good would it do to continue arguing her point?

"I will. It's my case."

His phone rang. He held Ava's gaze a moment longer, driving home his immovability on the matter.

She nodded. "You got it. Guess I'll roast marshmallows over the fire while I work."

"Good," he said. The ruddy color of his cheeks turned to a deeper crimson as his phone continued ringing.

She turned back to the desk, and he answered his phone. The thought of sitting in the chair for three more hours to only reach ten more dead ends was torture, but the case had to be solved. If she must investigate like a Luddite, so be it.

"James," Bale said.

Even if it was another argument, she was glad that she wouldn't be sitting again for another few minutes.

"Yeah?" She turned and strode back to his workspace.

"That was the medical examiner. The tox results are back."

"It was cyanide, wasn't it?" she asked.

"It was. Covey Cahill's death was definitely a murder."

"I was working off that assumption all along," she said.

"Me, too, but now we have reason to be more aggressive with our investigative methods." He grinned, and it seemed to be genuine.

Although a grade-A ass sometimes, Bale wanted the same thing Ava did: to solve the case and get whomever killed Ms. Cahill.

"What do you have in mind now?" She moved to his desk.

"Since Ms. Cahill was testifying against the upper echelons of Emerald Block, I want to go over all the info we have on all the known associates and members of the syndicate. There must be a connection somewhere. Working it from the passengers' side is slow, but we already have so much information on the syndicate members from prior surveillance, arrests, and court cases that it should go faster from that angle. Besides, they're the only ones who would go to such lengths and take such risks to shut Ms. Cahill up for good."

"I can go over the footage again to see if any of the syndicate are in the airport." Ava headed back to the computer. Her earlier angst at needing to be in the seat were forgotten.

"I'm ordering facial recognition for that. It'll be faster." He reached for his phone, stopped, and looked at her. "Don't say a word. The answer is still no."

"I said nothing." But she had started to. He had seen her face and knew what she was about to ask. "Just saying, if speed is a concern now, I know—"

"No," he said, dialing his phone and ignoring her completely.

After he hung up, Ava spun her chair to face his direction. "I want more footage from San Francisco. I want another angle. I put in the request already."

He stared at her for a few seconds. "Fine. We need more angles to be able to see faces in the crowds better. I'll send it to facial recognition when it arrives. How long? Did they say?"

"No. I'll let you know as soon as it's here, though. Did they say how long it'll be for facial recognition results?"

"I sent them a long list of faces to scan for. It's going to take a while. It usually takes a bare minimum of twenty-four hours to get results, but with the number of faces on the list and considering it's getting late… I would think it will most likely be day after tomorrow when we get results, or anything resembling results."

Ashton could have the results in several hours. Maybe less. She kept her mouth shut about it. She had figured out it was easier to not open it in the first place than to force it shut after the words started spilling out.

CHAPTER TWENTY-TWO

Different Angles

San Francisco sent the extra footage quickly. Less than an hour after she put in the formal request, the footage arrived, and a follow-up call came in to her phone.

"Impressive," Bale said. "Not often that happens."

"What, the call?"

"The request was sent, and less than an hour later, they're calling to let you know it's already waiting for you." He shook his head. "You'll have to teach me how you do that someday."

"It's easier to catch flies with honey than with vinegar, Bale," she said, imparting some of her grandmother's golden, if odd life advice.

She pulled up the video footage and motioned to Bale. "Want to help me scour through this?"

"I don't think so. That's all you, James. I'm working on the backgrounds still. Two more came through."

"Ooh, that's seven of the eighteen." She emphasized the last number. "One word for you."

"Yeah? What's that?"

"Ashton." She turned her attention and her chair to the computer.

"You know where I stand on that. My people will get the work done in their own time. They're good."

Ava nodded but didn't turn to face him and offered no verbal response. She could have argued that Ashton was better than his best, but what good would it do?

"Some of the best," he said after a long silence.

"Isn't that how we all feel about our units, though?" She said it with a lack of attitude, but she wanted him to think about it.

"Ha ha. She's got comebacks. A little fire never hurt anyone. Neither did a little attitude, but sometimes…"

"You know that every time you say something genuine and then follow it with 'but,' you've just negated everything you said before the 'but'?" She looked over her shoulder toward him.

"Just work and let me know if you come up with anything."

She turned away again, satisfied that she had gotten her point across.

"Like the tall woman who is apparently a shapeshifter."

She nodded without turning. His jab was only administered because she was making him think about things in a different way. It happened often around her, and she was accustomed to it.

The footage ran for almost two hours even with playback at fifty percent faster than normal speed. She only slowed the footage at points in which she could partially see the woman's face. If she saw anyone exit the restroom alcove who was tall, or even slightly resembled the woman, she would replay that part at normal speed, but there were only three instances of that—and they were all men.

After watching footage until she had practically memorized each person and each segment like a kid who watches a cartoon until it's dedicated to memory, she stood.

"Nothing, huh?" Bale asked as he stood and headed slowly for the door.

"Nope. I'm going to go talk to the attendants again." She moved toward him. "You quitting for the day?"

"No. Not by a long shot yet. I'm going to get something to eat, and then I'm back at it. What's got you piqued enough to go speak with the attendants again? We questioned all of them thoroughly already."

"I'm not sure. Call it a hunch, but something with the one switching flights and them having a trainee on 808 the same day a woman is poisoned to death doesn't sit right with me." She stepped into the hallway and her knee popped. The sound was loud and sharp. She kept moving.

"I was going to say something about hunches and how you're too young to have very accurate ones, but after hearing that knee, I'm beginning to wonder just how old you really are." He chuckled. "Better hope we don't have a ninja granny on the run; you'll never be able to keep up with that granny knee you have."

Ava laughed despite her best effort. They shouldn't be laughing. The case was terrible. What happened to Covey Cahill, the death she suffered, all alone even on a plane with so many passengers...

But weren't all the cases horrible in their own way? Wasn't that the reason she had become an agent? The FBI always ended up with the worst of the worst cases. The cases that showcased the banality, the cruelty, and the greed of the human race.

"I don't think we have to worry about her being on the run. She seriously never came back out of those bathrooms. There haven't been any deaths reported at the airport, and I don't know where she went, but she never came back out. One of the surveillance clips ran for a full three hours after she entered. Nothing. Not a single trace. Three men came out who were of comparable height, but that was it."

"She either stayed in there much longer than normal, or she was really good at disguising herself. If she was the poisoner, maybe she knew to lay low and do whatever it took to get back out of the place without being noticed."

"I don't know how she did it." She walked out the front door. "Maybe she did stay in there for much longer than expected, but wouldn't somebody have noticed?"

"Like who? If she had just poisoned a woman, it's not like she would have been there with her grandkids," Bale said.

Ava stopped at her car. "You're right. I hate it when you are, but I can't argue with that."

"I'll be sure to gloat after I've had dinner. What about you? Want something?"

She shook her head. "Thanks, but I'm going to see if I can catch Riley Moss and Asa Berry before they're gone on another flight."

"Good luck."

She got into her car and called Riley's number. She answered on the second ring, sounding out of breath.

"Riley Moss? This is Agent James. I was wondering if I could have a word with you?"

"About the case, I'm sure."

Of course. What else? The best place to get a manicure in DC? "Yes, about the case."

"That's fine. Whatever I can do to help, but make it quick. I need to get ready for my next flight." She stammered for a moment. "I am still free to go about my regular life, right? Nothing has changed?"

"No, nothing changed. Everyone is free to go about their life as normal. I needed to speak with you face to face, though. Do we have time? Ten minutes, and I'll be out of your hair. Promise."

"How soon can you meet me at the airport hotel?"

"Twenty minutes. Fifteen if I cheat a little."

"You better cheat unless you want to have that conversation in the airport," Riley said.

"Be there in ten," Ava said and hung up.

Twelve minutes later, she parked at the airport hotel. Riley let her into the room.

"I thought you were only allowed to cheat a little," she said, looking at her watch.

"We are, and only under certain circumstances. I just bent the speed limit a little here and there." Ava went inside.

Riley closed the door. "What did you want to talk about that couldn't be said over the phone? Please don't divulge anything that will put me at risk. I like my life and my job, as hard as that is for some people to believe."

"I just wanted to ask you about Tanzy Bruner, the other attendant."

"What about her? I already told you what I know." Riley's eyes shifted to the clock on the table and back to Ava.

"Do you know why she was so eager to switch flights?"

"It was between her and Melissa. Tanzy has two little kids at home, and I suppose, perhaps, it could have had something to do with them."

"Have you spoken to Melissa since the flight?"

Riley shook her head and looked back to the clock. "If that's all, I really need to head out now. It's not the kinda job where they forgive lateness."

"What about Tanzy's kids would make her want to switch flights?" Ava moved to block the door.

"All I know is that she asked Melissa to switch, Melissa agreed for whatever reason, and we got Tanzy Bruner. I wish Melissa hadn't switched, but she did. We had a trainee, and having an attendant we were unfamiliar with made it that much more stressful. If I know Melissa, though, something tugged at her heartstrings to make her agree to something so spontaneous like that. It was really last-minute." She looked at the door with mild panic. "Speaking of—may I go now? Please, I want to help, but I also don't want to be late for work."

Ava stepped aside. "Have a good flight, Riley."

"Thank you. I'm sorry I couldn't be more help. If I knew more, I'd tell you. Maybe you should talk to them. They're the ones who switched out."

"I will. Thank you again." Ava stepped out and went in the opposite direction to her car.

Ava called Bale.

"Is it possible that Tanzy Bruner found out about Covey Cahill's flight and prearranged to be on that flight so she could poison her?" Ava asked.

"I would think it's unlikely. I mean, I don't really think so, but at this point, I wouldn't rule it out, either. What about the trainee?"

"He was scheduled to be on the flight all along. Tanzy is the one who wasn't. She's the one who waited until it was almost too late to ask someone to swap out with her." She told him everything Riley had said.

"It's a maybe. Like I said, it seems unlikely, but I wouldn't rule it out."

So, she was left with more questions than answers.

When there were more questions than answers, there was only one thing to do: She needed to speak with Tanzy Bruner.

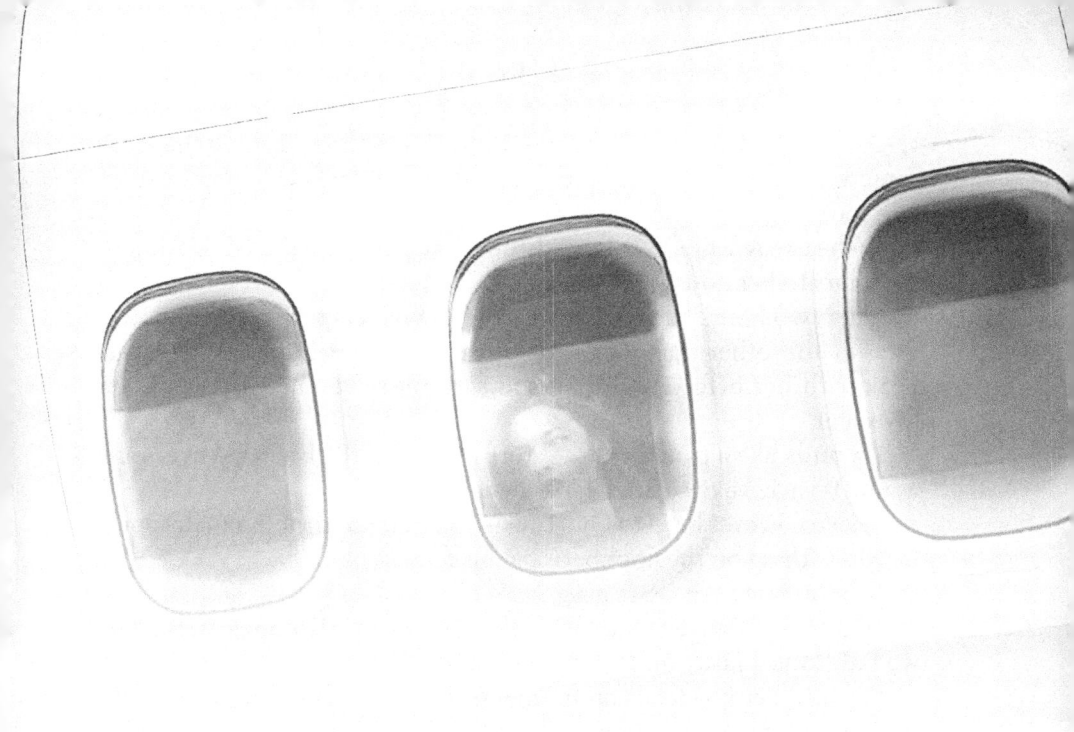

CHAPTER TWENTY-THREE

Tanzy's Story

B ALE FLIPPED THROUGH THE PAPERS ON HIS DESK AND PULLED ONE out. "Tanzy Bruner lives in the Old Town section of Baltimore," he said.

"Then that's where we need to go," Ava said. She picked up her things and went to the door. "Are you coming with?"

Bale picked up a folder. "Just getting the files together. Remind me again who's living in the Stone Age when it comes to technology?" He sifted through papers and put more into the file.

"Paper files are easier to add notes to and to keep safe. Keeping everything out of the computer for this case was your doing. Remember that."

"Don't remind me." He carried the file to the door. "I never thought I'd ever say that I wished for the electronic files, but here we are."

Ava laughed and nodded agreement. "Sometimes, I think the electronic version would be simpler, but I don't see me switching up anytime soon."

In the car, Ava plugged Tanzy Bruner's address into the GPS. "Almost two hours to her house."

"And two hours back." He consulted the papers for several minutes. "One of the other attendants lives just outside Baltimore. We could speak with her before returning and save ourselves another two-hour drive later."

"Sounds like a plan. I bet there are others on the lists who live close by, too. If we have time, we'll look them up."

"Have you ever been to Old Town?" Bale closed the file and dropped the whole thing on the floor between his feet.

"I have. Not such a safe place."

"One of the danger zones nowadays. Ms. Bruner is a single mother of two little kids. I just wonder why she stays in Old Town."

"Family, her financial commitments, there are several reasons a person chooses to remain in a less-than-desirable situation. Sometimes, they have no control over it."

"Old Town used to be safer," he said. "Maybe she moved there before it turned bad."

The remainder of the drive passed with discussions about the decline of all the major cities in the nation. In the span of ten years, they concluded, the whole of the United States had spiraled out of control. Ava hated that mindset, but there was little to do for it. It wasn't like she could deny the underlying truth of their conversation.

"I prefer to believe that there is hope in every situation," Ava said as she turned up the street to Tanzy's house.

"I prefer a lot of things, but I've learned that doesn't matter much in the face of reality."

"That's a cynical slant."

"Every cloud doesn't have a silver lining, and that's just the harsh reality of the world we live in." He unbuckled his seatbelt and retrieved the file from the floorboard.

"You're not going to carry that inside, are you?" She eyed the hefty file with papers sticking out the sides and top helter-skelter.

"I am. It's a good technique for sweating the suspect." He neatened the file.

"Intimidation on an emotional level." She cocked one eyebrow doubtfully at him.

"Whatever gets us answers. If she's intimidated by the size of the file, that signals to me that she has something to worry about. If she has something to worry about…" He raised one shoulder.

"That doesn't instantly make her guilty. Especially not of murder."

"No, but it's a good indicator that she might know something that we need to know. Are we going in, or are we just going to sit here arguing ethics?" He opened the door and stepped out without waiting for a reply.

The brick house stood two stories on a tiny spit of grass that could hardly be called a yard. The privacy fence around the property was in need of cleaning and a few repairs, but the house looked immaculate. Not a chipped piece of paint on any of the woodwork, and the bricks were in excellent shape—the sign of a newer construction.

"Nice place," Bale said as they stepped onto the stoop.

"Very," Ava admitted as she rang the doorbell and then knocked.

"Classic double-tap. Nice," Bale said with a wry smile.

"Learned it from a really good agent not so long ago," she said.

The woman who opened the door and stared out at them expectantly, at first, was a complete stranger. Kids yelled in the house, and a bout of high, childish giggles exploded into the doorway. The brunette was shoved violently to one side, and her attention was no longer on the two people on her porch.

"Jess, take your brother to the living room," she said sharply to the little girl, who was the obvious older of the two.

"Okay, Mama, but he's being a brat." Jess grabbed one of her brother's arms and half-dragged him away from their mother.

He screamed. It was a keen, piercing sound that sent the hairs up on Ava's neck. Bale bristled beside her.

The woman looked back to them. "Is there something I can do for you?" She directed her question to Ava and ignored Bale save for a glance in his direction.

"Tanzy Bruner?" Ava asked.

The woman sighed and ran a hand over her long, brown hair. "Yeah, that's me. Who are you?"

"I was on Flight 808. Agent Ava James."

Tanzy looked confused. "Yes," she said in a tone that said she didn't recognize Ava.

"You bumped me with the cart while I was sleeping."

"Listen, if you're going to file a complaint—"

"We're federal agents," Bale interrupted. "We're here to ask you some questions about the woman who died on that flight. Can we come in, or do we need to do this back at the station in DC?"

Ava inhaled deeply and let him have the lead. It was his case, and he had every right to handle it how he saw fit. That did not mean she had to like it, or even approve.

Tanzy's demeanor changed, and she looked at him for the first time. "I already spoke with the agent at the airport. Or, maybe it was a cop I spoke to. I don't really remember."

Bale opened the file, keeping it tilted so her view of it was restricted. "It looks as though you spoke to Agent Lin. I have your statement here." He flashed a paper and then stuck it back in the folder quickly.

Tanzy nodded. Her face paled and her eyes went wider. "Okay, then. What else is there? I gave my statement, and you obviously have it. Now, if you'll excuse me." She turned toward the racket of the kids playing in the living room. "Nancy is here, but the kids will just run over her. She's a pushover. I need to get back to them." She started closing the door.

"There is actually a lot we need to ask you," Bale said. "We are investigating a murder here, and as unfortunate as it is, you are in the middle of the investigation."

Tanzy looked at them with shock. "What? Why? I did what I was asked to do. I gave you all the information I had back at the airport."

"Here or DC," Bale reminded her none too gently. "Your choice, Ms. Bruner."

After only a brief moment of hesitation, she flung the door wide with irritation and motioned them inside. "Can we make it quick, please?" She motioned toward the screaming coming from the other room.

"We'll be quick," Ava said as they stepped inside.

Tanzy turned away from them. "Nancy!" she yelled over the din of screaming and laughing from the kids. "Nancy, please quiet them if you can. I have company for a minute or two."

A woman with deep auburn curls stuck her head out of a doorway. Her cheeks were flushed, and she was grinning. "Everything okay?"

"Business. Just keep an eye on them for a few, okay?"

"You got it." Nancy disappeared from view, and within three seconds, the kids had quieted as if someone had turned down the volume on a television.

Tanzy turned back to them. "In there." She pointed to a sitting room on the other side of the entryway.

Toys lay on the floor with two discarded blankets. One blanket had Disney Princesses on it; the other had a Lion King motif. A single shoe sat on a chair. Stuffed animals, balls of every color and size, and even clothes were strewn all over the house.

Tanzy entered behind them. She grabbed toys and clothes, and seemingly realized too late that her arms were full while more kid-debris remained. Her overwhelmed expression said it all when she looked from her full arms to the remainder of the room, and she dumped it all near a corner, sighing heavily.

"What did you need to ask me?" She crossed her arms and remained standing with the open doorway to her back.

Ava and Bale stood, also. They exchanged a look, and Ava understood that he wanted her to start the questioning process.

"Ms. Bruner, you traded flights with Melissa Rockford that day, didn't you?" Ava asked.

"I did. Last time I checked, it wasn't illegal to do that. Frowned on sometimes, but it broke no policies or laws."

"I am aware of that. I just wondered why you traded with her on such short notice."

Bale moved a well-loved floppy-eared stuffed dog from a chair and sat. He opened the file again and set his pen at the ready to record her answer.

Tanzy's gaze flitted from him to Ava several times. "Brady was sick. I needed to get back to take him to the doctor." She fidgeted and adjusted her hands and arms.

"Brady? He's your son we saw when we came inside?" Ava asked.

"Yes. He's three," she said. "He had a runny nose and a low-grade fever. I needed to get him to the doctor, and taking that flight would have allowed me to do that, but then… Well, you know the rest."

Bale wrote. Whether he was really writing what Tanzy said, Ava had no idea, but she hoped he was because she, for once, was not taking physical notes.

"And did you?" Bale asked, not looking up.

"Did I what?"

"Take Brady to the doctor after the delay at the DC airport?"

She shifted from foot to foot and shook her head. "No, he was better when I got back."

Bale continued to write.

Tanzy gave them wide eyes. "What? He was better."

Ava nodded. "That's fine, Ms. Bruner." She glanced at Bale, and he made no effort to add anything, or to stop her and take over the questioning. "How well did you know Covey Cahill?"

"Who?" Tanzy shook her head as if confused.

"Covey Cahill. The victim." Narrowing her eyes, Ava looked for signs of deceit. How could she not know who Covey Cahill was? "The woman you were questioned about at the airport—"

"You know, when you were delayed and couldn't take your son to the doctor for his..." Bale consulted his notes. "For his runny nose and low-grade fever. That same Covey Cahill." His expression remained unchanged from its former suspicious scowling frown.

Jess came screaming across the living room and down the hallway toward the door to the sitting room. She held a sock monkey over her head. The scream turned into a gale of riotous laughter as she passed their room and kept going. A few seconds later, Nancy, with Brady on her hip, trotted after Jess. Brady wailed and held out both hands in the direction his older sister had gone.

"Monkey," he warbled in a teary voice.

Nancy glanced in at Tanzy. "I'm sorry. She took his monkey again, and he won't play with the smaller one. Can you—"

"Monkey," Brady demanded in a louder voice as he tried to wiggle free.

Tanzy waved a hand for Nancy to go after Jess and the monkey. Nancy smiled apologetically and took off again.

Ava and Bale exchanged a look that said they were both glad they didn't have to deal with that all the time.

"I'm sorry," Tanzy said, running her hands down her cheeks and looking exasperated, worn, and exhausted. "Now, I know who you're talking about, but I didn't know her at all. Just from the flight, and that she sat next to you." She looked pointedly at Ava. "I see hundreds of people, sometimes more, every week on those flights. It doesn't mean I actually know any of them."

"Did you serve her anything to drink or eat?" Bale asked in a clipped tone.

"No, I didn't," Tanzy answered in the same sort of clipped, irritated voice. "She asked for a Coca-Cola, but I had run out. I went to the back galley to get her one, but when I came back, she was asleep, or something. She didn't answer when I spoke to her, so I left with the drink instead of bothering her further."

"Why not get her attention? She did request the drink, and I'm guessing that it didn't take all that long for you to go to the back and get her one," Bale said. "Or did it?"

"I served a few other people off the cart on my way to the galley, but no, it didn't take more than five minutes or so. I didn't want to wake her because she seemed like she needed the sleep or something when she first boarded. Her face was all red, she was sweating, and breathing kinda fast as if she was either really sick, or she had been running, though I don't know why that would have been because she was the first one on the plane. It's not like she was running late, or in danger of missing the flight, or anything like that. I sort of thought, or was worried, that she was going to be one of those passengers who get thirty minutes into the flight and freak the hell out, start seeing demons, shapeshifters, or hearing the voice of God. I was even ready to offer her some alcohol with her Coke, but like I said before, she was asleep, so I left her alone. I figured that was best for everybody including her."

Ava nodded. She had seen several viral videos in recent months of passengers freaking out on planes. She didn't begrudge the flight attendant's job.

"Did you happen to see anyone go into the bathroom?" Ava asked.

"No. Maybe. I don't know. It's a flight. People use the bathroom, and I'm not one to monitor it, but if you're asking if I remember anyone going in, sure. A handful of people, but they weren't acting suspicious or anything like that. Why?"

"Just wondering," Ava said. "Was this before or after I woke up and found that Ms. Cahill was unresponsive?"

"You mean, dead," she said in a monotone. "I don't remember. Lots of things happen on flights all the time, but the whole flying with a dead woman aboard was a new one for me."

Two cop cars zoomed by with their sirens blaring. Tanzy recoiled and then moved toward the windows a few steps, putting her right between Ava and Bale. The cruisers stopped a few houses down the street.

"There are too many big windows in here," Tanzy said, heading for the door. "Let's move to the kitchen." She didn't wait for them as she breezed out of the room and turned in the direction Jess had gone with the monkey.

"Guess we're moving rooms," Ava said to Bale as she followed Tanzy.

Nancy had the kids in the kitchen. They sat on barstools at the bay window with their plates on the wide sill. They giggled and played with the Teddy Grahams in between biting the graham cracker heads off, which brought on even more laughter. The large sock monkey sat in the corner of the windowsill smiling blindly at a point somewhere above Brady's head.

Nancy stood at the island behind the kids and was slicing a banana when they entered. "They were getting hungry," Nancy said. "Calmed right down when I gave them a snack. Wonder what's going on now?"

She carried the banana slices to the kids and motioned toward the flashing cruiser lights down the street.

"Probably another fight," Tanzy said, craning her neck at the window for a better view.

"Bang, bang, bang," Brady said, pointing a finger gun at the street. "Cops go bang, bang, bang, Mommy."

Nancy folded her hand over his and pushed it gently back to the plate. "Look, bananas. Brady's favey," she said, making a big deal out of the sliced fruit.

"They're not afraid of the sirens?" Ava asked.

"It's a regular—"

Gunfire ripped through the air. Bale ducked and reached for his pistol; Ava had hers out of the holster and to her side. The kids screamed and slapped their hands over their ears. Nancy grabbed one kid under each arm and ran toward the dining room. Everyone else followed close behind.

The dining room faced away from the street and the shooting. Nancy shoved the kids under a side table. "Stay there. Don't come out," she ordered sharply as she sat on the floor with her back to them in a shielding fashion.

Tanzy ran to the kids and scooted under the table to hold her crying, scared babies.

More cruisers came down the street. The two initial units left in front of them.

"Looks like they're chasing someone," Ava said as she stood in the kitchen doorway looking down toward the site.

"I hate this neighborhood," Tanzy said through gritted teeth, still clutching her kids to her. Tears wetted her cheeks. "I want out of here so bad I can taste it. All this stupid, useless violence. I can't keep doing this alone."

Nancy rubbed Jess' back. "You're not alone, Tanzy. I'm here. It's okay. It'll be over in a minute."

"It'll be over just long enough to make us feel semi-safe again, and then it'll happen again." Tanzy sobbed, kissing Brady on top of his head. "I just can't anymore."

"Where is the father?" Ava asked, walking close to the table to make eye contact with Tanzy.

"D-E-A-D," she spelled out. "While I was pregnant with Brady, he was caught by a stray bullet."

Jess turned to look up at Ava. "That spells gone to heaven. D-E-A-D. Gone to heaven. That's where Daddy went. There are angels up there who needed his help, and if I'm good, real good, one day that's where I'll go, too, and I can see Daddy again." She looked unsure and turned to her mother. "Right, Mommy?"

Tanzy nodded. Her chin quivered as she fought more tears. "Right, baby."

"Why don't you just sell the house and move away from here?" Ava asked.

"Because life is never that simple. It's amazing how simple you think everything is. If it was so easy, I wouldn't be here right now. I wouldn't have lost my husband. Try living in the real world for a while before you go throwing out your over-simplified solutions like I just overlooked them or something." She pulled the kids tighter and kissed their heads.

Ava stepped back to the kitchen doorway. "It looks like the situation is cleared up on the street. You can come out now."

Tanzy reluctantly allowed Nancy to take the kids, and she walked toward the kitchen with a sullen, deeply sad expression. The dark circles under her eyes had grown darker and seemed to have sunk in, giving her the appearance of being at least a dozen years older than she was.

"Jesus, aren't we finished yet?" she asked as she moved to the window and scanned the street.

Ava pulled out her pad and opened it to the back where there were small business card slots. She pulled four of the cards out and handed them to Tanzy. "These are some federal assistance groups who help women and kids in need." She spoke in a near-whisper and held up a hand to stop Tanzy interrupting. "Before you hand them back, or argue about it, just know that I have given out hundreds of these in the last year alone. These groups help with all sorts of situations, not just what you're probably thinking. Just check on them when you have a chance to do so." She put a hand on the woman's upper arm and gave her a slight nod. "We'll see ourselves out."

Tanzy looked at the cards, scoffed, slid them in her back pocket, and nodded. As Ava and Bale walked out, Tanzy headed back to her kids.

In the car, Bale gave her the side eye.

"What?" she asked as she buckled up.

"You gave her financial and abuse group cards?"

"I did. Hey, the way I figure it, she might be financially strapped and can't move, or maybe she's being abused or bullied by someone like a family member, or a lover, and she's afraid to try leaving. Domestic abuse comes in many forms, and it affects every person differently."

He shook his head sadly. "I hate to be the bad news bearer, here, but you can't save everyone. Some people don't want to be saved."

"I know," she said, turning her eyes back to the large house. As she turned the car around, she got a good look at the property again. "God, this is a lot of house even for a family of four."

"And do you see those two cars? That one is an Audi, and the other is a BMW."

"I wonder what an in-flight attendant's salary is?"

"Not enough to buy those cars," he said with a dry chuckle. "Or that house. Maybe she got a settlement of some sort when her husband was shot."

Even a settlement would not have sufficed for such car purchases. Tanzy did not seem the type to spend out of her kids' college funds or savings, either. Of course, who knew if they had either? They were still toddlers, and the father was killed before the youngest was even born.

Something was up with Tanzy. But up enough for them to have to dive even deeper?

CHAPTER TWENTY-FOUR

Melissa Rockford

SOMETHING ABOUT THE EXPENSIVE CARS AND THE OVERSIZED house bothered Ava as she drove. Something about her story felt off, too. "If the kid was sick, why not let Nancy take him to the doctor?" she asked aloud.

"I think you nailed it," Bale said. "The operative word in that sentence is 'if.' I don't think he was."

"Then why would she switch flights with Melissa Rockford in such a hurry?"

"Your guess is as good as mine. She acted shady as a maple, in my opinion."

"You think she had something to do with Cahill's death?" Ava thought she was hiding something, but she was unsure what.

"I don't know. But I'm not ruling her out just because she got weepy over her kids and dead husband, though."

"I'm not, either. I'm just trying to figure out if she was being truthful."

"Most people are not truthful. Not completely, anyway. That's just my experience," he said, leaning his seat back a couple of notches.

"I want to go talk with Melissa Rockford. That's the logical next step, and we're pretty close to where she lives, I think. Can you check the records for her address?"

"She wasn't on the flight; why do you want to talk to her today?" He pulled up a phone number on his mobile and dialed. "Lin, can you get me the address for Melissa Rockford, the flight attendant who wasn't on Flight 808?" After a few minutes, he scribbled the address on a piece of paper and hung up. "Got it."

"Why did you have to call for it? Isn't it in the electronic…" Ava let her voice fade. "Never mind." Realization hit her. Bale had put nothing of the case in the computer because of the mole.

He chuckled and entered the address into the GPS. "Sometimes, you're pretty slow to catch on."

"Sorry, I was trying to step out of the cave again." She grinned.

"Smart ass," he said. "Ready for me to hit start on the GPS?"

"Yes, please, and thank you."

"Hope this pans out better than the most recent interview. I'd hate to go back home with nothing gained from this excursion."

"It wasn't for nothing. We saw how Ms. Bruner lives, her kids, her friend, her super-expensive cars, and we have the story she gave us."

"I like my evidence a little more on the concrete side. We got nothing."

"Maybe because she is innocent and there's nothing to get on her. It happens. People aren't all nefarious. Some people are just people."

"Some, but not many. Given the right set of circumstances, anyone can turn into a murderer."

Ava tsked. "Cynical view of your fellow humans."

"Not my fellow humans. I took myself out of the murky waters of social circles many years ago. There's nothing to be gained from hanging around with groups of people—like-minded or not. Usually, it just causes grief in one form or another, and always sooner rather than later."

"No wonder you have that perma-frown stitched on your face all the time. If I thought like that, I guess I would be frowning, too."

"Perma-what? I don't have a perma-frown. This is just my face."

"Exactly," she said.

Melissa Rockford lived in a humbler house in the suburbs about forty minutes from Tanzy's neighborhood. Melissa's house was a ranch-style duplex. The house was white brick with glossy black trim around the windows, black gutters, and a black porch. It was different, but pretty and neat. The grass was trimmed low and neat, and not a blade of loose grass had been left behind on the concrete sidewalk or the porch. A tidy half-circle rug lay outside the door. 'Wipe your dirty paws' was written on it, and there was a likeness of a dog paw under the words. Unsurprisingly, the rug was a greyish-white, and the bold writing and paw print were black.

Ava raised her hand to knock but the inner door opened. A woman with dark blonde hair stood on the other side of the storm door's glass.

"May I help you?" she asked.

"Melissa Rockford?" Bale asked.

The woman barely nodded. "Who are you?"

Ava showed her badge. "I'm Agent James, and this is Agent Bale. We would like to speak with you about the flight you swapped with Tanzy Bruner a few days ago."

Melissa sighed and opened the door. "I heard what happened. Come on in. I don't want the neighbors hearing everything. They're nosy as hell, and they always eavesdrop if I'm outside talking to anyone." She scoffed and rolled her eyes.

"Ms. Rockford, we appreciate you speaking with us," Ava said.

"Please, just Melissa, or Missy is fine. Ms. Rockford was my mother, and I hated that witch. And, you're welcome. Please, sit." She motioned them to a sofa and chairs in the living room.

Ava and Bale sat, and Bale pulled out the notes and made ready to write.

"What would you like to know? As you're aware, I'm sure, I was on another flight entirely when that poor woman died, so I don't know how much help I can be, honestly."

"Tanzy Bruner," Ava said. "How well do you know her?"

"Tanzy is pretty private. I mean, I know she has two kids at home, and I think her husband died a few years ago, but that's hearsay. Gossip around work, you know. Personally, I know her on a professional level. We've never hung out with each other, we don't go out socially, she's never been here, and I've never been to her house, if that's what you mean."

"That's what I mean. So, you aren't friends outside of work?"

Melissa shook her head. "Just to be honest, Asa is the only person from work I've ever gone out with, and that was only because she started really hounding me to put myself back out there after my divorce. We became friends, but no one else."

"When Ms. Bruner asked you to swap flights with her, what was the reason she gave?" Ava asked.

"She just said she had some urgent business to take care of here in DC, and that she desperately needed to switch with me so she could get back here sooner."

"She didn't say what that urgent business was?" Bale asked in a disbelieving tone.

Melissa shook her head. "No."

"And you didn't ask?" he continued.

"No, I didn't," she answered, averting her eyes. "Well, I did, but she didn't want to tell me. I told her I couldn't switch last-minute like that, and that she needed to give me more warning if she ever wanted to do anything like that, but she kept on. Practically begging me to swap with her. She finally told me that her mother was in the hospital in DC and that she really wanted to come see her. She thought her mother might pass away. Said she wanted to at least have a chance to say goodbye in her own way."

Ava looked to Bale. His pen scratched furiously at the paper.

"Which hospital was her mother in?" Ava asked.

"She didn't say, and I didn't ask. That felt like overstepping. I felt sorry for her when the waterworks started. I don't deal well with people when the tear factory opens for business." She shook her head sadly and pointed at herself. "Damaged goods here. Thanks, Mom," she said to the air above her.

"I understand that," Ava said.

Bale gave her a side glance, and his unspoken question was written on his face.

"I don't deal very well with crying people, either. Not because I'm damaged goods; just because I don't like that raw emotion. So, Ms. Bruner didn't say anything else after she told you that her mother was deathly sick in the hospital?"

"No. I agreed pretty fast after that. I don't want to be the reason some woman doesn't get a chance to say goodbye to their mother. Just because me and mine didn't get along doesn't mean others don't. Besides, I'm bi-coastal. I have this little place, and an even smaller one out in San Francisco. The other flight was a short one, and it was returning to San Fran that evening." She grinned mischievously. "I got to spend some more time with a really good friend out there, so I'm not complaining."

"Boyfriend, huh?" Bale asked without looking up.

"Yeah. That must have sounded bad considering the situation. I'm sorry. I didn't mean to be—"

THE WOMAN IN THE WINDOW

"It's fine," Bale said. "A woman was murdered on Flight 808." He stood abruptly. "I'm glad you had a nice time with your boyfriend in California, Ms. Rockford. We'll see ourselves out."

Melissa stood. Her eyes were wide with shock, and her cheeks burned red.

"Have a good rest of your evening, Melissa," Ava said apologetically.

Outside, Ava caught up with Bale. "You didn't have to be so rude to her."

"Wasn't being rude. We were done. She didn't kill Ms. Cahill, and we needed to go. There's more to do than sit around listening to her talk about her boyfriend out in sunny California." He got in the car and slammed the door.

Ava slowed her pace. Bale was right. There was more to do. A lot more from the way it seemed, but she didn't like that he had been rude to a woman they were questioning. A woman who was not even on the suspect list.

Melissa might not have been on the suspect list, but Tanzy Bruner had claimed the number one slot on that list. Her story did not match the story she gave Melissa Rockford, and Ava knew before she and Bale checked, that Tanzy Bruner's mother had not been in the hospital at all.

"I'm checking the story about Bruner's mother," Bale said.

"Absolutely. We are thinking the same thing, though," she said as they pulled into the parking lot at Bale's office.

"She wasn't in the hospital at all." He got out without looking to see if Ava agreed.

CHAPTER TWENTY-FIVE

Buck Perron's Story

THE NEXT MORNING, BALE'S OFFICE WAS EMPTY. AVA SET A LARGE coffee at his workstation and went to her own. Tanzy's story to Melissa still needed to be checked out. It would not take long to find the woman's name and then check hospitals in the DC area to find out if she had been in one. It would also take very little time to get the mother's address and go speak with her.

Ava decided that would be the most efficient path to take.

Between the keyboard and the computer monitor, Bale had placed a note. *Tanzy Bruner mother, Gina Hopkins never in hospital in DC*, it read.

At least, the name was there. All she had to do was run it through the system, check that it was the right Gina Hopkins, and get an address.

A half-hour later, Ava walked out the door with a small piece of paper with a name and address on it. She put the address into the GPS, and a church symbol popped up near the marker. A church would be a good landmark, and it would make Gina's place easier to find.

The GPS said, "Your destination is on the left."

Ava stopped the car, and her phone rang. She looked to the left: a cemetery and the church. The phone continued to ring, and she answered as she looked for Gina's house.

"Agent James?" Bale asked.

"Yeah, yes, it's me."

"Where are you?"

"I would say at Gina Hopkins' house, but I think my GPS needs updating. Something is wrong with it. Keep talking, I'm going to roll down this street and see if I can find six-eighteen."

"If you're in front of the church, you're there."

"She lives in a church?" Ava looked at the old stone building in disbelief.

"Out back of it and to the right just a little."

Ava's eyes tracked to where he said. "That's a cemetery. Unless you mean she lives on the other side of the street." The number on the house directly across from the cemetery was six-nineteen.

"No, to the right. Plot number one-three-eight. I just came from there."

Ava closed her eyes and snorted. "Okay. Well, we know for sure Ms. Bruner was lying about her being in the hospital days ago because none of these graves are fresh."

"Nope. She died five years ago. When will you be back?"

"I'm heading that way now. Why?"

"I found something else out about one of our passengers."

"Which one?" Ava's mind recalled the bald man in the back on the left, the young jerk in the back on the right, and the older woman at the front after Covey had been discovered deceased. All three of them had sent up red flags for Ava by their actions alone.

"Buck Perron."

"Bald man in the back of the plane after I found Covey dead. I knew something was off about him. He was way too nervous. What did you find out?"

"He is a cousin to a man named Randy Jenkins, better known as RJ, who just happens to be in prison because of his involvement with Emerald Block."

"I'll be there in twenty." Ava disconnected the call and drove too fast through the morning work traffic. Buck Perron had garnered a reaction from her on an instinctual level. Tanzy Bruner was a liar, but maybe she wasn't a killer after all. Being the former didn't equal being the latter.

Bale was in the office with the coffee Ava had brought him. He raised it in semblance of a toast when she entered. "Thanks."

"It was cold a long time ago. What have you got on Buck Perron?" She rooted out her notebook and flipped through it. The paper she wanted wasn't in it. She went into the bag she used for casefiles and pulled out the file with papers she had acquired from the flight. It was there. She had noted Buck's name. She held it out to Bale. "I knew he had something to hide."

"I've not gotten anything new on him in the last..." He looked at his watch. "Fifteen minutes. You broke the speed limit, I'm sure, but how did you get through morning commute traffic that fast? Did you drive on the sidewalk, too?"

"No. What did Buck's cousin do to get put in prison?" she asked, steering the conversation away from her unsafe driving.

Bale handed her the report on Randy Jenkins, AKA: RJ. "His story is that he was set up by one of Emerald Block's muscle. A man who only goes by Vance; no last name. He says this Vance is the one who got carried away and beat a man to death, but the judge and a jury didn't see it that way, so..." He took a big gulp of the coffee and winced. "That is terrible." He set the cup aside. "Anyway, RJ went to prison on murder charges. Mr. Buck Perron is the one I'm really interested in." He handed her another report.

Buck Perron was a forty-year-old businessman. He had owned, operated, and lost a total of ten businesses in the last thirteen years. "Talk about down on your luck," Ava mused as she scanned the list. It continued on page two for a total of sixteen failed and lost businesses since the man was twenty. She looked up. "Sixteen businesses in twenty years?"

"That's not just bad luck, if you ask me."

Ava looked at the papers again. "Poor business skills, for sure. Looks like he would have given up a long time ago. Look at all the debt he's in because—" She looked up again. "Ah, I see. He might be into Emerald Block for money, and because they know RJ is his family, and RJ did work for them, maybe Buck would, too."

"Or, maybe ol' Buckaroo there is working for them. Maybe all those businesses are fronts for their illegal activities. Gambling, drug-running, gun-running, and who knows what else they're into." He stood.

Ava looked over the list again, and nodded, hoping Buck was the man who killed Covey, and that she and Bale could collar him.

"You ready to go?" Bale asked, dropping the cup of coffee into the trash bin on his way out the door.

She caught up to him. "Where, exactly, are we going?"

"To talk to Buck Perron. Where else? But first, I'm stopping somewhere and getting a real cup of coffee."

Bale's somewhere ended up being a Shell station at the edge of town.

"Gas station coffee?" she asked.

"One-stop-shop. Got everything you need." He sipped the coffee and said, "Ah, that's better. That's how a cup of coffee is supposed to taste. You should have gotten one."

"No thanks. It smells strong enough to make a beard sprout on my chin."

"Now, that would be a shame," he said and snickered.

Buck Perron's house was small. Seven-hundred-square-feet kind of small.

Bale parked at the curb and eyed the place. "At least it's brick."

"Less upkeep for the owner."

"I bet he has a landlord. From his history, Buck doesn't strike me as the type to own a home no matter the size."

"I don't know how he's affording rent, just to be honest. Anyone with his amount of debt would be strapped for money all the time." She leaned toward the idea that Emerald Block was footing the bill for Buck's house and probably everything else. That would be a dandy bunch of blackmail to hang over his head and get him to drop poison in a woman's drink or food. People were apt to do all sorts of things when they were threatened with homelessness and ruination.

"Unless this house is a front just like I believe his failed businesses have been. Puts on the appearance of being in financial woe, when in reality, he's living like a Rockefeller."

"Nah. No Rockefeller vibes from this one. Just wait 'til you meet him. It's not hard to imagine he would lose a business rather quickly. I'm just shocked he did it so many times. Not exactly a daring soul, in my opinion."

Bale and Ava got out at the same time.

An older Jeep Cherokee sat at the top of the short, paved driveway. There was no garage or carport. Bale stepped onto the concrete pad that played the role of a tiny porch. There was even a ratty wicker chair with peeling white paint sitting at the edge with its back to the house.

Buck opened the door before Bale knocked. "Can I help you?"

Bale nodded. "Buck Perron?"

"What can I do for you?" Buck looked from one to the other and then recognition settled on his face. "I remember you," he said to Ava. "You were on Flight 808. The FBI woman who had to hold hands with that dead woman until we landed. I'm sorry you had to do that."

"That dead woman is why we're here, Mr. Perron," Bale said, not giving Ava a chance for small talk with the man.

"Why are you here about her? It's not like I knew her. I certainly didn't kill her, either." He remained in the doorway, blocking their entrance.

"Could we come in and just ask you a few follow-up questions?"

"Well, I think we can discuss your business right here." Perron's hand on the doorknob tightened until his knuckles turned white.

"It's just follow-ups," Ava said with a slight smile. They needed him to cooperate, not clam up and shut them out.

Perron looked doubtful as he planted his other arm against the door frame and kept silent.

"Mr. Perron, we know about your cousin, Randy Jenkins."

Perron's face blanched and his eyes darted from Bale to Ava. He straightened and dropped his arm to his side.

"It would be in your best interest to let us in," Bale continued.

"Bastard," Perron muttered as he dropped his head and ran a hand over it as if to smooth the hair that used to be there.

"Excuse me?" Bale asked defensively.

"Not you." Perron shook his head and looked up. "That bastard cousin of mine." He glanced over his shoulder and then stepped aside. "Might as well come on in."

Bale stepped inside. Perron walked ahead of him. "Close the door, please."

Ava closed the door. He led them into a miniscule kitchen that had three cabinet doors under the sink and two above, a fridge that stood four feet tall and rattled loudly when the compressor kicked on, and an apartment-sized stove that looked in need of a serious deep scrubbing. Dirty dishes sat in both sides of the sink.

Perron indicated the kitchen table. "Have a seat, if you want; just push the crap out of your way. I don't get much company, so I haven't straightened up in a long time."

Ava took one look at the dirty plates, bowls, and cups on the table and decided to stand rather than touch any of it. If the table was that dirty, there was no telling what might be on the fabric of the chairs.

Bale pulled out a chair, armed the dishes toward the middle of the table, and flopped the notepad and folder onto the grimy surface without flinching. He wasn't much older than Ava, but she gathered right then that he had been in worse conditions often enough that Perron's place didn't much faze him.

"What about RJ caused you to come to me over this dead woman on the flight?" Perron picked up some of the dishes and let them clatter onto the dirty ones already in the sink.

"Mr. Perron, your cousin killed a man, didn't he?" Bale asked.

"He did. That's the reason me, and almost every member of my family, broke ties with him. None of us have had anything to do with him in years. I didn't hang around with him even before then, if I'm being completely honest."

Bale shifted in his seat. "For your sake, I hope you are."

"You hope I am, what?"

"Being completely honest. Because Randy Jenkins was tied in with a group of very bad people."

It was Perron's turn to shift in his seat. He cleared his throat. "Yeah, he was. That's on him. I didn't have a thing to do with that. Or with him."

Ava stepped closer to the table on Bale's side. "Mr. Perron, we have reason to believe those people were the ones—"

"The woman on your flight was murdered," Bale interrupted.

"I know. I gathered that when we were all detained and questioned at the airport."

"She was going to testify against the people your cousin was involved with," Ava said.

"Emerald Block, or Emerald Group?" Perron looked slightly confused.

"Yes. Are you associated with them?" Bale asked.

"No. I told you that was Randy's thing, not mine. I'm nothing like Randy. He's a savage without a conscience. The only person who still has contact with him is his degenerate sister, and the family disowned her a long time ago over drugs."

"Isn't that what Randy was into?" Ava asked.

Perron huffed and rubbed his bald pate again. "I don't know what all he was into," he almost yelled. "Why can't you understand that? I didn't hang around with him. I had nothing to do with him before he killed that guy, and I definitely haven't since then."

"You've started a lot of businesses over the past twenty years," Bale said, ignoring Perron's latest protestation as if it were nothing to him. "What do you do for a paycheck, exactly?"

Perron blinked at him stupidly for a moment.

"You know, how do you come up with the money to afford your day-to-day necessities? How do you acquire the money to start all these businesses that you ultimately end up losing?"

Ava cringed inwardly at Bale's gruff and crass interrogation. There was a softer way to go about getting answers.

"I get donations from people who believe in my businesses. I save money when the businesses are successful. That's where I get what little bit of money I have for this grand estate." He flourished with his hands and scoffed.

"Donations, you say?" Bale asked.

"Yeah, you know, investors."

"That's usually only enough for the initial start-up when there's even that. Doesn't it take two or three years for a new business to start running on profit? Even successful ones?"

"Yeah, most of the time it does take a couple of years. A couple of years of really hard work, I might add."

"Then you must be one really hard-working man, Mr. Perron, because from what I saw in your history, you've started sixteen businesses in twenty years, and none have lasted more than two years. When they were scrapped, none of them were making what I would call a considerable profit. Not enough to call them successful, and not enough to be saving any money from said profits. Now, how are you affording all this, really? I make decent money, and I don't have enough to start businesses. Especially not every few years."

"I'm in debt. Of course, I'm sure you already saw that in your extensive digging through my background. A metric shit-ton of debt to be more exact. After the sixth or seventh business endeavor, I didn't have much of a choice but to continue trying to start another one. It was the only way I could make enough money to keep the loan sharks at bay."

"Loan sharks?" Ava asked. "Which loan sharks, Mr. Perron?"

He scoffed again. "Totally legal institutions. At least, by the law's estimation. Bank of America, Citi Bank, and a bunch of smaller, local ones like Griffin's First National, Murdaugh's Credit Union. Didn't you check those records, too?"

"They're banking institutions, not loan sharks. Which loan sharks are you into for money?"

"I'm not. That's just a phrase I use for the banks. They're like lawyers. All of them are a bunch of crooks. If you'd ever taken out a mortgage, you'd know that."

"Are you into Emerald Block for money, Mr. Perron?" Bale leaned forward to stare hard at the man.

Perron imitated Bale's motions. "No, Agent. I am not into Emerald Block for anything. I have never been involved with them, and I never will be. *Capisce?*"

Bale sat back and flipped the notepad closed. He clicked his pen and stuck it in the inside pocket of his jacket. "How did you know Covey Cahill?"

"Jesus Christ, man. How many times do I have to tell you that I never saw her. I never knew the name until the flight. If she was going to testify against that ring of criminals, so be it. I didn't know that, and if I had, I wouldn't have cared. Let them fry. Every last one of them. I saw how they can ruin a person's entire life and tear a family apart. Do you think any of them batted an eye about what happened to my cousin and my family as a result?"

Bale nodded once and stood with a grim expression. "We'll show ourselves out. I wouldn't leave town, Mr. Perron."

"How would I, Agent? Dip into the fortune I've made over the last two decades?" Perron chuckled humorlessly and stayed in his seat. "Shut the door on your way out, please."

Ava walked ahead of Bale, glad to be out of the claustrophobic house.

In the car, Bale tossed his file to the backseat. "I don't believe him."

"About which part?"

"The money. Him and his family disowning Randy Jenkins. Oh, and that he has no ties whatsoever to Emerald Block. He stinks of guilt."

"I don't think he was being completely honest about the money, but I'm not sure if he would have the guts to get tied in with Emerald Block. Maybe a lower-rung group, though."

"Oh, you mean the ones without the predilection toward extreme violence? Yeah, we don't have many of those."

"Ones that might know him because of his predilection to starting up businesses that will fail. The ones who might have a use for such a fluid businessman. Perron can jump from one industry to the other without pause or hesitation. Another, smaller group might see that as a boon if they intended for his business to be a front for their illegal dealings."

Bale's eyebrows flicked up high and then dropped as his mouth turned down deeply at the corners and then his expression was neutral leaning toward angry again—his default expression setting.

He didn't need to say that she might be onto something. His expression and ensuing silence did that for him.

Regardless of the truth in Perron's story, the man was still on the suspect list. He and Tanzy were tied for the top slot, and neither Ava nor Bale had to voice that aloud.

CHAPTER TWENTY-SIX

Randy Jenkins

Ava and Bale sat in the interview room waiting for the guards to bring Randy Jenkins. The place smelled of some industrial cleaner that burned Ava's sinuses. The smudges on the table said that cleaner had not been used on it in a while, but it was still much cleaner than Buck Perron's kitchen table had been.

"You really think he'll give us anything?" Ava asked.

"It's worth a shot, isn't it? It doesn't matter whether or not he gives us what we're asking for, sometimes, what they refuse to tell you gives you as much information as you need."

Ava adjusted her seat and looked over her notes. For the moment, Tanzy Bruner seemed the most likely suspect, and Perron was right behind her. Given Perron's debt, and the ease with which a man in such debt could be persuaded to do things outside his nature, he should have been first on her list. There was something about Tanzy and her kids in that big house in a dangerous neighborhood that trumped Perron's situation. Also, she was shifty, and that her story about why she wanted that flight in particular didn't match with Melissa's story.

A buzzer sounded in the near distance. A few seconds later, the door opened. Two guards, one big as a mountain, and the other slim and short, escorted Randy Jenkins into the room.

Randy's black hair was long. It lay lankly over his short, furrowed forehead at a side-swoop. His small tight grin and dark eyes gave him the air of someone who was smart enough to know better, yet evil enough to not give a damn. He might have gotten a raw deal just like his defense said, but Ava highly doubted that upon seeing him.

The guards looked to Bale for confirmation. He nodded once to them, and they moved outside the door where the mountain-sized guy was in plain view through the high window. The whole crew looking only to Bale for confirmation chafed her like steel wool against bare skin. It was something she would never get used to, or accept as the norm. Just because Bale was a man, the guards had assumed he was in charge, and therefore only had to get his confirmation.

"Well, ain't I the lucky one today?" Jenkins asked, eyeing Ava salaciously. He smooched at her. "I ain't had such a pretty visitor since my sister visited last, and you know, society frowns on it if you get excited over your sister."

"Looks to me like you haven't been so lucky," Ava said. "You're the one in cuffs and stuck in a cell eighty percent of every day."

"Mr. Jenkins," Bale said, shifting in his seat hard enough that it scraped loudly against the tiled floor. "We're here to ask you about your ties to Emerald Block."

Jenkins threw his head back dramatically and laughed. It was a grating sound that denoted sarcasm at its highest level. He lowered his head and leveled a glare at Bale. "Then I think we're already done here."

"I didn't take you as a man who scared so easily," Ava said with a measured smirk.

"I ain't scared of you, Pretty Girl." He gave another oily grin and a wink.

"Who are you scared of, then?" She folded her arms and leaned them on the table as if totally relaxed in his presence despite his tactics to make her uncomfortable.

"Nobody. Except maybe Torres two cells down from me. Anybody with half a brain is at least a little scared of him. Dangerous Mexican. He likes to cause pain—"

"We don't care about him, Mr. Jenkins," Bale said. "Emerald Block. That's who we care about today."

Jenkins shook his head. "No can do."

"If Emerald Block wanted to poison someone, who would they have do it?" Bale asked, ignoring Jenkins' reluctance to speak about the group.

"Is this a hypothetical question?"

"If it helps you answer it." Bale wore his usual expression, but there was a measure of disdain in his eyes to go with it.

Jenkins grinned with one side of his mouth and chuckled shortly without breaking eye contact. "Listen, I'm doing my time. I'm not talking about them. Not to you, or anybody else who comes asking." His gaze shifted to Ava for a heartbeat, and then it was back to Bale.

"You're in for murder one, right?" Ava asked.

"Yeah. No secret there. You have nice hair. I bet it's nicer when it's down."

"It is. I like it, anyway. Now, did you really murder that man, Mr. Jenkins?"

"Mm. Hearing you say Mr. Jenkins in reference to me is a real turn-on."

Bale exhaled deeply and began tapping his pen against the paper.

"Did you?" she asked, nonplussed. Men like Randy Jenkins were manipulative, but it was simple to manipulate them, too. It would have been easy to get upset with his inappropriate words and actions, but she refused to give him the pleasure of knowing he was really getting under her skin.

"That's what they say." He held up his cuffed wrists. "These aren't a fashion statement, you know."

"I'm asking if you really did it."

"It's in the court records that I said I didn't do it. Vance is the one who whaled on that dude until he shit the bed. Not me." His face reddened.

The muscles in his jaws clenched, and all the flirty playfulness left his expression. His dark eyes turned icy, and if Ava had been alone with him, she would have had her hand on her gun.

"So, you're sticking to the story that you were set up by this one-name guy you call Vance?"

"That's exactly what happened, but I don't expect you to believe that. No one else did, and it's a moot point now." He sat forward and clunked his cuffed hands onto the table.

"Wouldn't you like to be able to get a little revenge on those guys who set you up?" Ava asked.

"Revenge? Against them? Are you mental?" He sat back and dropped his hands into his lap. "The prettiest ones always are the craziest."

And he was back. Ava took a breath. "If they wanted to poison someone on a plane, who would do it? Who could? Vance?"

Laughter burst from Jenkins before he could stop it. "Vance? That man is nothing but a bumbling piece of muscle with feet and hands. He ain't smart enough for any other position, which is why he's the number one muscle on the street. I was in the wrong place at the wrong time, and they threw me under the bus."

She nodded. "Okay, if not Vance, then who?"

He shrugged and looked over his shoulder at the huge guard outside the door.

"Come on. Give us something, Mr. Jenkins. These people set you up. Why would you protect them? Just a name. A first name is enough."

"I'm doing my time here, and I ain't talking about them. To anybody. I value my life, and I'd really like to live long enough to be released." He leaned on the table to get closer and lowered his voice. "You'll never find who did it. The Block has players everywhere. They're at every level in every service industry and beyond. They're like cockroaches with guns, knives, and money you can't even imagine. They're everywhere, and they scatter when the light hits them." He sat back, laughed, and turned to the door. "Hey, Briggs, I'm done in here, man. I want to go back to my cell now."

"Mr. Jenkins, a name," Ava said. "We could help you."

Jenkins turned to look at her with hope in his eyes.

Bale looked at her with mild shock.

She nodded at Jenkins. "Help us, and we'll help you."

The door opened, and Briggs, the big guard stepped inside. Jenkins glanced in his direction as he stood.

"Come on, Jenkins," Briggs said.

Jenkins looked at Ava, and the hope in his face had iced over. "You can't help me. Not enough to get what you want, anyway."

Jenkins left the room with the guard.

"What the blue hell was that, James? You told him we could help him? What were you going to offer him, a new mattress? An extra set of coveralls?"

"I was trying to get anything from him." She stood and closed her notepad before snatching it from the table angrily.

"Well, that worked like a charm. We got a whole lot of nothing."

"We got something," Ava said after they retrieved their things from the guard and walked out of the building.

"Yeah, what? A big dose of Horny Jenkins' attempt at flirting, and an admission that he has the hots even for his sister?"

Ava shuddered. "No. We did get that, but we also got that he is terrified of Emerald Block."

"That's not exactly groundbreaking news. Lots of people are terrified of that group." Bale got behind the wheel of the car.

Ava got in and buckled up. "Maybe not, but if we could find this Vance—"

"No reason. He's not tied to our investigation, and if we wasted the time to find him, he wouldn't give us anything. Muscle don't know the people who run the gang. The muscle know the least about the ones in charge, and that's for a reason. None of them are the brightest crayons in the pack, and if they're arrested, they don't have any information to give the cops."

Bale's phone rang before he could start the engine.

He answered curtly and held a short conversation in which he gave mostly monosyllabic answers and asked one-word questions. Where? When? Who? Right. Yes. Be there soon.

Good thing no one was judging his intelligence on his vocabulary variation.

"That was Dr. Pate," he said as he turned the ignition key.

"And?" Good thing no one was judging her on the same basis. She grinned. Being around Bale was rubbing off on her. He did not exactly elicit deep conversations from a person.

"And they found cyanide on the outside pocket of Covey Cahill's purse along with fingerprints from several different people."

"Several different people handled her purse? That's not normal."

"That was my thinking exactly. My mother would have knocked you one upside the head for touching her purse even though it was a huge clunky thing that was so heavy it felt like she carried lead in it."

"That's most women. It would be the equivalent of a man's wallet having fingerprints from a bunch of people on it. Did they run the prints yet?"

"No, he's waiting on us. He's been keeping everything out of the system as much as possible for as long as possible."

"We're going to run them?"

"That's the plan. Unless you have a better one."

She did not have a better plan. The prints had to be run if they had a hope of finding who handled that purse. No one else showed any symptoms of being exposed to the poison, so whoever the people were handled that purse before the poison ended up on it.

THE WOMAN IN THE WINDOW

That seemed a reasonable assumption, at least.

CHAPTER TWENTY-SEVEN

Stagnation and a Different Tack

Of the six sets of fingerprints on Cahill's purse, hers was one, Tanzy Bruner was another, and the other four sets remained a mystery.

"Two are all we identified?" Bale asked when he saw the fingerprint report.

"Afraid so. The others came up as no-hits in the system." She sat heavily in her chair. "Tanzy Bruner didn't mention that she touched Ms. Cahill's purse."

"No, she absolutely did not."

"What reason would she have to touch it?"

"Maybe helping her settle into her seat?" Bale sat and scowled at the fingerprint report again.

"She didn't mention that, either. Just that she saw Ms. Cahill board the plane looking as if she was out of breath, and that she went to get her a Coke later."

"A Coke that was never delivered because she didn't want to wake Ms. Cahill." He shook his head and closed his eyes briefly. "This is a dead end every way I turn. We have no idea who might have touched that purse before Ms. Cahill left for the airport that day."

"It should have been limited to her and her handlers and possibly some security people, right? I mean, she was in San Francisco for her safety, not to make friends. Do you really think she was out there partying and living up the social life?"

He chuckled shortly. "No. She didn't even go to the grocery store or restaurants. She opted to have everything delivered to her apartment building's lobby where she picked it up after the delivery person left."

"Then, there should have been a very limited number of people touching her personal belongings."

"What, you want to go fingerprint everyone on the plane? Everyone in the terminal at SFO? Here, at Reagan International? It's useless. Another piece of information that leads nowhere."

Ava took the stack of background reports on the passengers. "What if we set aside all the passengers who have priors of any kind. Their prints would be in the system, and therefore, they aren't the ones who left prints on the purse."

"Yeah, just like the hundreds of thousands of other people in the area." He scoffed.

"Then, that narrows the list significantly, doesn't it?" she quipped. His Little Debbie Downer attitude was annoying.

"That puts our Buck Perron in the presumed innocent pile, doesn't it?" he asked as he leaned back and stared up at the ceiling with his hands behind his head.

"It does, but it doesn't remove our in-flight attendants. There are four of them, and they are all squeaky clean from the looks of their files."

"Of course, they are. Just like the pilot, the co-pilot, and the stack of people you're looking at who don't have their prints in the system. Just like the four mysterious people who touched Ms. Cahill's purse, who, I might add, could be in San Francisco at this very moment digging their toes into the sand on some beach and ordering margaritas while we're wasting time and chasing our tails all the way out here in DC."

Ava shoved the pile of files to the side. "Okay, then. A different tack. Do you have any ideas about who the mole in the Bureau might be?

Anyone stand out to you as showing too much interest in the case when there's no reason for it? Anyone been acting shifty lately?"

Bale rocked the chair forward and brought his hands down to the desk. "No," he said, staring at the black screen of his computer. "Maybe." He sighed heavily and grunted. "I don't know. When something like this happens, everybody suddenly seems a little suspicious."

"But you had someone in mind when you answered that. Who?"

He turned to face her. His lips were pursed so hard there was nothing but a thin line where they should have been.

"Who, Bale? You're upset that we're not seeing progress, that we're stagnating and doing nothing more than chase our tails, so who do you think might be the mole?"

"An accusation like that could ruin a man's career and his life. Even if it's a false accusation, or one that simply turns out to be wrong. I don't want to name names."

"Not even if it means forward movement on this case?" She scooted her chair closer. "Just think about it. If Emerald Block wanted Ms. Cahill dead, they had to know where she would be, and when, and with whom. You know I'm right."

"I never said you were wrong. I said if I happened to be wrong, a man's life could be ruined for nothing. An accusation has a way of sticking to a person even if it's proven wrong. People have a tendency to assume that innocence was bought and paid for. Especially when it's an accusation against someone in any sort of law enforcement career."

"I understand that, but between you, me, and the walls, who do you think it was?"

"I know who I think it might have been. I have my suspicions, and I'll keep them to myself for now. Stop asking."

"That's fine, as long as you're actively thinking about it. Was the case-file secure?"

"Yeah. In the system as per Bureau protocol. To see it, someone needs to hack it." He ran his finger down the monitor screen and then checked it for dust.

"Have you had anyone check to see if it was hacked?"

He shook his head and reached for a bottle of aspirin beside the computer. "I've been busy on the case at hand, in case you didn't notice, and I haven't gotten to that yet. But it had to be hacked. That's the only way someone could get the information. That's why I've not been adding things to it since Ms. Cahill's murder." He turned to her as he shook three aspirin into his palm. "In case that slipped your notice, too."

Biting back was not as important as what she really wanted. "I know someone who can check the file, and not only check it, but can trace the hacker, if it has really been hacked."

Chewing the aspirin, he shook his head and made a sound as if trying to tell her no again.

"He has all the newest tech to do the job in record time, and he's completely trustworthy. His best friend outside the crew is his computer. But only if you're interested in finding out the truth about the casefile and who might have cracked it."

He gulped water from a bottle and held up a finger for her to wait a minute. He sloshed a mouthful of water and then swallowed with a grimace. "We've discussed this before, James. You know how I feel about it."

"No, we didn't discuss it before. I recall mentioning it, and you immediately shut me down. Are you afraid of what and who we'll find if you let my man do this?"

"I'm not Jenkins. Stop trying to manipulate me like you did him."

"Well?" she asked, ignoring his words the way he ignored Perron's and Jenkins' during questioning.

"What?" There was more exasperation in his tone than irritation.

"Let my man have a shot at it. Could put us on the right track with this case. At the very least, he can lead you to the person who hacked the file. You'll know who the mole in the agency is at last. No more wondering."

"Just stop. Stop badgering me about it and let me think it over." He huffed out a breath and reached for the water again.

That was a preferable response than the first one he had given her about bringing in Ashton. At least the absolute no had turned into a soft maybe.

If there was one thing Bale would learn about her, it was that she was persistent. Sometimes to her own detriment, and this was something she was not willing to let go.

CHAPTER TWENTY-EIGHT

Another Suspect

Ava dialed Tanzy Bruner's number for the second time in an hour. There was no answer again. If Tanzy had something to do with Covey Cahill's murder, or if she had guilty knowledge, a message about further questioning might have been enough to send her on the run.

She hung up and shook her head at Bale.

"Maybe she's out with the kids," he said.

"I really need to know if she touched Ms. Cahill's purse, or if she noticed anyone messing with it after boarding but before I got on. No one touched anything after I got on."

"Not that you're aware of. You slept for what, two hours, at least?"

Ava winced and nodded. "Yeah, something like that."

"Call her again and leave a message if she doesn't answer. The worst she can do is run, and there will be a record if she does. She's got two little kids. Surely, she couldn't get far with two toddlers."

"You'd be surprised," Ava answered, recalling her recent case in which the mother kept herself and her two young children hidden.

"She has babies," he said. "She'll have to use her debit or credit cards sooner or later to buy things for them: food, pull-ups, something, and we'll catch her. You want me to make the call and leave the message?" He reached for his phone.

"No. I got it." She rang the phone and waited for the voicemail to pick up. "Ms. Bruner, this is Agent James. I was wondering if it would be okay if we stopped by to speak with you again this evening or tomorrow. We just need to clear up something, and I think you're the best person to do that. Please give me a call when you get this." She left two numbers—hers and Bale's.

"All right, now can we do some more work here to whittle this list to a more manageable size?" Bale asked.

"I would be glad to do that." She wanted to tell him that it was not her who was delaying progress. It was the case and his unwillingness to allow her access to her team for help. "What do you have in mind?" She stood by his desk.

"I want to do deep dives on the remaining suspects. We can keep anyone who has anything that raises red flags in their past. Especially over the last five years." He pulled a list of names from under paper napkins from some anonymous fast-food joint and handed it to her. "This is a list of Emerald Block's people we are aware of. Look for connections to any of them as well."

The paper held a long list of names, many of which she already had. "Okay, then. This should be tons of fun."

"If people only knew how glamorous our jobs really are." He flashed a sardonic grin and then turned his attention to his computer.

"Did you just make a joke? Was that some dark humor peeking out?" She went to her desk.

"No. Absolutely not. Does this look like the face of a jokester to you?" He cocked an eyebrow at her.

She took one look at his Grumpy Cat expression and laughed. "Not really, no."

The work was tedious. Most of the suspects had at least one thing, one event in the past five years that landed their names in the keeper pile. After the third one came back with a massive debt relief from an unnamed source, Ava pushed away from the computer and tossed the paper into the keeper pile.

"This is getting redundant," she said aloud. "The first three have a red flag. At this rate, all of them are going to be keepers, and we've accomplished nothing."

"You've only gone through three?" He glanced at her.

"How many have you done?"

"Five, and this one makes six." He raised a paper and dropped it into a short pile with a smirk.

"That's your keeper pile, isn't it?"

He nodded and blew out a breath.

"All six of them are in it."

"Right again. But persistence pays off in the end." He popped his knuckles and went back to the computer. "That's what they say anyway."

"Sometimes, I would like to punch they in the nose. If I only knew who they were."

"Save the punches and put the energy into keystrokes. We're nearly done with the list."

"That's a silver lining, if ever there was one."

Ava worked two more names, and then pulled Stanley Tilson from the pile. Within twenty minutes, she had pulled so many red-flag events from his past five years that she kept digging. Thirty minutes later, she hit the print button on the file she had compiled and hurried to the printer to retrieve the papers.

"You act like you've found the needle in the haystack and might get a prize for it," Bale said, yawning and pushing back from the desk to look at her questioningly.

"Stanley Tilson. His red flags are amazing. He struggled with money and failed business ventures all through his twenties, and into his early thirties. Right now, he's forty-two, and he's set as far as money goes. He's lived from Arizona to Vermont, and finally settled in the DC area only three years ago." She grinned at Bale.

"Okay, that sounds like what we're looking for, but he could have just gotten his life together and finally made a good business decision."

"Three years ago, right after moving to DC, Stanley suddenly came into money, and guess what he did with it?"

"Bought his mother a house. I don't know," Bale snarked.

"Started a chain of hotels with restaurants. Over just the last three years, the business grew into a chain, Bale. Stanley Tilson is rich. Like really rich, and it happened in just three years. He's the owner of Tilson

THE WOMAN IN THE WINDOW

Platinum Suites hotels in DC, Maryland, Virginia, and Massachusetts. That doesn't happen in just three years. It's impossible."

"Did you double-check that you were getting the correct information?" He stood and walked to her, his hand out for the papers.

She gave them to him. "Of course, I did. I couldn't find how or where he came into enough money to reasonably buy the first hotel, let alone staff it and start it up. The original hotel is right here in DC, too. I think the money came from some big loan shark, you know, like maybe Emerald Block. Unless he tapped out a bunch of the smaller loan sharks in town and just hoped to make enough profit to pay them back."

"Emerald Block aren't loan sharks. They're a crime syndicate. Big difference." Bale continued looking over the papers.

"Exactly my point. It would take someone like that backing his endeavor to accomplish so much in only three years. I checked out the Tilson Platinum Suites here in DC."

"You checked it out? You mean online?"

"Yes. Virtual tour of the suites, pricing, restaurant, all the main points of interest. The place is way overpriced for what it offers, and most of the clientele are politicians, rich businessmen, CEOs, and the like. It seems to be a popular place among that echelon of citizens."

"Echelon of citizens, huh?" His grin was lopsided as he shook his head. "You definitely use odd wording sometimes, James."

"Echelon is—"

"I know what echelon means, James. I'm just wondering what echelon you're talking about."

She was glad he interrupted her because for a split-second there, she felt a lot like Ashton must have felt every time he got to explain one of his gadgets to her, or anyone with less knowledge about tech gadgets.

"The elite of our society. That echelon. Oddly enough, Tilson Platinum Suites doesn't seem to cater to celebrities. Most horribly overpriced hotels and the like cater to celebrities, but not Tilson."

"Maybe that's because of where it's located. Not exactly Hollywood. We don't get many celebrities out here in the capital city, but politicians and businessmen? They are everywhere. And they have bank rolls that rival celebrities. The lack of concern about how they spend it, too."

"He's worth checking out, then." Ava took the papers back.

Bale looked off into the middle space for a few seconds as if deciding about Stanley Tilson. He nodded. "Yeah. I suppose he is. Nothing is impossible." He took the papers back from her. "You mind? They go with the main file." He looked pointedly at his desk where the ever-growing paper file lay bloated and spilling out.

"Not at all."

"Delete it from the print history and the search history on the computer. We'll check him out, but I don't want anyone knowing about it just yet."

Deleting things from browsing and print history did not delete them as if they never existed. Ashton had proven that theory wrong more than once. Perhaps the deletions would keep the mole from picking up on Stanley Tilson for a while, though. She couldn't fault Bale for his cautions.

CHAPTER TWENTY-NINE

Tanzy and the Mole

B**ALE ANSWERED HIS PHONE AND HIS EXPRESSION SHIFTED TO ONE** of even more agitation than usual.

"How?" he asked.

Ava turned to stare at him when she heard the sharp edge to his tone. He motioned for her to move closer and then he punched the speaker button.

"Officer, you're on speaker. My partner needs to hear this, too."

Ava glanced at him in shock. He had called her his partner when his real partner, Agent Lin, was off working what he called the back channels of the case against Emerald Block.

"Tanzy Bruner is dead," the officer said.

"How?" Ava asked.

"Shooting, I'm afraid."

Ava and Bale locked eyes. "Damn neighborhood is so dangerous," Ava snarled. "She wanted out so badly." The two kids were left motherless and fatherless.

"She went the same way her husband did." Bale shook his head sadly. "Those kids."

"Did it happen anywhere near her house, or in sight of her kids?" Ava asked.

"No. She was parked at Jumpers waiting on her kids and a friend to finish their playdate."

"There was a drive-by at Jumpers, the kids indoor play park?" Bale asked in disbelief. "Tell me you have the bastard who did it, or the intended target, at least."

"No, sir. Tanzy Bruner was the intended target from what we can tell right now. This wasn't an accident."

"Not an accident?" Ava asked, feeling like a mockingbird.

"No. Nobody else was hurt, and there was only one shot fired. At close range."

"How close?" Bale asked.

"About ten to fifteen feet is what forensics is saying, but they aren't finished yet. It might have been closer. At that distance, and where Ms. Bruner was sitting, there's no way she wasn't the target."

"Thank you, Officer. We're on our way," Bale said. Thumbing the disconnect button, he glared around the room. "What the hell is wrong with people?" he asked.

It was a rhetorical question. Ava had no trouble discerning that. She grabbed her things and turned to the door. Bale stalked out in front of her, and again, she found herself following his lead.

Bale clutched the wheel tightly. It was easy to understand all the things that were probably going through his head. Two kids had been happy and playing inside, having a grand time. Their mother sat in the lot, probably just back from some errand, and waited for them to finish. Minutes before they were due to walk out, someone walked up to the parked car and shot their mother. They had no parents, and their lives had just been twisted and turned until they might never recover even though they were young. The trajectory they had been thrust upon was a bad one. It was one shared by many criminals that populated jails and prisons all over the world.

Cruisers sat around a car in the parking lot with their lights strobing swaths of anxiety-inducing red and blue onto the building, trees, and passing cars on the road to the left. A crowd pushed closer to the police line, and officers shooed them away, and sometimes had to physically remove them. Some people were only rubbernecking out of curiosity, but a few, as always these days, held up their phones and small cameras to try recording the morbid, tragic scene.

Bale's rhetorical question tumbled through her mind as she and Bale got out of the car. *What the hell is wrong with people?*

The detective met Ava and Bale at the back of Ms. Bruner's car. The body had been removed already, and Ava was glad.

"Agents," the detective said by way of greeting them. He held out a sheet of paper with a few names written on it.

Bale took the paper. "What's this? Witnesses?"

"Yeah. We put them inside there." He tilted his head backward, indicating the Jumpers building. "They're shut down. Sent all the kids home. Before you ask, the security cameras were dummies put up to deter any would-be vandals from spray-painting the place or breaking in."

Ava looked toward the building. "Wouldn't have done much good. The trees would have blocked the cameras' views of this area, anyway."

"Mm." The detective turned to check the view. "Yeah, probably, but we might have been able to see who the shooter was, or at least the direction he left." He tapped the list in Bale's grasp. "Most of them are useless. Preoccupied and noticed nothing until the shot, and then they panicked. Unfortunately, around here, the people are used to ducking and taking cover when they hear a shot because single shots are rare as hen's teeth. But that's exactly what this was. One solitary shot, and one dead vic. She had to be the intended target. Anyway, I underlined the ones I thought had anything useful to say."

"Thanks. We'll question them. See what we can get," Bale said.

Inside, two couples and eight women sat separated across the playground. Some in chairs, some sitting on equipment. Some were pale and wide-eyed. A few actively cried and continuously swiped at the tears.

"Divide and conquer?" Bale asked in a low voice as he scanned the open play area.

"Yeah," she answered, holding out her hand.

Bale tore the list in half and placed one piece in her hand. "Don't get caught up in their stories, just find out if they saw anything. If not, move to the next one."

She agreed, but the people were scared and nervous. There was no way around hearing their stories. Once she asked the first question, it would be like opening the floodgates.

Working through the list as efficiently as possible, Ava moved from the second woman on the list. She had seen nothing of use but had heard the shot. "Tatiana Estan," Ava called.

"Over here," a woman answered.

Ava walked between brightly colored snails wearing saddles and poised on large springs to the woman sitting on an equally bright-colored mushroom in the toddlers' climbing pit.

"Mrs. Estan?" Ava said as she took a seat on a short platform in the shape of a stump.

"Just Miss. I'm single. Never married, but I brought my daughter here today. She's only three." Tears welled in her eyes. She pulled in a deep breath and tilted her head back slightly.

Ava knew and understood the change in posture. Miss Estan was trying to keep the tears from starting. "Miss Estan, did you see anything? The shooter, the victim, anyone who stood out like they didn't fit in? Anything?"

The woman nodded. "I was outside walking to my car when it happened. I was parked on the opposite side of the lot, but I'm vigilant when I'm with my daughter. I'm always afraid someone will try to snatch her, or there will be a drive-by and she'll get hurt."

Ava nodded, wanting to commend the young mother, but not wanting to get tangled in an off-track conversation.

"There was a man at the other end of the parking lot. He was in a suit. I noticed him, and then turned to unlock my daughter's door. I put her in the car seat before I looked again. He was walking near the car when it happened."

"Did you see a gun?"

She shook her head. "But I heard the shot. I saw him near that car and thought he was walking toward my end of the lot. I wanted to be in the car and get it started before he got that far. I don't trust people. Especially not men walking alone in the parking lot of a kids' place like this. He didn't look like someone who had a kid, either. He just didn't fit in. Look how we're all dressed. Plain. Casual. It's a kids' playpark, and it's not the cleanest place in the world. Who would come here in a suit like that?"

"Is that all?"

"No. He's the only person who didn't panic. After I heard the shot, there were screams, people running, and people crying as they ducked behind anything they could find. That man acted like he was going to duck beside the car, as if he was scared, too, but when everyone else was down, he straightened his tie and just walked off long before the cops and the ambulances showed up."

"And how did you see all this?"

"I had opened my door and was getting in when the shot happened. I jumped in the car and slammed the door. I guess I kinda panicked like everybody else. I grabbed the steering wheel with both hands, and just froze like that for the longest time. I was looking toward where the sound came from, and that's how I saw what he did. It might be bad, but I was just glad he didn't notice me staring at him."

"Can you describe him?"

"He was too far away to get a good look, but he was kinda tall. Taller than your partner. His hair was really dark, almost black, but it was short. Clean-shaven, and he walked with confidence, like he knew he'd never be suspected, or something. Like you see these rich criminals act in the movies. It was weird."

"Was he skinny, fat, average?"

"Average. And I'm pretty sure the car he drove off in was a silver one. It looked expensive, too."

Ava wrote everything down. "Thank you, Miss Estan." She got Estan's contact information and gave her a card with her own.

Ava walked back to the front doors. "Reuben, Sonya Mabry?" she called.

Within another hour, all the witnesses were sent on their way, and Jumpers stood empty except for Ava, Bale, and two female employees, who had also been questioned.

No one had more information than Tatiana Estan. Ava showed her notes to Bale. "She's the only one with anything useful, and it isn't much. She was too far away to get a good look at the guy."

"Tall, dark hair, average build, wearing a suit, and driving a silver car," Bale said with a huff. "That narrows the suspect list down to a manageable five- or ten-thousand just in a five-mile radius."

A young girl shoved open the door and walked in. The detective was on her heels. She was holding up her phone, and almost immediately homed in on Ava and Bale.

"Miss, you can't just—"

"I have a video of the shooter!" the girl yelled, hurrying her steps to avoid the detective getting hold of her. "I was across the street waiting on my mom to get out of a doctor appointment, and I heard the shot. I recorded him." She shoved her phone into Ava's hands. "The detective said there were FBI in here. You're them, right?" She held to the phone tightly.

"I told her to wait," the detective said.

"It's okay," Ava said. "We were finished in here."

The detective looked to Bale. Bale nodded, and the detective straightened his jacket as he turned to walk out.

"I'm Agent James. Come over here and sit down."

"What's your name?" Bale asked.

"Brandy. Brandy Weiss. My mother is Linda. I was over there." She pointed out the window to a building past the parking lot. "It was a straight view but not very close."

"How old are you, Brandy?" Ava asked.

"Seventeen."

"Where's your mother now?"

"She's in the pharmacy down the block a bit."

"We need her in here, Brandy. You are a minor," Bale said.

"No. I don't want her here. She'll be pissed if she finds out I put myself in the middle of something like this, but I couldn't sit there and do nothing. I'm so sick of all these senseless shootings around here and nobody ever gets held accountable. When they do, they get a smack on the wrist and sent home with barely any time served. He killed someone. If she was here, she had a kid, and now that kid don't have a mom." She glanced around nervously. "Or a father, whichever one was sitting in that car. I heard the crowd say it was a woman."

"It was a woman, Brandy, and I appreciate what you're trying to do, but we really need your mother here. Like it or not, you're a minor."

Brandy bit her lip and looked out the window toward the other side of the intersection where she had been. She nodded. "Tell you what." She turned back to Ava. You keep the phone. The video's on it. I'm leaving. I'm not telling my mom what I did, but I'm not taking that phone, either. I want you to use that video to catch the man who did this."

"Brandy, we can't let you do that," Bale said.

"So what? You gonna arrest a minor for trying to help?" She stood and held his gaze boldly. "Maybe that was a phone I found and it just happened to have that video on it, and I turned it in to you two. It's a burner, by the way. All I could afford working part-time at the McDonald's two days a week." She flashed a tight smile as she took two big steps backward. "Good luck with your case." She turned and bolted out the door.

Ava watched her cross the parking lot, giving the site of the shooting a wide berth.

"Well, that was totally unexpected," Ava said, eyeing the phone in her hand. She pushed the button to brighten the screen, and a grainy video was paused on the screen. She flipped it so Bale could see it.

He shook his head, but his eyes didn't leave the screen. He squinted and leaned closer. "We need her mother's consent."

They walked to the car where Brandy sat. Her horrified expression would have been comical if it had not been so genuine.

"What are you doing?" she asked out the open window. "I gave you the video."

Bale held out the phone. "We need your mother's consent to be able to do anything with this, Brandy."

Quick as a streak of heat lightning, Brandy snatched the phone from Bale and tapped the screen. When he instinctively reached for it, she held it out the window with the screen facing him. The video was playing.

Unable to do anything else, he and Ava moved in close and squinted at the screen in unison. Ava shaded the screen with her hand. It didn't help much, but she could see that the recording was horrible quality, but it was all they had at the moment.

A woman came down the sidewalk carrying a large purse and a pharmacy bag. "Hey, what are you doing? Get away from my daughter!" she yelled.

Ava stood straight and faced her. "Linda Weiss?" she asked.

"Well, yes, but I don't know you," the woman said, stopping between Brandy and the agents defensively. "And I would suggest you get away from my daughter immediately before I call the police."

Bale side-eyed Brandy in the car, and Ava watched the girl's face redden as she shrank against the seat guiltily.

"Ma'am, we are federal agents," Ava said, showing her badge.

The woman's eyes went from the badge to the parking lot where there were cruiser lights still warbling. "What's going on?" She spun to her daughter. "Brandy, what's going on?"

"Well, at least you gave us your real first name," Bale said.

"I'm sorry, Mom. Some guy shot a woman over there, and I was just trying to help. They won't take my video without your permission."

"Give me that phone." The woman tore the phone from Brandy's hand and watched the video. Her face paled. She looked at her daughter and then Ava. "Take it." She shoved the phone toward Ava and let go.

Ava barely caught the phone before it hit the concrete.

"Ma'am, we need your information so we can return the device after—"

"Keep it. We don't want to be involved." The woman rushed around the back of the car and to the other side to get in. She started the car and pulled out in front of a Prius. The driver laid down on the horn and yelled angrily as he slammed on his brakes to keep from hitting her.

"Well, now what?" Ava asked.

"We work with what we have," Bale said, turning on his heel and heading back to the car.

CHAPTER THIRTY

Forward Momentum

B ALE USED THE LAPTOP TO RETRIEVE THE VIDEO FILE FROM THE phone. He played it on full screen. The quality was worse than they had initially believed while watching it on the sidewalk.

Ava cast the screen to a large monitor at the back of the office. The quality looked even worse on that screen.

"He looks like the robber on that old Atari game," Bale said. "Can't tell anything about him or the car he drove off in." He cursed and thumped his fist against the desk.

"Ashton could clean it up in no time," Ava said. "He could get a clean shot of the man's face, I'm sure of it. And the car? That would be easy as pie for him."

"My team will work on it. I've already compiled the file on a thumb drive for them so it doesn't have to go online." He turned a sour expression to his desk again.

"How long will it take them to get us something useable, do you think?"

"Jesus, James, I don't know. Did you see the quality? She recorded this on a toaster instead of a phone." He threw his hands up in frustration. "A couple of days, okay? Probably. Maybe three."

"Ashton can have it done in hours, Bale. Hours. Just a few hours, and then we'll have pictures and a video to work with. A few hours versus a few days."

He turned his angry mug to her. "Okay, stop deifying this Agent Ashton and just bring him in. He'll have to bring his own equipment, or it will take him just as long as it would take my team. Is his crap mobile? This new-fangled, updated, out-of-this-world equipment he supposedly has."

"As a matter of fact, I think almost all of it is mobile, and the stuff he will need for this definitely is." She turned to go to her desk, excitement building. She would finally have part of her team to help.

"He can come, but only if he works where he can be watched at all times. I mean every keystroke will be monitored by one of my trusted agents, and he better be every bit as good as you say, or—"

"He is. He's better than what I've said. Most people can't even understand what he's saying when he tells them what he's doing or how a piece of his equipment works. And he's trustworthy. I trust the man with my life all the time, and I have no qualms about it."

"Doesn't matter if you trust him, or not. I don't. Not yet. I have no reason to. If he agrees to be watched closely while working, he can come, but my guys are going to continue working on it, too."

"That's fine. He won't have a problem with that," Ava said, hoping she was telling the truth, and if she wasn't, that she could convince Ashton to be okay with it.

Sal answered the phone. "Ava, everything okay?"

"It is. Kinda."

"I was afraid something happened when I saw your number. What is it?"

"Nothing happened in that sense, Sal. It's just that I need some help from one of the team on this case."

Silence ensued for the next several seconds. "You can't get help from DC's expansive roster?"

"Not the quality of help I can get from Ashton."

"I'll approve it. We don't have the time to dig into it. I trust your judgment, so if you say you need him, he'll be on his way now."

"Thanks, Sal."

"Just promise me you'll nail these bastards," she growled.

"That's the plan."

Sal hung up before Ava could say more.

With Ashton on his way, Ava's mind relaxed a bit. It would be good to have him there; someone she knew and trusted and understood—the opposite of Bale and his team.

As soon as she stepped back into the office, Bale stood. "I've got to walk around for a few. I'm setting up like concrete. Is your tech-god coming?"

"He is. Hopefully he'll be here later this evening."

"Good. I'll leave it up to you to prepare a file for him."

"Bale?" Ava said as he stepped out the door.

"Yeah?" He leaned back in.

"What about the Covey Cahill casefile in the system?"

"What about it?"

"Ashton could trace the hacker if it was hacked." She took her seat.

"I am almost a hundred-percent sure it was. There's no other way that information could have been leaked unless it was one of her detail, and I would trust either of them with my life." He stopped and looked at her as realization dawned on his face.

"Oh, just like me with Ashton, huh?" She smiled.

"Yeah. We'll see after he gets here." He disappeared from the doorway.

Ava pulled the deep dive papers to her and saw that Bale had put all his with hers.

He popped back into the doorway. "Maybe."

"Okay," she said, a little shocked.

"If he can pull off this super-fast video clean-up, then yeah, he can work on the hacker."

"Sounds good."

He was gone again.

There was no question. Ashton had cleaned up worse files. Way worse, and he always did it faster than any other tech.

She worked to prepare all the files for Ashton. He could better tell her if and how he could apply his skills to help them once he arrived, but he would need the files to do that.

One of Bale's deep dives caught her attention. It was the report on Judy Edwards, listed as being thirty-four. Her background check was suspiciously empty. It was void of all the normal things on background checks, and made it seem as if the woman sprang into being only a year prior.

Ava set the report aside to wait on Bale's return. Why had he not noticed the lack of anything in her background? The utilities were in her name, as was her apartment, but they had only been added twelve months ago. She worked at a coffee and pastry shop on the same block where she lived. There were no credit cards in her name, no debit cards, and no bank accounts. Who lived in this day and age using only cash? And how?

The Blueberry Bistro where Judy Edwards worked was an old, family-owned business that barely made enough money to keep its doors open. That might explain the cash-only lifestyle Judy was able to sustain.

The Birch Street Apartments where she lived were old and humbled by age and progress—just like The Blueberry Bistro. Judy lived in a one-bedroom that was less than six-hundred square feet, and there had never been a complaint filed against her. Being there only a year might explain that one, but most people had at least one complaint for something—being late on rent, playing their TV or music too loud, having visitors too late at night. But not Judy Edwards.

Bale returned looking refreshed and carrying two cups of coffee. He set one on Ava's desk. "Be kind to your body while you're young, or you'll reap the effects when you're old." He stretched his back.

"You're not old by a long shot, and I'm not that young." She tapped Judy Edwards' report. "Didn't you notice anything unusual about her background check?"

He leaned to read over it and shook his head. "There's nothing to see."

"Exactly. She's thirty-four and there's nothing prior to a year ago. Where's she been for thirty-some years of her life?"

"I said look for red flags in your stack of reports, not go over mine and quibble about people who have been good all their lives." He went to his desk.

"There's nothing. No bank accounts, she lives by cash apparently. No credit cards, and the only records are her workplace and her apartment with the utilities. She doesn't even have streaming services or internet in her name."

He looked up from his coffee. "Who doesn't have internet?"

"Or a cell phone? Or Netflix, or Hulu, or whatever?"

"No bank account; no online services," he said distantly.

"No internet; no online services."

Ava told him about the apartment building and The Blueberry Bistro.

"God, how long was I gone?" He looked at his watch.

"About forty minutes. That's all it took me to look up these places. They're older establishments. There's not much to search through to get names and property history."

"I must admit that you've hooked my interest. Maybe I didn't look closely enough at Judy Edwards. She was a nobody, a ghost until a year ago. That's around the time Covey's case started."

Ava nodded. "She goes into the suspect pile."

"She was already in the keeper pile," Bale said.

"But you hadn't marked her at all. You dropped everything in the keeper pile, remember? I say we promote her to suspect since the time of her appearance lines up with the Cahill case."

He rubbed his chin. "You do know that women's preferred method of killing is by poison, don't you?"

"I've seen them use a lot of other methods, too, but yes, poison seems to be the preferred method."

"I want to speak with Stanley Tilson, the hotel mogul, before we talk to her. I thought about him a lot while I was walking, and he's dirty. Has to be in bed with some bad people to get where he is so fast."

Ava couldn't agree more.

CHAPTER THIRTY-ONE

Tilson's Tainted Platinum Suites

Stanley Tilson smiled tremulously at Ava and Bale. "May I help you with something?" His smile continued to falter and glitch. His gaze jumped from Ava to Bale continuously as he waited for an answer.

Bale flashed his badge. "Agents Bale and James. We need to speak to you about the flight again. You were questioned by—"

"Stevens. At the airport, yes." He stood so abruptly that his chair shot back and hit thin metal signage that clattered and rattled. Tilson sucked air in through clenched teeth and scrunched his face. Turning to check the signage, he groaned. "That only cost a small fortune so I can use it once a year. If that." He moved from behind his desk.

"Mr. Tilson—"

"Yes, if you don't mind, could we walk while we talk? I really need to check on tonight's special in the restaurant. Chef Fischer won't be thrilled, but you are federal agents." Tilson stepped into the hallway and tittered nervously.

Bale glared at being cut off in mid-sentence a second time.

Tilson's actions seemed off. He didn't look like a man who tittered at anything, nervously, or not. He had the square chin and broad shoulders of a man who stands on business. Not a nervous nellie.

"Most people have no idea what hard work it is to run a successful hotel and oversee everything yourself. I don't do this for all my hotels, of course. That would just be madness, but this one." He patted the corner molding as he turned left. "She's special to me. She is the matriarch; the one who started it all; the one who lifted me from a lifetime of bad luck, worse choices, and a growing desire to give up on it all."

"That's all well and good, Mr. Tilson," Bale said. "But we need to ask you some follow-up questions about Flight 808."

"Of course. Ah, here we are." He pushed a door open and walked inside.

The smell had drifted down the hallway, and Ava knew the kitchen was close before he touched the door. Thick, rich, mouthwatering aromas wafted to her. Whoever Chef Fischer was, he wasn't being paid enough.

The stainless white backdrop dominated the large kitchen. The room looked empty with only the large, fortyish man in chef's whites standing at a prep table and a slim, harried younger man hurrying behind him to get to the oven. He glanced up and then continued working with the food in front of him. The deep stainless pan held a roast that must have weighed in at fifteen pounds.

Tilson walked straight to the chef and began talking about the menu.

Ava and Bale exchanged an irritated glance. Why were they having to chase Tilson around? Was it not clear that the matter they needed to discuss was important?

Ava stepped to the end of the prep table. "Excuse me, Mr. Tilson."

Tilson stopped talking to the chef in mid-sentence and exhaled deeply as he held up a finger for the chef to hold on. He turned to Ava. "This will only take a few more seconds, if you don't mind, and then I'll be clear to hear you out." He turned to continue his conversation with the chef. "Now, Chef Fischer, as I was saying—"

"No, Mr. Tilson, as I was saying. We need a word. Now. This is important. Quite possibly even more important than tonight's special."

Tilson paused, waited for Ava to finish, and without glancing her way, continued once again. It was the last straw.

"Mr. Tilson, did Emerald Block fund your Tilson Platinum Suites startup? Is that where you got the money? From a crime syndicate?"

Chef Fischer jerked toward her, knocking a large stainless bowl to the floor. "Christ almighty. Sorry, Mr. Tilson." The chef bent to the task of cleaning up the mess.

Tilson's eyes widened and his mouth dropped open at Ava's blunt question. He motioned for Ava and Bale to follow him. "This way," he hissed as he sped toward the exit door.

In the hallway, Tilson kept up his speed-walking pace. "What the hell do you mean asking a question like that in front of my staff? I would advise you not to do that again. Our business is private. It's nobody's business where the money came from." He stopped suddenly and spun to face her. "Including yours, Agent James." He turned away and walked again but at a slower pace.

"It is my business, if it came from Emerald Block."

"How? How does that make it your business? I can borrow money from anyone I please. Including Emerald Block, if I so choose. This is my business, my livelihood, my life."

"If it came from Emerald Block, the money was obtained illegally, Mr. Tilson. It's probably blood money. One woman is dead because of them, possibly two now. Do you really want your name tossed into the same pile as Emerald Block after learning they killed a woman?" She did nothing to keep her voice down, and it carried in the wide hallway with its high ceiling.

Tilson stopped at a door, flicked a card over the lock and shoved the door wide. "God, get in here and lower your voice," he said through his teeth.

Ava and Bale strode into the room and eyed him.

He stuck his head out the door and looked in both directions before shutting it. He stepped close to them and talked just above a whisper. "If he sent you to see if I would rattle under pressure, you go back and tell him to go to hell. I don't appreciate being tested to prove my loyalty. You tell him that. I did what I was told, so you can all leave me alone."

"What? Him who, Mr. Tilson?" Ava asked.

Tilson blinked stupidly at her for a split-second but recovered quickly. "No. No, don't you play that card with me. Tell him I did what I was supposed to do, and you can all leave me the hell alone."

Bale shook his head. "What exactly did you do, Mr. Tilson? And who did you do it for? Porter Ambrose?"

Tilson took a big step back. "You're not with him?"

"We are with the Federal Bureau of Investigation, Mr. Tilson," Bale said, flipping his badge again. He held it so Tilson could get a good look.

Tilson took another step back and propped his hip against a dresser. The disbelief twisted his expression and narrowed his eyes. "You're really not with him?"

"No, we're not with anyone," Ava assured him.

"How do I know? He's one of you, so I know most of the tricks." He wagged his finger up and down at them in a naughty-naughty-kids kind of gesture and wore a half-grin as he did it. "You almost had me there. You really should look into an acting career. Both of you. So genuine."

"Who is one of us?" Ava asked. The mole had made a mistake in using Stanley Tilson. The man was a ball of nerves, and he was scared as witnessed by the beads of sweat forming on his reddening forehead and his temples.

"My contact. You know damn well who," he said with a short, high chuckle. "You can stop now, really." He flapped his hand and chuckled again as he wiped sweat from the side of his face.

Bale stepped forward, closing most of the distance between himself and Tilson. "What's your contact's name, Tilson? And no bullshit. I want it straight. Who the hell is your contact?" Bale's fists clenched at his sides and his shoulders stiffened. His expression could have melted the stainless steel in Chef Fischer's kitchen.

Tilson held his hands up, palm-out near his shoulders as he gave a compensatory step away from Bale. "I don't know his name. Jesus, you two are telling the truth. You really aren't with him, are you?"

"How do you not know his name?" Bale continued.

"Because he never gave it to me, and he certainly never flashed his badge so I could read it. I guess dirty agents don't want to advertise their identities, do they?"

"If I find out you're lying to me, Tilson—" He grabbed Tilson's shirt and tie in one swift movement and yanked the man forward so they were almost nose-to-nose. "I'll beat—"

Ava stepped in before Bale could finish his threat. They were losing control of the situation, and it could cause big trouble for their investigation. She gripped his forearm. "Bale," she said sternly, leaning close to his face. "Bale, let go. Not worth it."

Bale's glare shifted from Tilson to Ava but his grip remained firm. He wasn't letting go of Tilson.

"I mean it, Bale," she said in a low voice, holding his glare. "Think of the case and what this could cause down the road. You're not this man. You're better than this."

For a brief instant, the muscles in his forearm bulged farther, and he shook Tilson one good hard time before letting go and stepping away.

Ava turned to Tilson. "If you know anything about this contact, we need to know. If you know anything about Emerald Block and Covey Cahill's death, you damn well better tell us, or you'll go down for it, too."

"If you'll just leave right now, I'll give you information in a day or two. They'll kill me if they know I'm talking to feds they don't have in their pockets." He headed out the door.

Ava and Bale let him go.

Bale turned on Ava. "First things first. You don't know that I'm not that man, and don't ever do that again. Ever. I could have had him talking to us right now instead of letting him walk and possibly warn everyone involved." His face flamed.

"You could have had him talking at what cost to the integrity of the investigation, Bale? Did you even pause to think about that aspect of it? You can't brutalize information out of someone and expect it to stick in court. You know that, and so do I." She swung past him and jerked the door open.

CHAPTER THIRTY-TWO

Judy Edwards

BALE HAD NOTHING TO SAY ON THE WAY BACK TO THE OFFICE, AND Ava didn't mind. She was happy to go over all that Tilson had said, and all that still needed to be done to connect the dots in the investigation. As far as she was concerned, she would be more than happy to get the case over with and get back home. Bale's uneven temperament had frustrated her enough to last her a lifetime.

Ashton texted that he would arrive within fifteen minutes just as Bale parked the car on Fourth Street NW, in front of the field office.

Bale got out of the car and headed inside. Ava followed but at a much slower pace. She let him sling the door open and storm inside while she paused in the sunshine slanting down through a tree directly in front of the flagpole. The wind ruffled the flags, and a sense of pride and duty washed through Ava. The flag wasn't a thing of beauty. It was quite mundane, as most flags are. But what it represented was glorious, beautiful, a thing to be treasured and protected at all cost. More than one thing; many things. Even though the country was navigating rough seas at the moment, the values of that flag still coursed strong and true through her being.

A group of people walked out, laughing. They stopped at the side of the entrance. Ava walked past them and was greeted with smiles of camaraderie. They recognized her as a fellow agent, a fellow citizen who fought to make the world a better, safer place for all. That sense of belonging bolstered her even as she entered Bale's office.

After checking that they were alone, she approached his desk, where he sat staring at something on his computer and wholly ignoring her. His face had lost most of the angry red coloring, but the steel remained in his eyes.

"I know why you were so upset with Tilson," she said. "I know why you did what you did."

"Really? Good for you. What do you want, a gold star? A pat on the back?" He never looked at her.

"No, I just thought you should know that I understood, but I couldn't let you risk the integrity of the case. Not after you've worked so long and hard on it. It doesn't matter who the mole is as long as we catch him."

His gaze shot to her. "Doesn't matter? How can you say that? Of course, it matters."

She nodded. "It matters because you think you know him, and that you might be associated with him when everything comes out. You won't be implicated. You had nothing to do with Covey's death."

"It goes deeper than that, and I think you know that." Some of the hostility had ebbed from his tone, and the steel in his eyes softened just enough to notice.

"I'm not disagreeing with you on that. It does go deeper, and I'm sure of it, too. But whoever this mole is, he'll pay for what's happened. Whoever leaked that information will pay, and no one is going to think you had anything to do with it."

"You can act so relaxed about it because it isn't you who will inevitably be investigated." Even more of the anger had gone. His expression morphed back to its default grumpy-cat setting.

"Ava?" A familiar voice called from the doorway. Ashton stood there holding two big cases. There was another in a bag hanging to his hip, and two more on the floor on rollers.

"Hey, Ash," she said. A weight lifted off her as she moved to help him. "Let me get something for you."

"The wheelies," he said, tapping the side of one of the floor cases with his foot. "Thank you. Where should I set up?"

"Agent Bale, this is Agent Ashton," she said as she rolled the wheelies into the office.

"Ah, the god that walks among us," Bale said, standing.

Ashton looked at Ava questioningly.

She cleared her throat. "Ashton, this is Bale. Don't worry, I don't think he bites. If he does, at least he's had his shots." She smirked at Bale and walked past him.

Bale extended a hand and a millisecond smile. "I do bite, but only when someone gives me a damn good reason."

Ashton shook with him. "The far back corner will be fine," he said, maneuvering past Bale and giving him a wide berth.

"I'll be right back. Don't start anything with all your toys until then." Bale stalked out of the room.

"Is he always that pleasant?" Ashton whispered.

"No, sometimes he is even more pleasant." She grinned. "He's fine. It's just this case. There's a mole, and he can't be sure who to trust."

As they set up the equipment and moved furniture to accommodate it all, Ava briefed him on the investigation.

Bale returned while Ashton was still working on getting the plugs and adapters hooked up.

"I want the cellphone video started first, and then you can work on facial recognition in the airport terminal footage," Bale said sternly. "James informed you that you will be working under strict supervision at all times?"

"Yes, sir, she did. I'm fine with that."

"You'll have to be. This is my case, and I'm calling the shots."

The tone gave Ashton pause. There was a brief interlude in which Ava feared another confrontation instigated by Bale. The moment passed, and Ashton, ever the congenial man, smiled and nodded.

"So it is, and so, you are. I'm just the borrowed help." He glanced at Ava and then sat in front of his equipment as it powered on. Within minutes, he pulled up the cellphone file. His fingers flew over the keyboard and then he tapped screens, moved, and pulled command strings and graphs from one screen to another. After a couple of minutes of that, he smiled up at Bale.

"What?" Bale asked.

Ava patted Ashton on the shoulder, grinning, and walked to her desk.

"It's started. The cellphone footage. It should be rendered and clarified within two hours. It's horrible footage. Looks like it was filmed using a radish instead of a cellphone, but I've done the best I can with it."

Bale's eyes widened as his gaze shifted between the screens and Ashton. "That's it?"

Ashton nodded. "Until it's finished, yeah."

"So, you're just going to sit there for two hours and do nothing?"

"Unless you have something else you'd like me to do while that's working."

"No. No, that's what I want you working on. Can you run multiple files through simultaneously?"

"Not advisable. It slows the whole process. It's quicker to run one at a time."

"The other agent will be here in a minute to supervise you," Bale informed him. "James and I need to be doing other work."

"Yes, sir," Ashton said. The inward look of satisfaction was unmistakable.

"Are we going to talk to Judy Edwards now?" Ava asked.

"That's the plan. Just waiting for Masters to get his butt in here."

Ten minutes later, Masters was in place, having received his orders from Bale.

Ava took her bags and shot Ashton a thumbs-up as she went out the door.

Birch Street Apartments looked as old and dismal in person as they did in the pictures online. Window units jutted out the windows showing off their grimy, rusted backs. The bricks underneath them were painted with the rusty color in runnels. A piece of wood had been tacked over one of the entrance doors, and someone had hand-painted *Please use other door* on it in bright orange.

"And I moan about my own place," Bale said.

"Probably one of the only places in the city that still takes all-cash payments. Most places require a credit card, or bank card, of some kind."

Bale stepped in front of Ava and opened the door. He walked in first.

The dim interior took some time for her eyes to adjust to. The glass entrance doors had allowed outside light to enter before one of them had been broken and blocked off with wood. The old-school incandescent lights hanging under their metal domes did little to alleviate the shadows and dimness.

They found Judy Edwards' apartment, and Bale motioned for Ava to knock on it. "She's more likely to answer for a stranger, if that stranger is a woman."

Ava knocked and held her badge under her chin so the woman could see it when she looked through the peephole.

"What do you want?" a female voice asked through the door.

"FBI, ma'am. We need to speak to you about Flight 808. The flight you were already questioned about a few days ago."

"I can read the badge, and I know how long it's been." Two chain locks, a deadbolt, and the regular lock disengaged one by one. She opened the door and pulled her thin sweater tighter around her. "I suppose you want to come in?"

"If you don't mind," Ava said, glancing at Bale.

She sighed softly and stepped aside. Bale came into view, and she stiffened markedly. "Who are you?"

"I'm Agent Bale," he said, stepping in and past her.

She looked out the door, and then closed it. "Any more of you hiding somewhere?"

"I wasn't hiding, Ms. Edwards, and no, there's no one else with us. Does the thought of that worry you?"

"No, of course not. I just didn't want to slam the door in some agent's face."

The apartment walls were devoid of any pictures or home décor. The only thing on the walls was a simple calendar. The days had been marked off with a single, precise diagonal black line in each block.

The living room sat to the right of the entrance. Situated in front of the window that didn't hold the air conditioner unit, there was an old sofa chair, a ragged foot rug, an end table that looked to be from a second-hand store, a small lamp, and an ashtray. There were no knick-knacks, nothing extra, nothing to make the place look or feel homey.

"Kitchen," Ms. Edwards said as she passed them. "There are more chairs in here."

Indeed, there were four folding chairs. Not the padded kind, either. The table was a thirty-six-inch folding table that could be picked up at any Walmart. There was an empty dish drainer on one side of the sink with a dishtowel draped over its side and a sponge in the utensil holder. On the other side of the sink, there was a four-cup coffeemaker.

"Do you want coffee?" Judy asked as she pulled out her chair.

"No," Ava said. "No, thank you."

"Good because I'm almost out. What did you need to talk about? I have one day a week off, and this isn't how I want to spend it."

"And we don't want to spend the day interrupting your day," Bale said. "So, did you know Covey Cahill?"

"No, I don't know her. Didn't know her, whatever. She's the dead woman from the plane, right?"

"Yeah, that's her. Dead. Murdered," Bale said.

"Are you married, have any kids?" Ava asked in a more genteel manner.

Judy turned untrusting eyes to her. "Why? What does that have to do with anything?"

Ava and Bale held their silence.

"No, I'm not married, and I've never had kids."

"Did you know any of the in-flight attendants?" Ava asked.

"No. I was a passenger just like everybody else. Why would I know any of them?"

"We don't know, Ms. Edwards," Bale bit. "That's why we're asking. It's our jobs to ask these questions."

"We're just following up," Ava said. "Do you live here alone?" She glanced around the sparse, cramped room.

"Yeah. I told you, I'm not married, and I don't have kids. Don't want any. I live simply, quietly, and I enjoy that very much."

"Must not have many visitors, either," Bale said, also glancing around. "No family visits from Aunty Jane, or Grandma?"

"No," she said in a tone that indicated she didn't trust them or their line of questioning.

"And why is that?" Bale asked as he looked back to her. "Most people have someone that visits them every now and then."

"Because I don't have any family. Not to speak of, anyway." Her gaze dropped to the side.

"Not to speak of, or you don't have any family?" Ava asked.

Ms. Edwards pulled in a deep breath and let it out slowly. She clasped her hands on the table in a slow, deliberate manner. "To speak of, Agent James, was it?"

"Yes, ma'am. Agent James and Bale." Ava pointed to Bale.

Ms. Edwards nodded. "They threw me out when I was sixteen, and I haven't talked to them since. We lived in a nice house in a nice neighborhood back in Florida, but those days are long gone."

"You've lived on your own since you were sixteen?" Ava asked.

"Yeah, I have. Plan on it staying that way, too. At least, for the foreseeable future."

"But, on paper, it looks like you didn't even exist until a year ago. Why is that?"

"I don't know what you're talking about, and I don't see the relevance, anyway. I'm a US citizen, and I've obviously existed for a few decades, plus."

"No bills in your name ever came up until a year ago. No driver's license, no social security card, nothing. You can see how that would look suspicious, right?"

"I think it's time for you to leave now." Judy stood and pointed to the door they had entered. "I have things to do, and you're done here."

"No, we're not. We're investigating a woman's murder, and you're on the list of people who look suspicious to us," Ava said.

"I'm a suspect?" Her eyes flew wide and she leaned forward as she put her thumb in her chest. "Me? Because you couldn't find records on me from farther back than a year ago?"

"And you'll move up that suspect list unless you have a good explanation for why you just appeared twelve short months ago, and why we can't dig up anything on you before that," Bale said. "And trust me, we did some serious digging. You've changed identities, and we can't figure out why. A woman on your flight ended up murdered, and you look real suspicious. Like someone who might be able to change her identity again at any time and disappear."

"This is ridiculous," she said, thumping back into her seat. Tears shone in her eyes. "You're not leaving until you get an answer, are you?"

"If we do, you're coming with us," Bale said.

Was it a bluff? Ava couldn't tell. Neither could Judy Edwards.

"If my cover is blown, it's on your head," she hissed as a tear streaked almost simultaneously from each eye.

"You're not undercover, Ms. Edwards, or whoever you really are. We checked that," Bale said disbelievingly.

"Not that kind of cover." She swiped the tears away. "I witnessed a high-profile murder in another state, and I was put into witness protection. Now all this shit? Do you have any idea how much trouble this could cause me? If the wrong person gets wind of your stupid investigation, I could be the next murdered woman that you have to investigate. Is that a good enough answer for you, Agent Bale?" More tears ran down her face unchecked. "If my cover is blown because of your asinine ignorance, Agent, then my blood will be on your hands."

Bale deflated. "Witness protection, you say?"

"I didn't stutter, did I?" she asked.

Ava got up and walked around Bale. "Ms. Edwards, I'm sorry. We checked, but that didn't come up, either."

"And it wouldn't, would it? That's why it's called witness protection. I had to leave everything and everybody and every place I ever knew. I was ripped right out of my own life and now I'm here in this godforsaken dump of a city because they thought I'd be safe here. Do you have any idea how many times I've had to move because of this? Are you finished wrecking my day and endangering my life?" She looked at each of them in turn with determination behind the tears.

Something else lurked in her stare. Something unnamed for the time. Something Ava couldn't quite make out, but that seemed familiar.

"Yes, we're done," Ava said.

Bale stood. He stared down at the crying woman a moment longer, and then turned on his heel toward the door.

Stepping onto the sidewalk again was like having rods shoved into her eyes, and Ava sucked in a breath as her eyes shut in response to the sudden brightness.

"Hurts like hell, don't it?" Bale asked, thumbing the unlock button on the key fob.

"You think she's telling the truth?"

"I don't know, but I'm going to check her story. I don't trust her."

Ava scoffed. "Isn't that like your grumpy expression?"

His expression changed to one of confusion. "What?"

"You not trusting someone is like your grumpy expression—a default setting." She raised one eyebrow and grinned as she buckled her seatbelt.

CHAPTER THIRTY-THREE

The Mole

Ava's phone rang, and she reached for it in her pocket.

"Saved by the bell," Bale said, keeping his eyes on the road and grinning.

Holding in a chuckle, and a bit shocked that he even participated in her bantering, Ava answered the phone.

It was Ashton. "The cellphone video is finished. I'm working on trying to clean it up a little more manually, but it's good already considering what it was before."

"We're on our way. Thank you, Ashton. I appreciate the quick work." She hung up. "The cellphone footage is finished. Ashton is working on cleaning it up some more, but we should go take a look. He says it's good for what he had to start with."

"The guru has spoken, eh?" His mouth twitched up on the right side.

"Ashton isn't the enemy, Bale. He's finished already with that footage. For your case. That has to be worth something. Wouldn't kill you to toss some respect his way."

"I don't grovel to my team the way you're doing with your tech support man. Everyone has to know where the boundaries are. They have to know who's in charge. If you coddle everyone on your team the way you're doing with him, you are in for a hell of a wake-up call when you're out in the field and a team member thinks he can ignore an order just because you're his buddy instead of his boss."

"I don't grovel to anyone, first off. And I don't coddle anyone. I show them all due respect. Maybe you should take notes."

He scoffed lightly. "It's a thankless job. One that will eat you alive if you expect a pat on the back every time you do your job. The people we help don't even thank us most of the time."

"All the more reason, as superiors, we should do exactly that."

After several minutes of silence, Bale glanced her way. "You're not so bad, James. At least you'll stand your ground for what you believe in."

"Isn't that the way it's supposed to be?"

He grinned. It was a wide, genuine smile.

She thought about Jason Ellis. His smiles were just as rare, and twice as contagious as Bale's. Would they get along? Would they be at each other's throats because they were so much alike?

"Better watch," she said in a flat tone.

"For what?"

"My grandmother used to tell me that if I made a face, it might freeze into place, and then I'd be stuck that way forever."

"What the..." His head jerked toward her. "Ouch. That was uncalled for."

She shrugged. "Just saying. It'd be awful if your face froze with that smile on it. I can imagine it might scare some people; make them wonder about your sanity." She shifted in her seat. "More than I'm sure they already do."

"And the hits keep on coming," he said. He parked and took the key from the ignition. "I'm not going to lie. I'm anxious to see if boy-wonder in there can impress me."

They walked briskly to his office. Masters shot from the seat next to Ashton when Bale walked in.

"Having a chummy time, there, Masters?" Bale bit as he approached the man with a scowl.

"No, sir. I was just taking a load off for a few minutes."

"Well, do it over there somewhere." Bale motioned toward the other side of the room.

Masters dropped his head and walked away red-faced.

"Ava says you have turned the cellphone video into something marvelous." Bale rested his hands on the back of the recently vacated seat beside Ashton.

"That's not what I said." Ava walked to the other side of Ashton and crossed her arms. "I told him exactly what you told me, Ashton. What have you got?"

Pushing his chair back, Ashton tapped at a keyboard as he continued to get into a standing position. "You can watch it for yourselves."

"Where are you going?" Bale asked.

"Right here," Ashton stepped around Ava, pulled his chair with him, and sat in front of three monitors. "Just got into DC's traffic-cam system."

"For what?" Bale asked, his brows nearly meeting above the bridge of his nose.

The video popped up on the screen, and Ava hit the play button. "Hey," she said to redirect Bale's attention. Ashton worked best when he was left to do his thing.

Bale turned his attention to the monitor and leaned closer over the back of the chair.

"I thought this was supposed to be a praise-Jesus miracle," he said three seconds into it. "Look at this. You can't see who's doing the shooting. You can't make out anything. That would never hold up for an identification."

Ava kept her eyes on the screen and let Bale fuss to the air. The video was good. It was miraculous considering the quality they had before. She could make out Tanzy Bruner's car just fine. The man holding the gun was too grainy to make an ID, but the video was clear enough to get a good measurement of him. He was around six-three and weighed probably two-fifty or two-eighty. The man was no lightweight. Someone of that stature would stand out in a crowd.

"I can't be sure of his car, even," Bale continued. "It's silver. Or, is that bad quality white?"

The video ended and Bale turned to Ashton. "Is this all you have?"

Ashton shook his head and kept working. A second later, he spun sideways in his chair and pointed to the monitor screen in front of Ava again, and then he turned back to his work.

Bale looked confused but turned to the monitor again. "James, he's one strange guy. You are aware of that, I hope."

"Aren't we all a little strange?"

Pictures came up on the screen, starting in the top left corner and filling the page.

"There," Ashton said. "The man's face is still obscured, but…"

Bale's face drained of color as he studied the picture of the silver 2024 BMW 3-Series at a red light. The angle showed the car's front and driver's side to the tail. He tapped the picture on the screen as he squinted at it.

Ashton tapped a few keys. All the other pictures disappeared, and the one Bale pointed out jumped to full screen.

"What is it?" Ava asked, leaning in to see if the driver was visible at all.

Bale turned on his heel and walked out of the room without explanation.

"And he says I'm strange," Ashton said in a semi-low voice.

"Thank you, Ashton. Print this one, please." Ava headed out the door to catch up with Bale. He was only a few paces ahead of her. He seemed to only want out of the room, not to get anywhere specific. "Bale," Ava called.

He kept walking, but his pace was slow, ambling, as if he were in deep thought.

She caught up to him. "Hey, what was that? You recognized something in that picture, didn't you? What was it?"

"It's not who I suspected." He held his phone in his hand and looked at it as if unsure what to do with it.

"The mole?"

"Yeah. It's not who I thought. It's his partner."

"You recognized the car, right?"

"Yeah. And his build. I just wanted to see his face to be sure, but I don't have to now. It was Max King. Griner's partner for the last eight years. Not the most likable guy, but who is in this place? I never thought about him. He was never even on my radar, and I bet he was never on anyone else's, either. Big guy with an attitude that made people want to stay away from him, but he was a good agent." He laughed sarcastically. "Well, I guess he wasn't such a good agent, after all. A good actor."

"Are you going to call Griner?"

He shook his head. "No. First, I need to know when anyone saw him last, and then I'll call the boss."

Ava went back to the office to get her things and the printed picture. She gave Bale enough time to make his calls, and then went back to the hallway to find him pacing with the phone stuck to his ear. He motioned her to follow him.

He kept talking into the phone as they walked out to the car. Ava got in and waited on him. He finished his call and got behind the wheel, a look of grim determination on his face.

"Griner and his boss haven't seen King in two days, but he was working undercover. His next contact is supposed to be two days from now. I asked why, but all I got was 'why do you need to know?'"

"And did you tell them why?"

"No. I just said I needed to ask him something about a case I'm working and hung up."

"If no one knows where he is, where are we going?"

"I know a few places he likes to frequent. Figured we'd go check them out; see if we luck out and spot him. If not, we're going to his house in Manassas."

"But if he's working undercover—"

"Did that video look like he was working undercover? He's not working on an official federal case. He might have been assigned to one, but that's not what he's doing. He's using his unsupervised work time to do this crap for Emerald Block. Who knows who else he's doing it for?" He slammed his palm against the steering wheel when the first red light caught him.

"If it's him, he's doing it for himself. They have something on him, and he's doing it to save his own butt."

"Or for money." The car leaped forward as soon as the light turned green.

They drove for over an hour to different bars, parks, and hangouts, and there was no sign of Max King. Bale questioned a few people at two different bars, but no one had seen him in several days.

Bale drove toward Manassas. "If he's not at his house, I'll try a couple places I know near there."

"Shouldn't you call this in to someone in charge? Your boss, maybe?"

He gripped the wheel and bared his teeth in a show of ultimate frustration. "Don't tell me how to conduct my investigation, James. This is my case. I'll deal with it my way."

"Hey, I'm not telling you how to do anything. By all means, it's your ass in the sling when this goes sideways and your bosses haven't even gotten a quick heads-up."

Bale called SSA Dee Gambel who put him in a conference call with SSA Rosa Esposito. Bale told them what was going on with the Covey Cahill case, and what he had found out about Max King. When they hung up, he glared at the phone perched on its dashboard holder.

"You heard that. They don't believe me about King. How am I supposed to go easy with this?"

"That's not what I heard. I think they don't want to believe King is the mole, and if he is, they will have to start an internal investigation into him, Griner, and everyone else on the team to make sure they weren't involved or had no knowledge of what King was up to. Nobody wants to think about the implications like that. They just don't want you to jump the gun and maybe land yourself in hot water, too."

"Well, look at you being all understanding and female-brained about the whole situation," he snapped.

"Female-brained, or not, you know I'm right."

Bale walked to the door of King's house in Manassas. It was nothing to write home about. Small house on a tiny lot in a semi-urban, semi-rural neighborhood. It was what Ava thought of as a suburb playing at being rural. Two blocks away, the city was in full view, and even the traffic noise infiltrated the little community.

Bale knocked and rang the doorbell several times before going around to the accessible windows and cupping his hands against the glass to peer inside. Walking back to the car, he kept looking up and down the street. Did he expect that King would pull up, or walk up while they were there? Ava couldn't hold it against him for hoping.

He got in the car and slammed the door. "It's like he's disappeared into thin air. Wherever he's at, it isn't any of his usual places that I know about."

He must've been laying low, Ava guessed. It was common for criminals to have a place to be far away from all the ruckus their deeds caused. Being a federal agent, King knew how to lay low and stay out of sight as long as he needed.

CHAPTER THIRTY-FOUR

Deceptions

ASHTON PULLED UP WHAT LOOKED LIKE A DOZEN SMALL SCREENS of data on the monitor. He pointed at one. "This is the Covey Cahill casefile. See this?" He pointed to an alphanumeric string on another of the miniature screens. "That's the path to the casefile. It's secured behind an encrypted password wall."

"Wait," Bale said. "I'm not a geek god, you're going to have to talk to me in layman's terms."

"It just means that to access the dedicated system, one needs a valid password. To get into that particular case, one would also need a valid password. A password that is created by the person asking permission to see the file. If they are in the main system, and their clearance is sufficient, they can get this far. But you secured the main file with yet another password, didn't you? You had to enter three passwords to get into the file, correct?"

"Yes, I did secure the main folder. I do that for my bigger cases like this one. Anyone who needs access gets that password from me."

"Unless they hack the file. Like someone did here." Ashton pointed to another screen. "This happened ten days before Ms. Cahill got on Flight 808."

Bale held up his hands in askance. "And what does that tell us other than someone hacked the file ten days before the flight? I know that means that someone leaked the information to Emerald Block, but I need to know who hacked it. Can you do that?"

Ashton brought more screens to the foreground. "I back-traced from the security breach and followed the path to the hacker's login screen." He pointed to it. The username was visible but not the password.

"That's King's login username." Bale cleared his throat. "Can you tell where the login took place? Which computer was used?"

Ashton maneuvered the screens, found the one he needed, and tapped it with one finger. "Birch Street Apartments. Unit 3B."

Ava and Bale exchanged a knowing look.

"Thanks, Ashton," Ava said as she moved to keep up with Bale.

"Don't you want to know how I back-traced it? Don't you want to know how…"

His voice faded as she turned out the door and toward Bale's retreating back.

Apartment 3B was empty. The ashtray, rug, and lamp were gone from the living room, and the calendar had vanished from the wall. The few dishes Ava had seen before were also gone. The woman in 3B had disappeared just like Max King had.

"We know this is where it happened," Ava said.

"Yeah. I knew something was wrong with this whole situation when we were here. Has an address ever been wrong in Ashton's work before?"

"No. They're always accurate."

"Then Emerald Block got their information after Judy Edwards, or whoever the hell she is, hacked into our secure system from this crappy little apartment."

"It might not have been Judy who hacked into it. It was King's secure login. You said that."

"It was." He stopped. "King did it from here. That's what happened. Maybe that woman helped him, but he put his login details on that page. He's the one who had access to the system."

Ava nodded. "They were in on it together. I bet they even had that witness protection story in place from the beginning."

"And it worked long enough for her to pick up and go. She's in the wind. Probably as soon as we left. What I don't get is what does King get out of this from Emerald Block? Why would he be helping them? He's federal. He has the backing of the whole Bureau."

"The possible answers are too many to list," Ava said. "Let's search around and see if there's anything that might give a hint as to where she was headed."

Bale snorted laughter. "Yeah. What, you think she wrote it in the dust on the floor? There's nothing here."

"Checking off the boxes. Leaving no stone unturned. Why waste time coming back later when we can get it done now?"

He walked into the bathroom and flicked on the light, unwilling to discuss it further or argue about it. "Maybe he's in with Emerald Block. Maybe he got his foot in the door, and he's working his way up."

"I doubt he's working his way up. But I'm not saying they wouldn't like the idea of having a federal agent at their beck and call. That would be a boon to any crime syndicate," she answered from the kitchen.

Bale walked into the bedroom. He opened the closet door as Ava moved to the living room. "I just wonder if that dirty bastard was hiding in here while we were here?"

"That would be too dangerous. He's smarter than that."

"He was dumb enough to get messed up in Emerald Block's business."

He was right. King might be smart, but he couldn't be a genius, or he would have never gotten involved with a crime syndicate.

As they finished searching, Ava had another idea. "Can you get me King's cellphone number?"

"Work or personal?"

"Both would be perfect." She dialed Ashton and put him on hold while Bale got the numbers. She gave Ashton the numbers as Bale called them out. "Ping the locations for the last several months on both phones."

"Will do. It'll take a while, and there's not much I can do about that."

"I expected that. Pull any personal information from the phones that you can on King. Any rush you could give it would be much appreciated, though."

They hung up.

"Ping the locations for the last several months?"

"Yeah. Criminals often have a safe haven. Somewhere they're comfortable laying low and hiding out for long periods of time after they've stirred up trouble in whatever form. If we ping his location over a few months, it might reveal where he's visited most often, how long he was there each time, and we can go check that place. I'm betting it's a place no one at the Bureau knows about if he was working with Emerald Block for very long."

"How long will this feat take your man?"

"He said it would be a while. There's red tape to cut through to get the ping locations—"

"I know that. I've waited upwards of eight weeks before."

"Oh, it won't take that long. Not for Ashton. The man has skills." She didn't want to say that Ashton knew how to work around all that red tape and then cover his butt on the way out. She had long suspected that was exactly how he got some information so quickly. However he obtained information, he had been doing it since he had started in the Bureau. He always had the necessary permissions before doing anything, and that kept his work legitimate.

CHAPTER THIRTY-FIVE

The Mansion

BALE RETURNED FROM A SHORT MORNING IN COURT WHERE HE HAD to testify in another case. Ava had spent the morning going over her notes and all the compiled files of the case. In the office, Ashton had been bent over the keyboard with coffee and an energy drink since before daylight.

Masters yawned and stretched in his seat. "Heard anything from Bale?" he asked Ava.

"Not yet, but I probably won't. He's coming back here after court." She was prepping notes in order when Bale entered the room.

"Speak of the devil," he said.

"And he shall appear," Masters said, standing. "I need a break. I'm glad you're back."

"Don't take all day," Bale said.

Masters scoffed and nodded as he walked out the door stretching his back.

"I'm glad you're back, too," Ashton said. "And your timing couldn't be better if it was planned. I just got the location where King has been going most often. Besides his house in Manassas, which I'm guessing you knew about."

"Yeah, been there," Bale said, walking over to him.

"He's been going to a place in McLean, Virginia. He's been there several times."

"How many is several, and over what time period?" Bale asked.

"Twenty-seven times over just the last two-and-a-half months. His phone stayed there for two to four days at a time on twelve of those occasions."

"Do you have the address?" Bale grabbed his pen and paper, ready to write it down.

"Yes." Ash handed Bale a paper with the address and coordinates on it.

"I need to get there as soon as possible." He turned to leave.

"I don't know where he is right now because his phone's been off for days," Ashton said loudly so Bale could hear him as he went for the door.

"Got it." Bale disappeared into the hallway.

Ava sighed and picked up all her things. "Thank you, Ashton. Anything else you find, just send it to my phone."

"You got it."

She nearly ran into Bale head-on as she stepped through the doorway.

"Sorry," Bale said, sidestepping her. "Hey, Ashton."

Ashton spun his seat around. "Yes?"

"Thanks. Thank you." He flashed a smile and turned back out the door, nearly hitting Ava again.

She followed him with a small smile, and yes, it was satisfaction.

Bale was already in the car and waiting impatiently as she put her things in the backseat and then climbed into the front. He pulled out before she was buckled.

"Not a word," Bale said.

"About what?" Ava asked as if she didn't know.

"You know what. I don't want to hear it. I just thought since he was so accustomed to getting pats on the back from you that it might hamper his ability to concentrate fully on his work if he didn't get it from me. It is my case he's helping with, and Masters has had nothing but good reports on him." He put his brake on hard.

"Jeez, what?" Ava asked, annoyed and startled.

"Masters wasn't back in the office when we left. I'll turn around."

"No, don't do that. Just call him. Or, give me the number, and I'll do it. Ashton isn't the mole. He found the mole. Remember?"

"Crap," he exclaimed. "You're right. Still…" He pulled over to the shoulder and dialed a number. A few seconds later, he barked, "Masters, if you're not back in that office with Agent Ashton, get there immediately." He paused as if listening for a few more seconds. "Get someone to bring you lunch, or take him with you when you go." He hung up. "That man is already thinking about lunch."

Ava glanced at her watch. "It's almost time for it."

"Yours is going to be late. I hope you're not hungry."

McLean was a twenty-five-minute drive. Less than half the time it took to drive to King's Manassas house. If he was there, Ava wouldn't be thinking about food even if she was starving. The case always trumped the desire or need for a lunch break.

Bale rolled into a neighborhood with huge, fine houses spaced far enough apart that the residents had plenty of privacy. There would be no hearing the neighbors argue, or seeing what they were watching on TV from a window.

"Nice neighborhood," Ava said.

"And up there is our address. Are you sure his addresses are always accurate?" Bale looked at the mansion skeptically.

"Always," Ava answered, eyeing the house with a measure of disbelief. "Family home?" she asked when Bale turned into the paved drive.

"No, I don't think so. There's no way this is his."

"He couldn't afford it on an agent's salary, that's for sure," Ava agreed.

"And definitely no way he could afford this and his house in Manassas. That one, I can see him being able to afford. Maybe easily. But this? No way."

The mansion sat far back from the road on a small, gentle hill. The pavement ran straight up to the front entrance and looped around a fountain that stood twenty feet tall if it stood one. There was ample room for parking on either side of the loop, but there were no cars to be seen. The three-door garage was closed. Perfect place to keep King's car out of sight.

Bale got out of the car and walked to the garage first. He looked through the windows in each bay door and then in the walk-through door. Ava took in the manicured landscaping of the front yard. She couldn't afford the landscaping. A theory began to take shape in her mind about King and Emerald Block, but she kept it to herself.

She knocked on the door and rang the doorbell three times in rapid succession. She held her badge at the ready as Bale joined her.

Three seconds passed. Then five more. She rang the doorbell three more times and knocked louder.

The door opened and a svelte woman with long, dark, wavy hair stood there with a metered smile and ice in her eyes. "You don't have to break anything. I was on my way. I heard you the first ten times you rang the bell and beat on the door like a caveman."

Ava opened her mouth to retort but closed it again and held out the badge instead. "Agents James and Bale," she managed. A smile of civility was asking too much. The woman had just called her a caveman in a manner.

"Agents? Ooh, sounds so…" She looked Bale up and down appraisingly. "So mysterious and intriguing. Would you two like to step into the parlor and out of the dreadful brightness of the sun?"

"Yes, thanks," Bale said, stepping in front of Ava.

"Would you like something to drink, Agents? Sweet tea, mint julep, plain ol' water?" She smiled as she moved gracefully to the wet bar.

"No, thanks," Ava said. "We're on duty."

"Well, sweetheart, I didn't think this was a social call. I was merely minding my manners. You always offer your guests a seat and something to drink." She smiled as she made herself a drink. "I'm having a little mint julep before lunch."

"Ma'am, who are you?" Bale asked.

"Margueritte. This is my house. Since you came here and knocked on the door, I was under the impression that you already knew me."

"Margueritte who?" Ava asked.

The woman's smile fell away, leaving only the ice in her gaze. "Fiore. Margueritte Fiore, Agent James." The smile returned. It was warm enough to melt glaciers and as genuine as costume jewelry. "Now that we're all introduced, what, may I ask, is the nature of this visit?"

"Ms. Fiore, is this your house?" Bale asked.

"Yes, it is, Agent Bale. All mine." She looked up and motioned with one hand. "I know, it seems far too big for just one person, but it's just me. And there's a small staff here a few times a week to make sure everything is in good repair. I have a cook who comes in the mornings to prepare meals, but he's gone already, so it's just me. And now you."

"Do you have any paperwork to prove this is your house?" Bale continued.

Ms. Fiore looked as if someone had slapped her. It took her a goodly moment to recover, and then she giggled as if he had made a joke. "I assure you this is my home, but I don't have to prove that to you at all."

"You're correct, Ms. Fiore," Ava said. "But I would warn you that we are federal agents conducting an investigation, and if you lie to us, you could go to jail for it."

Fiore laughed. "Investigation into what? Whether or not this is truly my home?"

"Where's King?" Bale asked bluntly.

"King? You mean Max King?" Her good humor dried up.

"That's who I mean," he said.

"Again, if you lie, you could go to jail. Just tell us where he is," Ava said.

Fiore laughed and took a large drink of her mint julep. "He isn't here. We're not steady. We're on and off, and for the longest time, we've been off. He hasn't been for a while. I haven't seen him in ages. I don't know where he is." She turned to look out the window. Somehow, she managed to make the space around her look like the cover of a romance novel. Maybe one in which the heroine is pining for her lover.

"That's not the truth, Ms. Fiore," Bale said. "Try again."

Spinning to glare at him, she shook her head. "I didn't lie to you. I just told you I haven't seen him in ages."

"And we know his phone pinged here just a few days ago. So, he was here only days ago," Ava said.

"His phone might have pinged here, but I didn't let him in. Besides, I've only just returned from New York City. I was there for the last seven days. You can check. I was at a charity function: Healthcare for the Underprivileged Charity Dinner and party. It was ten-thousand a plate, and another five to stay and enjoy the after-party. There was a small fashion show that was total rubbish, and some college kids put on a short play that touched on the social struggles for underprivileged kids and the homeless population. It was pretty good, but that fashion show?" She groaned, rolled her eyes toward the ceiling, and flapped a hand. "A waste of their fabric and my time."

"Would you mind if we had a look around, Ms. Fiore?" Bale asked.

"I most certainly would. You have shown me no warrant. I invited you in out of the sun, not to go fingering through my private things. I told you: Max King is not here. You want to look through my house, show me a warrant. Until then." She sipped her drink.

"Thank you, Ms. Fiore," Bale said tightly. "We'll check your story about the charity function. We may get back with you about that warrant, too."

"Yes, sir, Agent Bale." She showed them to the door and opened it wide. "You drive safe out there. It would be terrible if you got in an accident. Toodles," she said in an overly saccharine voice as she twiddled her fingers at them and smiled broadly.

Bale grumbled about Margueritte Fiore for the entire length of the drive back to the office.

Ashton looked up as Ava entered. "I pulled up all the information about that house in McLean. I thought you might need it if no one was there."

"What did you find?" Ava asked, glad to be away from Bale's grumbling for a brief moment.

"It belongs to a Margueritte Fiore. She has owned the house since it was built ten years ago, but there's something else." He flipped through printouts and pulled one to give Ava. "That list of Emerald Block names you gave me?"

Her gaze ran over the paper. "Yeah?"

"Margueritte Fiore is the niece of Ruby Vos. There's Porter Ambrose who runs the outfit. Then there's Logan Ayres as second-in-command. Ruby Vos is listed as third-in-command."

Ava let that sink in for a moment. "Covey Cahill's boyfriend was the fourth. Callum Horne."

Bale walked in. "Anything new and useful?"

Ava took him the paper. "Ashton already checked the house information. It does belong to Ms. Fiore. But look at this. Margueritte Fiore is the niece of the third-in-command in Emerald Block."

"Ruby Vos," he read aloud.

Ava nodded. "Callum Horne was under her, and he was Covey's boyfriend."

"This is all twisted up and bordering on making me crazy." Bale's phone rang. He answered and walked toward the door. He stopped, hung up, and came back. "Tilson is dead."

"Stanley Tilson? Our hotel guy?"

"Yes. Shot through the head. Still in his car in his garage at home. At first, they thought it was suicide, but it wasn't. He was shot in the head through the passenger side glass."

"I don't mean to interrupt," Ashton said excitedly. "I found something on the terminal footage, and you're going to be shocked."

Ava groaned. "We've got too many balls in the air."

CHAPTER THIRTY-SIX

Dummies

Ashton motioned for Ava and Bale to watch the left-hand monitor. "This is where the mysterious, tall woman in the terminal has just walked away from your victim, Covey Cahill."

The tall woman walked easily toward the restroom alcove and disappeared.

"That's where we lost her," Ava said. "I must have watched the footage from here until the end twenty times trying to pick her up again, but I never saw her come out."

"Just wait. She does. And that's where you're going to be shocked." Ashton hit the fast-forward on the footage. When he put it back into normal speed, he put his finger on the screen again. "Watch right here."

A man with a mustache and a ball cap sauntered out of the restroom alcove, looked over his shoulder toward the people heading to board their flight, and then walked past Ava at the counter with a smug smile, and continued out the door.

The self-satisfied smile as he passed by her was odd, and Ava's skin prickled. Did he know her? Had he also gotten the last-minute information about her flight, or the well-orchestrated seating snafu choreographed by Bale? How much did he know about her? Was she being paranoid?

"Ashton, that's a man with a mustache," Ava said. "Where's the woman?"

"I think your nerd fried a circuit," Bale said in a stage-whisper. He made eye contact with Ashton. "Just yanking your chain, man. It was a joke."

Ashton did not laugh. Neither did Ava.

"I thought it was funny," Bale said defensively. "Either way, the question remains: Where is the woman? And why did we just watch a man walk out of the terminal?"

"That's two questions," Ashton said, turning to the second monitor. "To answer both, the man you watched walk out was the woman in question. The woman was never a woman. It was a man." He played a video of the man heading for the parking lot.

A very tall man of average build walked with his back to the camera. He swung one arm free while the hand of the other was stuck in the pocket of his dark jeans. He adjusted the ball cap several times as if it were uncomfortable, and then he was out of the camera's sight.

"That was the woman? How did you come to that conclusion?" Bale asked.

"Facial recognition. I scanned her face into the system, and this is what came back. I also compared his gait with that of the man in the cellphone footage." He prompted the third monitor to play a split screen of that footage.

Ava's heart fell. "Agent Max King," she said.

"Unbelievable," Bale said, backing away from the monitors.

"But once you see it like that," Ashton said, playing the footage again.

"Yeah," Bale said. "It's kinda hard to miss."

"We weren't looking for a man, though," Ava added.

"I have more," Ashton said.

"Play it," Bale ordered, moving close again.

Max King returned, sans the mustache and ball cap, to the airport later and caught a flight to DC.

"He flew under his own name back to DC," Ashton said. "Do you want to see more, or should I just tell you what happened once he got back?"

"Just tell me," Bale said disagreeably. "I'm not a big fan of mysteries or cliffhangers. If I need to see it afterward, then play it."

"He left the airport here and drove back to Manassas. I don't know for sure where he went. I lost him on the traffic cameras a few miles from his home address. He took back roads where there were no cameras shortly after arriving in town."

"He was headed back to his house. I'd bet my boots on it," Bale said. "I'm going to put a detail on that house and the house in McLean, too. He'll return to one of them soon enough, and when he does…" Bale turned and started punching numbers into his phone.

"Ava?"

"Yeah?" She turned to Ash, proud that he had surpassed anything Bale had hoped for. He always went above and beyond.

"I'm in the process of pulling King's financials." His fingers flew over the keyboard and screens popped up on two of the monitors in cascading layouts.

"What is this? What am I looking at, Ash?"

"He has received payouts from a company in DC. That company, Faison Coin-Op Laundromat, is a dummy company used to filter money; to make it anonymous." He grinned. "At least, to most people who care enough to notice it at all. It just looks like he owns the laundromat, but things are never what they seem in DC, are they?"

"You're right about that."

"Faison Coin-Op Laundromat is a dummy company. King is listed as the owner so that the payouts from it seem legitimate, but nearly a hundred percent of the payouts originated from politician slush funds."

Ava furrowed her brow. "Why would politicians be paying King?"

"I don't know. The list of possibilities is practically endless. You can believe that not one of those reasons is good because they're hiding the payouts."

"I want you to follow every lead on this. Every lead, no matter how insignificant it seems. Can you have that by tomorrow morning?"

"Is my name Ashton?"

Ava chuckled and clapped his shoulder. "I don't know. That depends on who you ask." She tilted her head in Bale's general direction.

"Well, to him, I am the Great Geek God, Techie."

"Also known as the Guru of Geekdom."

He laughed. "Seriously, I'll have the financial traces by tomorrow morning, no problem. I've been working on them for a while already."

"Of course you have. You are Ashton, after all."

Ava waited for Bale to get off the phone and told him about the dummy company and the payouts.

"I had no idea he even owned a laundromat."

"If I don't miss my guess, none of his coworkers knew. It is solely for the purposes of filing taxes and keeping his finances looking legit. Ashton is working on tracing more of the money trails. We'll know more about Max King and his income than we ever wanted to know by tomorrow morning."

"That soon, eh?"

"Yeah. Hey, did your guys ever get that footage done for you?"

He smirked. "You mean the footage that Ashton already gave us? No, my guys didn't get it finished. I pulled them off it just now and put them on the stakeouts at the Manassas and the McLean houses."

"Are we going to check out Tilson's death?"

"Yeah. The investigator in charge said he'd meet me at the scene and walk me through what they had before giving me the files, if I wanted. I agreed. It's okay to have their point of view and their opinions out of the way before I start investigating."

Thankfully, the ride was more relaxed than some of the others she had taken with Bale. Maybe he had come to terms with the whole Max King being a criminal situation.

CHAPTER THIRTY-SEVEN

Bodies of Evidence

Detective Ruiz was a short, skinny man in his early fifties. Life had not been kind to Ruiz. His thick hair was silver to the roots and tinged with brassy yellow near the end. His dark eyes were sunken, and his face had so many lines that it resembled a topographical map of Texas.

"The victim pulled into his garage, and the shooter…" Ruiz let the word shooter linger in the air as he gave Bale a hard look.

"What about the shooter?" Bale asked.

"He was apparently already in here, waiting to ambush the victim. Tilson never even raised his arm, which is a normal reflex when someone sees what's about to go down. His hand, however, was still clutching the gear shift from when he put the car in park." Ruiz stared at Bale. "The shooter was, uh…" He did the weird pause in the middle of the sentence thing again.

Bale made a rolling gesture with one hand. "What is it about this shooter that's bothering you, Ruiz?"

The detective's dark eyes narrowed, and he slipped a hand toward his hip. Ava bristled and stepped to the side. She put her hand on her gun.

"He's one of your guys, Agent Bale."

"Ruiz, take your hand away from your gun," Ava warned.

"Yeah?" Bale asked. "And how do you know that?" His eyes kept darting toward Ruiz's hand near his gun.

"Because there was a little spot of blood over there by the roll-up door that didn't belong to the victim. There was another right behind you, in the darkness. He would have been hidden there. We ran that blood, and it came back as a match to—"

"Max King," Bale finished for him.

"How did you know that?" Ruiz's fingers rested on the butt of his gun, and he never looked away from Bale.

"Ruiz, last warning," Ava said, pulling her firearm from its holster and keeping it at her side.

"Because he's a suspect in a case we're working. Just like Tilson was."

"Yeah?" Ruiz asked, his fingers lifting away from the gun.

"Yeah, but I need you to keep that information to yourself for a while. If he gets wind that he's been fingered, he'll run. Being an agent, he knows what we'll be looking for, and we'll never catch him."

Ruiz considered that for a moment and then stood straight, letting his hand drop back to its normal place at his side.

Ava cautiously slipped the gun back into its holster, relieved that she didn't have to point it at the detective.

"Ballistics match with the recent shooting of Tanzy Bruner, and if I'm not mistaken, that was your case, too," Ruiz said.

"You're not mistaken. Bruner's death was part of this case, too." Bale held out his hand for the files.

Ruiz handed them over and then produced a thumb drive. "That's all we have for now. I'm handing it over to you. My boys are off this one. Good luck, Agent Bale." He turned and gave a small two-finger salute off the top of his forehead to Ava. "You, too, Agent James." He pointed to her gun and flashed a smile as he walked out of the garage.

Ava and Bale looked around the garage, getting an idea of how things went down. "That's three down. I wonder how many more are on his kill list before he's done?"

A shudder ran down Ava's spine, and she sidestepped so the brick wall was at her back instead of the open door. "I don't know, but let's focus on catching him before there are any more deaths." Was she on that list? Was Bale?

Bale's phone rang as they walked back to the car. He answered and gave Ava the new files to put with the growing stack in her bag. She opened the back door and leaned in for the bag. Another shudder ran down the length of her back. Turning, she looked at the windows in the house across the street. Was he there? Watching her, taking aim?

A curtain dropped back into place in an upstairs window, and Ava imagined Max King standing there with his gun pointed down at her. It was an unobstructed view. She and Bale were like the proverbial sitting ducks on that street. Not even a tree offered a place to take cover.

Paranoia was a merciless mistress, and one which Ava did not appreciate being in the company of. Putting the car between her and the house, she peered through the window to keep watch as she placed the files in her bag and fastened it shut again.

The front door opened a crack. Was that a gun glinting sunlight in the darkness beyond?

She backed up and shut the car door, keeping her eye on that suspicious glinting.

"Bale, get a move on, would you?" she said as she pulled her gun again.

Seeing her pull the gun, Bale hung up and ducked and moved toward the car as he pulled his own weapon. "What is it? What do you see?"

"House across the street. The door opened. I see something glinting in the sunlight. Looks like a gun."

He turned to peer through his door window and the passenger door window simultaneously.

Just then, an elderly lady stepped partially out the door, wearing glasses, and looking warily over at them. "What's going on over there?" she called in a raspy voice. "You better leave before I call the cops."

Bale gave a low laugh and holstered his weapon before standing straight. He held up his badge and walked to the front of the vehicle. "Ma'am, we're federal agents. I'm Agent Bale, and the woman peeking around the back of the car at you is Agent James. This is part of an official investigation."

Ava stood straight, shoved her gun back into place, and walked around the back of the vehicle. She forced a smile and held up her badge. "We could come over and show you, if you'd like."

"No. You just stay over there. Whatever's going on, I don't want any part of it."

"Did you see what happened here this morning?"

"No. I was gone. I already gave my statement to the police." She went inside and slammed the door.

Bale laughed again as he got in the car and started the engine.

Ava slid into her seat, knowing it was going to be a long ride, no matter where they were headed.

"Don't let it bother you, James," he said through yet another hearty chuckle. "Those glasses really were glinting dangerously."

"Who called?" she asked sharply.

"Metropolitan PD. Judy Edwards was shot dead at a bus stop this morning. From the reports, she was shot about thirty minutes after Tilson. Investigator is going to send me the files as soon as ballistics is confirmed. I would bet my paycheck it's a match to the gun used to kill Bruner and Tilson. I figure we can go ahead and start driving toward the house in Manassas. By the time we get there, the reports should be ready. I already have enough to get a warrant to search King's house."

Tossing King's house in search of any evidence sounded great. Nothing better to relieve the tension. "There won't be anyone there to serve the warrant to."

"I wish there would be. I wish he would show up so I could arrest him and tell him what a piece of bottom-feeding garbage he is."

Sure enough, when they reached his house, King was not there.

Bale briefed the two men he had on stakeout near the house, and they met him on the front lawn.

"Be thorough," Bale said. "I want all the electronics, any calendars or day planners you find, any scraps of paper with notes scribbled on them—I want those, too."

His men nodded and headed inside. One went to the farthest room, which was the kitchen, and the other took the living room. Ava took the bathroom, and Bale went to the bedroom.

A minute into searching, Bale called out, "Ballistics are a match to our gun. Look for a nine-millimeter."

Ava took everything from under the sink, noting that there were significantly fewer bottles and tubes under a man's bathroom sink than under a woman's. When she finished, she stood and repeated the process with the medicine cabinet above the sink.

King had three prescription bottles. Two were labeled as antibiotics. She shook the first one and looked through the amber plastic at the capsules. He had taken about half of them. The other one looked as if he had taken almost all of them. She dropped them into evidence bags and placed them in a large paper bag on the floor. As she reached for the other prescription bottle, she knocked a razor, a tube of lip balm, and the last prescription bottle off the shelf and into the sink.

"Save the pieces," Bale called. "They might be evidence."

"Nothing broke," she replied.

But something had sounded off about the plastic bottle from Wayne's Pharmacy. She picked it up and shook it as she had the other two. When no pills rattled, she held it up to the light.

A small glass vial containing a dusting of powder up one side was nested in there. Her heart pumped harder.

"Bale, you better come see this," she said, staring at the bottle.

Bale appeared three seconds later. "What?" He reached for the bottle.

"Don't open it," she warned. "What if it's cyanide? Do you think it could be?"

He carefully tilted the bottle side to side. "If we're lucky, it is. I'll have Dr. Pate run a test strip on our way back to the office." He slid the bottle into a plastic bag and put that plastic bag inside another. "Can't be too careful."

She shook her head.

They finished collecting everything. Ava and Bale left. Bale's men resumed their former stakeout position. Surely, King would arrive at one of the houses soon.

Dr. Pate suited up and shooed Ava and Bale from the room while he tested the powder in the glass vial.

Bale paced like a man in the maternity ward waiting room.

Pate returned. "It's cyanide." He gave Bale the report and the vial, which was back in its double plastic bags.

"I knew it," Bale said, rushing for the door.

"Thank you, Dr. Pate," Ava said, following Bale. So much for him showing appreciation. It obviously wasn't going to be something that was easy for Bale to remember.

"Gotta let them know before they open any of the evidence and handle it without gloves." He said over his shoulder as Ava caught up to him in the hallway.

Ava's phone rang. Expecting Ashton, she answered and stepped away from Bale in the parking lot. "Agent James," she said.

"Is Agent Bale there?" a man asked.

She glanced at Bale. "Who's calling?"

"Warden Eller. I need to speak with Agent Bale. He didn't answer his phone."

A more distant male voice said something.

Eller came back. "Did you say this was Agent James?"

"Yes."

"I'm calling on behalf of Randy Jenkins, an inmate at the prison. He is in the infirmary and is requesting to speak with Agents Bale and James immediately."

"What happened to him? Why's he in the infirmary?"

"I'm afraid he's in bad shape. Speaking to you two is his last request. He won't last much longer. There's nothing they can do for him. His injuries are quite grievous."

"How long do we have?"

"Maybe a few hours," Eller said, lowering his voice. "If you intend to come, do so right away."

"We'll be there in half an hour." She hung up. "Bale, we need to go. Give me the keys."

Still on the phone and irritated at being interrupted, he fished his keys from a pocket and tossed them to her as he went around to the passenger side of the car.

Ava drove for ten minutes before Bale was off the phone.

"Where are we heading?" he asked.

"The prison. Randy Jenkins wants to speak with us. Warden Eller said it was his dying request."

"Dying? What happened to him?"

"I don't know. Eller didn't give many details, but he said the injuries were grievous."

Had someone gotten to Jenkins in prison? Had King gotten to him even in there?

CHAPTER THIRTY-EIGHT

A Last Request

Randy Jenkins lay on a bed in the infirmary staring at a blank, pastel-green cinderblock wall. He had his back to the other prisoners in their beds, of which there were five.

The guard pointed to Jenkins. "The doc gave him something to calm him down. He's cuffed to the bed rail. I don't have to tell you the rules?"

Ava shook her head.

"Been down this road a few times," Bale said.

"Mr. Jenkins," Ava said as they approached.

Jenkins shifted on the bed and looked at them. He looked pretty bruised and beat up, but otherwise okay.

"I don't see any grievous wounds," Bale said, frowning deeply.

"'cause they haven't been administered yet," Jenkins said with a sleepy smile. "I'm glad you're here." He pulled a small wooden box from under his pillow. "I made this in here. I want you to give it to my mother for me. I don't trust Eller to do it."

Ava took the box and set it on the edge of the bed. "Mr. Jenkins, what happened? The warden said you wouldn't make it, but I'm not seeing a man dying from his injuries."

"Oh, and can you give Mom this, too?" He pulled a letter from under his side and held it out to Ava. "Please?"

She held the letter. "I'll deliver this stuff if you'll tell us what's going on."

"Emerald Block. That's what happened. They had me beat to a pulp this morning."

"Why?" Bale asked.

"Because they found out I had talked to the two of you. When word got out that you visited me, that's all it took. You know everything we talked about was recorded, right? I mean, you know that much, surely."

"We know that, but it's also confidential," Ava said.

Jenkins scoffed. "No, it's not. And now I'm in the infirmary with three broken ribs and a messed-up face as proof. When they find out about my cousin, Buck Perron, and that he was on that plane, they'll kill us both to make sure we don't talk."

"You mean, Emerald Block admitted they had Covey Cahill murdered?" Ava asked.

"The boys giving me the beating didn't talk much, but yeah, that was the gist of it. They said Emerald Block's business was Emerald Block's business and that I better keep my mouth shut. They said no more talking to you guys, too. Said next time, they'd finish what they started."

"Then why did you call us in? Now that we've returned to see you, it's surely a death sentence."

Jenkins shrugged. "Doesn't matter. I just wanted to make sure you knew about Buck. Keep him safe. He had nothing to do with Emerald Block. Heck, he barely even glanced in my direction even before I got tangled up with them. Buck's a good man. Whole lot better than me. You think Emerald Block will care about any of that when they find out he was on that plane? No, they won't. They'll kill him anyway. He'll be a liability in their eyes. Just like me."

"We'll do what we can to keep him safe," Ava said, unsure exactly what they could do. King had been moving through the list of liabilities quicker than a wildfire in a high wind.

"Tell him I'm sorry, too. I'm sorry that I caused all this. I was stupid. Tell Mom I love her, and I never stopped regretting all the grief I caused her." He stretched gently and grimaced. "At least I won't have to look over my shoulder forever. It'll all be over sooner rather than later. So much for staying alive long enough to get released."

"Mr. Jenkins—"

"And don't let anyone know you're giving her that stuff for me. They might go after her. Wait for a long time, like maybe several months, after I'm buried." He put his head on the pillow again with an expression as blank as the wall at which he stared.

Ava tried again. "Mr. Jenkins, we can get you some security in here."

"Maybe keep you alive until your release date," Bale said. "Maybe even get that moved up, if you would testify—"

"Forget it. I'm done," Jenkins said with finality.

"Even without agreeing to testify, we could get you a cell to yourself and offer you some safety while you serve out the rest of your sentence," Ava said. "We could have you put on suicide watch, so it wouldn't be as noticeable."

"No. Thank you for the offer, but no. It doesn't matter if I live under a blanket of security in here. When I get out, they'll find me. I don't want to live that way. I don't want the constant threat of them hurting my family just to get at me, either, and if I go into hiding, that's exactly what they'll do. You don't understand the lengths they'll go to, or the cruelty they can inflict for even minor infractions."

Ava slid him a card. "If you change your mind, I know people who can help."

As she and Bale left the prison, he called for an agent to visit Buck Perron at home and to remain there until further notice. The man was to be protected until they figured out what to do.

A half-hour later, Mr. Perron rang Bale's phone to thank him personally.

"Mr. Jenkins said he was sorry for the trouble he's caused, and that he was stupid," Bale said.

Ava shot him a look. He could have left off the last part. Her mother would have said Bale had no bedside manner at all. Ava could verify that.

After he hung up, he heaved a weighty sigh and rubbed his cheeks with both hands. "He says he'll go to Maine. He's leaving first thing in the morning. He has a friend up there he'll stay with until he can find another place, preferably farther away."

"Is he going to change his name? Anything to make it harder for Emerald Block to track him down?"

Bale shrugged. "Didn't say. Maybe moving away will be enough."

"I hope so. For his sake. I wish we could do more for him, though." Ava tried to concentrate on driving to keep her mind from overloading her with ideas on how to keep Jenkins and Perron safe.

"You can't save them all, James. You can't even help them all. They're adults. They'll figure it out and make up their own minds."

Ava's phone rang.

"Would you?" She nodded toward the console.

Bale picked it up.

"Just put it on speaker, please," she said.

He answered and pressed the speaker button before attaching it to the holder on the dash.

"Hello? Ava?" Ashton asked over the phone.

"It's me," she said.

"I followed up on the money trails."

"What did you find?"

"Lots of dummy companies. Land Trust LLC, Midas Real Estate, and Stratton Delivery Service are the top three."

"We're on our way back. I want to see the trails and who's at the other end of them."

"I'll have it ready."

The line went silent.

"He's really on it, isn't he?" Bale asked.

"I told you he was good."

"You didn't tell me he could accomplish more than an entire team."

She smiled. "Mm, I believe I kinda did, but now you know it for yourself."

"Sometimes, seeing is believing."

She parked at the curb and gave Bale the keys back. She took the files inside. It was time to sort through them and determine their next step until King was located. There were angles to consider that might give them a hint of his location and his next target.

In the office, Bale's desk phone was ringing. He hooked it with one finger and put it to his ear.

Ava dropped the bag containing the files on her desk before walking to Ashton's area. He pulled up the three dummy companies he had mentioned in the call, and started pointing out how the money was filtered through them in the same way it was filtered through the laundromat.

"Hey, stop whatever you're doing," Bale said, walking toward Ashton and Ava. "Just got a call that a DC cop, Officer Mason Hudson, was shot and killed during a routine traffic stop just now. The witnesses said the shooter drove off in a sporty silver car, and one man said it was a BMW. Can you get me anything on that?" he asked Ashton.

"Where did the shooting take place?" Ashton cleared the screens with a few keystrokes.

"Intersection of Fourth and Adams, heading south," Bale said.

Ashton worked furiously at the keyboard. Multiple screens and pictures flashed across two of the monitors. His eyes moved from keyboard to monitor. Suddenly, he stopped typing, pulled a screen to the foreground. "There," he said. "It's Max King's car."

Bale was already heading for the door. "Send the location to James's phone." He jogged out the door with Ava right behind him.

By the time they were in the car, Ashton had sent the street name.

"King is on M Street, getting ready to cross over Rock Creek, heading toward Key Bridge," Ava said.

"He's heading to one of the houses in Virginia." Bale threw on the lights and siren and stepped on the gas.

"Or just running."

"Call for backup. King is going down today."

CHAPTER THIRTY-NINE

Fishtails and Dirty Agents

K ING MANEUVERED THE BMW SMOOTHLY, WEAVING IN AND OUT of traffic, going over to the other side into oncoming traffic, and back again without decelerating. Horns blared and brakes squalled on the Francis Scott Key Bridge as civilians compensated for King's reckless movements.

Bale took advantage of the halted cars and moved between them with an ease and speed equivalent to King's. Adrenaline pumped through Ava's veins until she was almost numb to the bite of the seatbelt against her collarbone.

King slid sideways at the steep left-hand curve after the bridge, and Bale caught up to him by cutting a straighter line through the stopped cars in King's wake.

With the horsepower of the BMW proving useless in the heavy traffic, Bale was on his rear. They blew through the red light in the curve, and King accelerated.

Bale swerved and almost lost control of the car as they sped through the second red light. He corrected and aimed for the driver's back of the BMW.

"Hold on!" he yelled as he hit the accelerator.

It was a pit maneuver. But there was too much traffic. Ava opened her mouth to protest, but it was too late. The impact jarred her against the seatbelt, and the BMW's backend broke traction, skidded to the right, and into an opening.

Bale followed and hit it again, sending it into an out-of-control skid that shot gravel and debris into the air in a pelting cloud.

The BMW hit a support beam for a canopy where gas pumps once stood. The Exxon station had been closed for a while, and the concrete had already been removed. All that was left was a gravel lot, the canopy, and the small, squat, empty building at the far end.

"Cover him," Bale barked as he bolted from the driver's seat.

Ava was out with her gun in her hands, advancing on King's position. He had fled the car and ran to the right as more agents pulled in behind Bale's car.

There was nowhere for him to go. A high block retainer wall ran the length of the lot to the right, and above it was a steep, unscalable incline. To the left, traffic. To the front, the old Exxon building.

"King, stop!" Bale yelled. "Don't make this any worse on yourself than it already is."

The other agents fell in line with their weapons drawn.

King turned to face Bale with a wide grin, holding his gun tightly at his side.

"Drop it!" Bale yelled, advancing in long strides, gun pointed at King. "Don't give me a reason. Drop it and kick it over, King."

Laughing, King dropped the gun, looked around as if for a possible egress, and then shook his head as he kicked the gun away.

Ava and the other agents moved in swiftly. King put his hands up and dropped to his knees.

Bale rushed to get behind King and cuff him.

THE WOMAN IN THE WINDOW

King sat in the interview room as if he had no worries in the world. "You've got the wrong man, and you're going to regret this, Bale."

"I don't think so," Bale replied coldly.

"I'm a federal agent, not a murderer."

"And we have evidence to the contrary," Ava said.

"Bale, you know me, man. I'm a fellow agent, and you're just going to let this random agent with her wild imagination come in here and do this to me? What the hell? You know what this will do to my career, my life, my reputation. I'll be ruined. You're ruining me. Come on, man."

"I'm not doing anything to your reputation or your life or your career. You did that when you started taking payouts from Emerald Block. You finished it off when you started killing for them. How deep are you into the syndicate? How long have you been involved with them?"

"I'm not! I'm telling you that you have the wrong person!" he yelled.

Ava pulled papers out of the folder and spread them on the table in front of him. "Know what that is, King?"

He stared at the pictures of the cyanide in his prescription bottle. "Whatever it is, it was planted."

Bale shook his head. "No. Your fingerprints are on the vial. That vial contains cyanide. The same thing that killed Covey Cahill." He dragged out a photo that showed King with the mustache. "And that's you in the San Francisco airport after you dropped that cyanide into her drink."

"What? You're crazy. I didn't poison anyone. I don't even know any Cahill."

"I bet you recognize these," Ava said, showing him his own financial reports. She pushed another set of papers toward him. "And these are the people who funded the payouts from all those different companies."

"Dummy companies," Bale added.

Ash knocked at the door before opening it. He handed Ava a piece of paper and walked out. Her blood ran cold as she read it and then let Bale read it.

"What's your relationship with Margueritte Fiore, King?" Bale asked.

"That's personal."

"How personal?" Ava asked.

"Personal enough that I don't think it's any of your business."

"Well, she's missing," Bale said. "And that big mansion of hers over in McLean? It burned down. Care to enlighten us on how that happened?"

King blanched. "You're lying. Lying bastards. That's what you both are."

Ava opened her tablet and pulled up news footage of the housefire. She turned the screen to King and let it play long enough that he knew it was real.

He covered his face and bent so that his head was between his knees. His breaths came faster and shallower.

"You aren't going to—"

King grabbed for the tiny plastic trashcan and puked.

Bale and Ava recoiled in disgust.

King heaved several times before settling back in his seat with tears in his eyes. "They'll come for me next."

"Who will?" Bale asked.

"Santa's eight little reindeer. Who do you think? Emerald Block." He bent and grabbed the trashcan again.

CHAPTER FORTY

Broken King

KING SAT STRAIGHT AGAIN, BREATHING HEAVILY AS HE WIPED HIS mouth on his sleeve. "Okay, okay, I'll talk. I will give you information, but you have to keep me safe. That's all I'm asking in return. Just keep me safe from them."

"You make me sick, King," Bale said. "I can't listen to any more of your whining pleas knowing what you did." He flipped his folder closed and stormed out of the room, leaving Ava to deal with King alone.

"I'll do what I can for you, if you will give us more information," she said.

"Whatever you want, just promise you won't let them kill me."

"Who was responsible for Covey Cahill?"

"She was Callum Horne's girlfriend. Callum is one of the higher-ups of Emerald Block under Porter Ambrose, which I'm assuming you already knew if you did an ounce of homework."

"We do know. Tell me something I don't know."

"Then you know the story of the raid gone wrong in which she was shot."

Ava nodded. "Like I said, tell me something I don't know. Who ordered the hit on Covey Cahill? Was it Callum Horne? Porter Ambrose? Ruby Vos?"

"Logan Ayres. He's second in command. Right under Porter Ambrose. If something happens to Porter, Logan is set to run Emerald Block. He's Callum's uncle. Callum didn't have the stomach to order the hit. He knew Covey was a liability, but he still had feelings for her. Logan has no feelings for anyone. The man is an iceberg, and he has venom in his veins instead of blood."

"That's something new," she said, noting it in the file. "Who runs the dummy companies? Is it Emerald Block, one of their people, multiple, who?"

"I couldn't say."

"You don't know, or you won't say?"

King shook his head and bobbed his shoulders.

"What you've given me isn't enough to ensure your safety, King. I need to know who runs the dummy companies that have been injecting your bank account for the last five years with all those huge payouts, and why they were paying you."

"I told you, I can't say."

She put down her pen and smiled. "You know, King, I will set you free right here and now, if you don't give me some name to work with. Who was paying you from those companies? Who all was involved? Unless you'd rather walk out of here a free man right now."

He shook his head again. "No. You can't do that. Bale wouldn't let you anyway."

"Bale wouldn't stop me if I told him you clammed up and refused to give us any information. And we'd have a big media show with it, too. Your release, I mean. We wouldn't want it to go unnoticed."

"You could work for them, you know. You're cold enough."

"Time's flying by, King. I'm giving you about another thirty seconds, and then I'm pulling the plug and walking out." She closed her folder and put her pen in her pocket.

THE WOMAN IN THE WINDOW

"No. Dammit." He heaved a noisy breath. "It's too big for me. Too big for you and Bale. I can't give you that information or they'll kill me for sure, and they'll make me suffer before they do it."

"And just how long do you think you'll live if I escort you back to your house and let you go?" She stood and grabbed the folder. "I'll give you two hours to decide how badly you want to live." She walked out of the room.

"Don't do this to me!" he yelled as the door closed.

Bale was on board with Ava's plan, but he was impatient as well. They let King sweat it out for the full two hours before Bale sent Ava back in.

"Ready to talk, or do I need to get my keys?"

"I'll talk. You win. I'm ruined either way this goes."

"Smarter than you look," she said as she sat. "Now, tell me about Covey Cahill and how she became a murder victim."

"She was going to testify against Callum Horne, Logan Ayres, and Porter Ambrose. She was privy to dealings in the highest rank of Emerald Block, and they weren't having that. Logan ordered the hit, Porter backed it, and Callum stood by the decision, but he couldn't carry out the murder. That's when they contacted me. They blackmail people into doing what they want. Trust me, when they tighten the thumbscrews, you'll dance to their tune."

"I would like to think I wouldn't find myself in a position where that was even remotely possible."

"Then you would be surprised just how easily it can come about."

"What did they blackmail you with? Surely it wasn't just some money payouts over the years."

"Yes, that's exactly what it boils down to. Money and lifestyle."

"Lifestyle? I saw your Manassas house, and that doesn't qualify as blackmail material."

He laughed. "You also saw the mansion in McLean. That was mine, too. So was Margueritte. Ruby Vos is her aunt, and I'm assuming you know her, too."

"Yeah, I've heard a thing or two about Ms. Vos, and I met Ms. Fiore. Classy, elegant woman. I don't know what she saw in you, but I suppose if you're raised around criminals, that's what you're used to."

"The Block was maintaining my lifestyle in return for services I could offer them. Let's say, special services that someone in my position within the Bureau can offer."

"Such as confidential information about anyone they want it on," Ava said.

"Yeah, such as that."

"You did leak them the information from Bale's file on Cahill, then."

"I thought she was the end of it, but you and Bale had to stick your noses into every hole and every corner until you got a bunch of other people killed."

"We didn't get anyone killed. You did that, King. You, and you alone. You're the one who pulled the trigger, and now I need to know why. Why Tanzy Bruner? Was she in on it?"

He nodded. "She was one of the contingency plans in place in case I failed at the airport."

"How did Emerald Block get to her?"

"I'm not sure, but if I was guessing, I would guess it had something to do with money. Maybe even threatened the safety of her kids." His voice dropped on the last part.

"So, you know more than you're willing to admit to."

"That's how they operate. They hook you in with money, do things for you, and then when it's time to repay, they stop at nothing. Kids are not off-limits to them. They'll kill them, or worse, to get what they want from parents."

"And those are people you willingly stayed involved with for five long years. How did you sleep at night knowing all that about them?"

"It's called insomnia. I haven't slept more than three hours in a stretch for at least four years."

"And that was three hours too long. What about Tilson? He was on the plane, too."

"Another backup plan. He had too much knowledge about it, so he had to go."

"How did they get to him? Or, are you unable to say?"

"He got his startup and continuation money for his hotels from the Block. They saw an opportunity that couldn't be passed up in that. They could always count on luxury rooms and fine food. They conduct business out of those suites. All of it illegal business."

"That's a given. Now, what about the money? Where's it coming from, exactly, and who's running the dummy companies?"

He dropped his head and shook it. "You're the one investigating. You figure it out."

Ava stalked out of the room with more information than before, but not with enough to satisfy her. King called her bluff about letting him go, and he had won. She couldn't, and wouldn't if she could.

The battle might have been lost, but the war was still in full swing.

And King was locked up. He wasn't going anywhere anytime soon.

CHAPTER FORTY-ONE

The Big Picture

Ash helped Ava with her continued digging into the dummy companies. They worked for several days on the spiderweb of trails that led from one fake company to another; from one false name to another. In the end, they all looped back around on themselves, and they made little progress at finding the person, or persons, who actually ran the companies and made the payouts to King.

"If we could find the person who initiated the payouts to King, it would lead to a whole laundry list of people getting payouts," Ava said.

"You're not going to believe this," Ashton said in response.

"You just won the Jackpot Lottery," she said, only half-joking. Even that revelation would have been welcome after days of staring at leads which amounted to dead ends.

"Dolend Corp," he said. "I've checked three times to make sure I had this right. Dolend Corp has been paying into the laundromat that was paying King. They supply all the cleaners to Tilson's hotels, too. Free of charge, and it's listed as a gift to guess who?"

She shook her head and shrugged.

"Manny Greene, Ford Blevins, Stacy Kilmer, and Tara Haight."

"Who?"

"They are the main assistants to Porter Ambrose, Logan Ayres, Ruby Vos, and Callum Horne, respectively."

Ava smiled. "And I'm betting those assistants have no use for free cleaning supplies in Tilson's hotels."

"And I'm betting Dolend Corp had no idea anyone would ever uncover that connection to Emerald Block," Ashton said, smirking.

"Emerald Block didn't, either. God, you are amazing."

Ashton grinned and leaned back. "I am Techie, the Great Geek God."

"I still like Guru of Geekdom." She patted his arm and laughed.

"You know, this might link Dolend to Emerald Block, but as for the killings?" He sighed.

"Yeah, I know. It would never stand up in court. The best-case scenario would be circumstantial at best."

"At worst, it would get tossed as being too flimsy. Dolend Corp is the top company for household cleaners in the United States and most of Europe. Their products are everywhere from residences to industrial settings. No judge would even want to consider such a case against them."

"Still, we know what's going on, and I'm going to see if I can make a difference." She went to find Bale.

He was in another office, talking to a fellow agent. She motioned to him from the doorway.

"What's up?" he asked.

"I say it's time to bring Logan Ayres in. We have King's confession. He's given us enough to run Logan in for questioning at the very least."

"You talk to King and see if you can get anything else out of him after he's had a few days to think about his situation. I'll go with Lin and pick up Logan."

Ava nodded. She wanted to go with him and bring in Logan Ayres, but she also knew King needed to be questioned further. He also needed to know Mr. Ayres was on his way to the office for questioning.

"See if you can get him to name another mole in the agency. If there was one, it's possible there are more."

"Will do," she said.

He clapped her on the shoulder and smiled as he walked away.

Ava went back to question King, but he wasn't in much of a talking mood.

"Give me the name of a corrupt politician, King. I know you know many of them. You were getting money from their slush funds."

"You know I can't do that. It would be a huge scandal in the capital."

"Were there other moles in the agency?"

He snorted laughter. "What do you think?"

"It doesn't matter what I think. The truth matters, King. That's all I want."

"Next question. Preferably one you don't already know the answer to."

"Then there is at least one more mole that you know about. Who is it, King? Talk to me. Don't you have an ounce of integrity left?"

He shook his head. "I tossed that out the window years ago, in case it slipped by you."

Taking a deep, calming breath, she thought and stared at him. "Okay, name one corrupt official. Doesn't matter how high or low the office is. Just one. Give me something to work with, and maybe I can do something for you. I'll tell the lawyers and the judge that you were willing and helpful. It would be a boon to your case if they could see that you helped bring down someone who is corrupt."

King laughed.

Ava stood to leave, clutching her folder tightly in one hand.

He laughed and couldn't stop. "It's too big for you, Agent James. Just like your ambition. Just like my ambition, and you see where it landed me," he said through the laughter. He continued to laugh even as tears formed in his eyes. "I'll be dead before any of this goes to trial. You know that, right?"

She turned at the door. "I take that as a threat of suicide. You'll be put on suicide watch until the trial." She pulled the door open and smiled back at him. "I'd hate for anything to happen to you before your sentence is read."

CHAPTER FORTY-TWO

Good to be Home

I T WAS GREAT TO BE OUT OF DC AND BACK IN HER FAIRHAVEN HOUSE. It was small, but it was hers, and it was quiet—something DC had forgotten how to be.

At work, she and Ashton continued to dig up anyone involved with the dummy companies, but they hit dead ends every time. It was a new disappointment every day with that case.

Sal came to Ava's office door. "Hey, what are you scratching your head over today?"

"This case. It goes to trial in less than three weeks, and I have to go back to DC to testify. I just want to get more of it worked out before then, if I can." She exhaled and looked up at Sal. "And I'm still working on the Margot Carter case, too."

"That's why I stopped by. Anything new on that case?"

"Not really. I've set up an interview with a woman who might have witnessed something odd before Margot was killed, though."

"Legit or just someone talking?"

"I don't know yet. She sounded scared when she called, so it might be legit."

"Might be paranoia, or drugs, too."

Ava nodded. "That's what I'm afraid of."

"Did you find any links with the San Francisco murders? What was it that Agent Ellis called them?"

"Housewife Murders. The M.O. is shockingly similar in most of the cases, actually."

"Mm. I'm going to take that as my cue to exit stage left." Sal backed out of the door.

"I know, you don't want to talk about a bi-coastal serial killer."

"Nope, I sure don't."

"Doesn't mean he doesn't exist," Ava called after her.

"Doesn't mean he's real," she called back from farther down the hall.

No, it didn't mean he was real, but Margot Carter, the victim, was as real as they came. So was her family. Someone had killed her. And whether Sal, or anyone else, liked it, or not, whoever killed Margot seemed to have ripped a page right out of the Housewife Murders book.

Thinking about those particularly creepy and gruesome murders conjured up thoughts about Jason Ellis. It stirred up questions about him that she would have rather left untouched for a while longer.

Had he lied to her? Had he told her he was in one city, when he was really in another? Had he been in the city when Margot was murdered? Was it a coincidence that none of the Housewife Murders had been solved in San Francisco? Jason had an excellent solve rate. Better than Ava's, except when it came to the murders that were so similar to the Housewife Murders.

Two hours later, after hitting another dead end with Bale's case, Ava was ready to scream. Even Ashton had grown weary of the case and had moved on to another of the older cases.

Sal came back to Ava's office. "You look like you could seriously use a break right about now."

Images of cheeseburgers and large black coffees filled her mind. Smiling, she nodded, and pushed back from the desk. "When did you dust off that crystal ball?" She stood. Coffee and burgers with Sal would be an awesome distraction from all that was running wild in her mind.

"I thought so." She stepped close and handed Ava a thick file across the desk. "A brand new case just for you."

Ava's heart fell. She took the file. "And here I thought we were going to go somewhere and get something to eat." Her tone sounded dejected even to her own ears.

Sal laughed. "After work, maybe."

Ava plopped back into her seat, banishing the shiny images from her mind.

It wasn't bad to have a new case. It was actually quite nice to be able to put the other cases away for a while.

She smiled and opened the folder, ready for a new challenge.

AUTHOR'S NOTE

Dear Reader,

I am thrilled to have shared with you the twelfth installment in the Ava James FBI Mystery series, The Woman in the Window! Imagining a murder mystery unfolding at 36,000 feet was an exhilarating challenge, and I'm grateful for the opportunity to take Ava on this high-flying adventure. From the cramped confines of the airplane to the psychological complexities of the investigation, I hope I accomplished my goal of keeping you on the edge of your seat until the very end.

But the excitement doesn't have to end here! I invite you to experience the latest installment in my Dean Steele Mystery Thriller Series, The Convict. This adrenaline-filled adventure finds Dean in Ashford Prison, facing riots, bloodshed, and a daring undercover mission that will keep you guessing until the final page. As the situation intensifies, a bloodthirsty inmate seizes control, holding guards hostage. And not even Dean could have predicted what would soon follow.

As an indie author, your reviews and support are invaluable to me. If you could take a moment to leave a review for The Woman in the Window, I would be enormously grateful. Your feedback allows me to continue to grow and improve as an author, and it ensures that Ava and the team can keep solving mysteries and catching criminals.

Thank you for your support and for joining me on this journey. Ava and the team are counting on you, and I can't wait to see where our adventures take us next.

Yours,
A.J. Rivers

P.S. If for some reason you didn't like this book or found typos or other errors, please let me know personally. I do my best to read and respond to every email at mailto:aj@riversthrillers.com

P.P.S. If you would like to stay up-to-date with me and my latest releases I invite you to visit my Linktree page at *www.linktr.ee/a.j.rivers* to subscribe to my newsletter and receive a free copy of my book, Edge of the Woods. You can also follow me on my social media accounts for behind-the-scenes glimpses and sneak peeks of my upcoming projects, or even sign up for text notifications. I can't wait to connect with you!

ALSO BY
A.J. RIVERS

Emma Griffin FBI Mysteries

Season One

Book One—The Girl in Cabin 13*
Book Two—The Girl Who Vanished*
Book Three—The Girl in the Manor*
Book Four—The Girl Next Door*
Book Five—The Girl and the Deadly Express*
Book Six—The Girl and the Hunt*
Book Seven—The Girl and the Deadly End*

Season Two

Book Eight—The Girl in Dangerous Waters*
Book Nine—The Girl and Secret Society*
Book Ten—The Girl and the Field of Bones*
Book Eleven—The Girl and the Black Christmas*
Book Twelve—The Girl and the Cursed Lake*
Book Thirteen—The Girl and The Unlucky 13*
Book Fourteen—The Girl and the Dragon's Island*

Season Three

Book Fifteen—The Girl in the Woods*
Book Sixteen —The Girl and the Midnight Murder*
Book Seventeen— The Girl and the Silent Night*
Book Eighteen — The Girl and the Last Sleepover*
Book Nineteen — The Girl and the 7 Deadly Sins*
Book Twenty — The Girl in Apartment 9*
Book Twenty-One — The Girl and the Twisted End*

Emma Griffin FBI Mysteries Retro - Limited Series
(Read as standalone or before Emma Griffin book 22)

Book One— The Girl in the Mist*
Book Two— The Girl on Hallow's Eve*
Book Three— The Girl and the Christmas Past*
Book Four— The Girl and the Winter Bones*
Book Five— The Girl on the Retreat*

Season Four

Book Twenty-Two — The Girl and the Deadly Secrets*
Book Twenty-Three — The Girl on the Road*
Book Twenty-Four —The Girl and the Unexpected Gifts*
Book Twenty-Five —The Girl and the Secret Passage*
Book Twenty-Six — The Girl and the Bride

Ava James FBI Mysteries

Book One—The Woman at the Masked Gala*
Book Two—Ava James and the Forgotten Bones*
Book Three —The Couple Next Door*
Book Four — The Cabin on Willow Lake*
Book Five — The Lake House*
Book Six — The Ghost of Christmas*
Book Seven — The Rescue*
Book Eight — Murder in the Moonlight*
Book Nine — Behind the Mask*
Book Ten — The Invitation*
Book Eleven — The Girl in Hawaii
Book Twelve — The Woman in the Window

Dean Steele FBI Mysteries

*Book One—The Woman in the Woods**
Book Two — The Last Survivors
Book Three — No Escape
Book Four —The Garden of Secrets
Book Five —The Killer Among Us
Book Five —The Convict

ALSO BY
A.J. RIVERS & THOMAS YORK

Bella Walker FBI Mystery Series

*Book One—The Girl in Paradise**
*Book Two—Murder on the Sea**
*Book Three—The Last Aloha**

Other Standalone Novels
Gone Woman
* Also available in audio

Made in United States
Orlando, FL
24 March 2024